Titles by Robert Adrian

Destination Citadel

Target Citadel
(Coming soon)

THE SAM AUSTIN CHRONICLES

DESTINATION CITADEL

—

ROBERT ADRIAN

ISBN: 0990610403
ISBN 13: 9780990610403
Library of Congress Control Number: 2014912699
Cambrian Park LLC, San Jose, CA

To Un-hi,

Who smiles gently through adversity and
knows the future will be brighter

ACKNOWLEDGMENTS

I would like to acknowledge the gracious and insightful feedback on this book provided to me by Jason and Geri Winters.

CONTENTS

INTRODUCTION

S am Austin considered himself a lucky man. As part of the Apollo space program, he and his best friend, Matt Jackson, were on the surface of the Moon, relying on surprisingly fragile systems and materials to protect them from the cold death of space. They'd traveled from "home" to this spot in the lunar rover, with Austin steering. "Home" on the Moon was the lunar module, which was referred to by its initials.

This was their second trip in the rover since they'd touched down. After finishing their first trip, they'd been pissed to learn that one of the dust guards had fallen or been knocked off the rover. Austin thought about the dust that had sprayed over everything in spite of the jury-rigged dust guard that they had tried to install. Jackson grumbled, "That damned dust coats everything and is impossible to brush away. We've already found out the hard way that this crap will be all over everything when we get back to the LM."

Austin, who always called his friend Jack, chuckled, saying, "Remember what it looked like the first time,

Jack? Two minutes after leaving the LM, our suits looked like hell compared to when we left Earth."

Jackson gritted his teeth and said, "It's a good thing we only have one-sixth of Earth's gravity to worry about, because this ride is anything but smooth."

They always started by traveling to the farthest point away from the LM that they would visit during that shift. They'd move closer to home as the shift wore on and their supplies of oxygen were depleted, so that they'd have the best chance of getting back to their temporary quarters if a problem arose with the lunar rover. Although they weren't particularly far from the LM, a bleak-looking rock formation, with jagged edges that were splashed with shades of black and gray, blocked their view of it, giving them a feeling of being even more alone than usual.

They'd just finished unloading everything from the rover when Austin noticed something about the pile. "Jack!" he called out, pointing. "What do you see?"

Jackson cursed, "Damn it, I see an idiot named Jackson who missed a piece of equipment!"

"We can't do this experiment without it," Austin said. "One of us has to go back and get it."

"That would be me," said Jackson. "It was on my checklist, and I missed it while we were screwing around with that damned dust guard. Besides, I'll get a chance to drive that buggy. Being an old man, you drive it much too carefully, and somebody has to see what it can really do." Even though he couldn't see Jackson's face, Austin knew there was a twinkle in his friend's eye. Ever since Austin had turned thirty over two years ago, Jackson had called him an old man, even though the smart ass was only twelve months younger!

Austin grinned. "Just make sure that putting it through its paces includes getting us back home without walking. See you in a few minutes, Jack."

As Jackson drove the rover back to the LM, Austin set up the equipment as best he could and then smiled upon realizing that he actually had a few minutes with nothing to do. Most of their time was scheduled very tightly, and they had all heard the lectures about staying with the schedule and not simply gazing into the sky. A couple of them had been so focused on their tasks that they had little idea of what the Earth looked like from the Moon, because they'd never looked up! Austin felt differently; with an unexpected gift of free time in hand, who in hell wanted to pass up the chance to take in a billion-dollar view? He turned away from the moonscape and gazed upon that extraordinary blue orb in the sky. No matter how many photos of the Earth taken from the Moon he had seen, there was nothing like looking at the real thing. The colors were so vibrant and messy that the Earth looked like a living organism, which it was, in a way. The stars didn't twinkle in space, of course; against the black background, they looked ready to touch.

Austin never saw the approach of the intense blue light that engulfed him. He froze, although he wasn't sure whether that was due to a property of the light or because he was simply surprised. He knew that he hadn't screwed up somehow and looked straight at the sun; that white ball of fire was in another direction and couldn't possibly have concealed such a shade of blue within its rays.

He wasn't sure whether he could actually see the light through his suit or if it was just a sensation of it passing through every part of his body, as if each particle in every cell was being inspected. He could see the light reflecting *inside* his helmet, as if it were radiating outward from his body. Although there was no pain, he felt an intensity that was like having a full stadium's worth of lights trained on one spot—and he was the spot. He had no sense of how long the light lasted. He just knew that it was there and then it wasn't there, without any fadeaway.

Austin was overwhelmed by the experience, and some time passed before he realized that Jackson was talking to him. He felt the tugging on his suit as he made out the words. "Sam, answer me, damn it!" Jackson shouted. "What the hell's the matter? Do you have a failure in your suit? Can you breathe? Can you move?"

Austin found that he could talk again and said, "I'm OK, Jack. I can't believe what just happened. Did you feel it?"

"Feel what? The only thing I felt was worry when you didn't respond when I called to let you know I was returning. The whole time that I was driving up to you in the buggy, you were like a statue. I haven't gotten a response from you at all until just now. What the hell happened?"

Austin shook his head slightly, as if to clear something from his mind. "There was the most intense light I've ever seen. It was blue, I was in it, and it was in me. Didn't you see it?"

"I didn't see anything, didn't feel anything. There's nothing around that could have generated a blue light. We're out of direct sight of the LM from here, and I'm pretty sure no one on Earth has a flashlight with a blue gel on it that can reach this far." Jackson's voice calmed down a bit as he continued, "Are you sure you're OK? We can scrub this walk while we check out the equipment to make sure there wasn't a malfunction."

"No, I'm fine. There's nothing we can do about it now anyway. Let's do the shift like we planned and talk with Houston about it when we're back in the LM."

"Suit yourself, old man."

COUNTDOWN

CHAPTER ONE

*A*nother *perfect summer day,* Sam Austin thought, as he gazed through the massive picture frame window at the Sierra Nevada. His eyes were as blue as the sky above, and he smiled as he listened to the complete quiet surrounding him. *I guess I'd better join my guests at the lake.* He moved away from the window with an easy, fluid grace, strolling lithely to the transport powered by one of his Austin Power Cells, a tall man apparently in the prime of his life and in superb physical condition.

There was no noise, save for the sound of the breeze as it fluttered through his dark hair. His face broke out into a smile. The sun kept dancing across his face in changing patterns as he passed by green-clad trees and faded gray boulders. The air was so fresh at that altitude that even breathing felt invigorating.

Austin liked to drive quickly over the trails, so in less than thirty minutes, he was at the lake. The mountains formed a natural basin for the lake, which was fed from a stream that coursed down from the peaks, runoff that came straight from the snow that hardly ever seemed to leave the tops of the highest mountains in the range. Even in the heat of summer, the lake was cold as hell. No one seemed to mind, though.

Most of the people were at varying levels of submersion in the lake, although a few less hardy souls were sitting or lying on their towels while they got warm again. Farther out, people were rowing themselves around in canoes or cruising around the lake in powered boats. The only noise from those boats was the sound of the gentle waves that made their way over from the boats' expanding wakes.

Several people saw Austin, and someone called out, "It's about time you put the work aside and got your ass up here!" Austin spotted a woman whose chestnut hair was darker than usual because it was wet. He grinned as he stripped and dove into the water. He swam toward her. He went under the surface and marveled, as usual, at the clear images under the water. The lake had never been polluted, and it always seemed that things that were far away were still in clear focus.

Very shortly, he had another reason to smile as he approached the woman. Like everyone else at the lake, she wasn't wearing a swimsuit, and the view was very nice to behold. She grinned when she saw him burst through the surface and gave him a playful splash, which he was happy to return. Later, after they got out of the water and stretched out on their towels, the woman smiled at Austin and said, "I'll bet it wasn't like this when you were younger."

Austin laughed and said, "If you mean what we called 'skinny-dipping' when I was a kid, you're right. Back then, while it was OK for kids to skinny-dip around lakes and streams, it was absolutely *not* OK for adults. They'd have been thrown in jail for public indecency! Things didn't change for most women in the US until well into the twenty-first century, when going topless became the norm." Austin smiled as he continued, "Now that we're around a couple of decades into the twenty-second century, a lot of people no longer worry much about swimsuits at all."

Later that evening, most of his guests were somewhere else on the property. Austin found himself having a private conversation with one of his guests, a man named Bret Yabuno. Yabuno was one of Austin's closest friends. He was also an expert in the design and integration of systems for use in space, as well as space-based propulsion systems.

"Sam," he said, "I don't know if I could have managed to move on with my life the way you have. It's been two years since you buried Suzie, yet you've refused to just sit around the place and forget about living."

Austin's eyes took on a melancholy look as he said, "The fact that she basically died from old age means that we were blessed to have been together for a long time. I'm not going to pretend it's been easy, Bret, but I'm at a good place as far as Suzie is concerned. Life goes on, and Suzie understood it."

Yabuno shook his head as he said, "I don't know how you deal with the fact that you'll always need to move on at some point, considering your life-span."

"I've come to terms with the fact that a serious relationship for me may be way different than what it is for other people. I don't get bogged down by worrying about what I want when I start seeing someone. I also don't drive myself nuts by asking if I'm prepared to watch someone I love do something that I can't share with her, such as die from old age. I just enjoy the relationship and see where it will lead."

"It's good that you're seeing Teri. She seems like a nice girl."

"She is," Austin replied with a smile. "I have no idea what will happen down the road, but I learned a long time ago the importance of staying in the present."

"The future isn't necessarily a bad thing to consider."

Austin's face took on a wry look as he said, "Why do I have the feeling that we're talking about something else now, Bret?"

Yabuno grinned and said, "You knew we'd be talking about it at some point. I've known you long enough to know that even at what's supposed to be a gathering with no talk of work, you'd want to hear about the status of the project."

"Why don't you tell me about it?"

Hours later, the conversation continued. Yabuno stood in front of a large display, moving images around like he was finger-painting. He pulled an image out and said, "We've come a long way from our first attempt with a warp-field generator, Sam. No more horrible situations with unstable warp fields that take out labs and people like they were blobs of clay waiting to be re-sculpted. Remember this one?" Yabuno brought the image to full size, and the room was filled with a lab in space, looking at an early prototype of a warp-field generator that was well off in the distance.

The countdown reached zero, and people stopped breathing while they waited for something to happen. Suddenly, a highly irregular bubble of space time rippled out from the location of the field generator, wiping out many of the cameras. Other bubbles reached out in different directions. In spite of the distances taken as a precaution, some of the viewers were knocked off their feet as one tendril of distortion reached across several miles of vacuum toward the lab and twisted several modules around and apart like warm taffy. The image was 3-D and vivid, so Austin and Yabuno had to fight the urge to duck as tendrils seemed to reach for them.

The distortions continued, threatening to reach other parts of the lab. Most people were now far less interested in watching the show than ducking for cover. As the distortions continued, things that should have shattered and fabrics that should have ripped instead deformed into grotesque shapes. When the tendrils distorted hatches, modules became prisons. Sometimes the seals on those hatches failed, and the prisons became coffins.

The generator finally failed, and tendrils that a few moments earlier had been reaching for more modules to use as playthings began to fluctuate and recede. As the space-time bubble collapsed, many of the pieces it left behind were twisted into misshapen wreckage. Emergency systems were screaming as the lab tried to seal itself off from areas that were exposed to space directly.

Yabuno made a quick motion, and the image returned to a folder. He grinned and said, "Thank God those days are long in the past."

As Austin chuckled in agreement, Yabuno pulled out a more recent image showing their progress and continued, "You already know that we've been able to manipulate a warp-field generator to sustain a warp field for six months. We're just a week away from getting confirmation that we can sustain one for at least twelve months. Within six months, we'll probably have it fine-tuned to be able to sustain it for at least two years. As we've planned, twelve months is the magic number as far as being able to reach Citadel is concerned."

Austin frowned, saying, "There's a big difference between being able to sustain a warp field in a lab and doing it in the field with a ship."

"Yes and no. We know that during any run that long the generator has to be monitored regularly and fine-tuned from time to time, which makes it pretty hard to rig an effective test drone. However, we've made the tests pretty challenging for the generator in the lab. We've been hammering it with more gamma radiation than it's likely to encounter for real during a run. It's still humming along."

"You haven't been able to include a simulation of the distorting effects on the warp field from a large body with an equally large gravity field of its own?"

"No, but we *have* dealt with those effects when doing shorter runs in our own system with test drones. Besides, we know where all of the bodies with significant gravity effects are located between here and Citadel. We can set our course to avoid those bodies, or at least minimize their gravitational effects."

The skepticism stayed on Austin's face as he replied, "I still wonder how well people would be able to function after a year in a microgravity environment. We've been in space for over a century and a half, and we haven't solved the problem of developing an effective artificial gravity. We're still stuck with poor men's substitutes like spinning and increasing acceleration. They sucked when they were first invented, and they still suck."

Yabuno countered the skepticism with another image, which looked like a flight suit. He said, "I believe we'll solve the artificial gravity problem sooner than you think. At least we have a better understanding of how gravity works than anyone did a hundred years ago. We don't sit around and say, 'It can't be done because gravity is a function of mass and ships can't generate gravity because they can't generate extra mass,' and that's the end of the conversation. I think we'll be able to translate that understanding into a practical result in a few more years. For now, your resistance suits, combined with a little time each day in a mini-centrifuge, should do the trick. As you predicted many years ago, the suits now aren't any more bulky or awkward to wear than a fairly thin flight suit."

Yabuno stopped and pulled out an image of a sleek ship nestled within a bay in their space yard. He gazed at it for a moment and said, "We're ready, Sam. *Pathfinder* is a fine ship. The past three months have confirmed that she's everything we hoped she'd be. It's time to install the warp-field generators and see what she can do. Everything that we've seen so far indicates that she can journey to the stars.

Austin finally grinned and said, "Let's do it, then. I agree that she's a hell of a ship. I'm satisfied that with the warp-field generators installed and the ship having been run through shakedown procedures, it'll be in good shape to visit another planet. Let's talk about whether that planet is still Citadel."

Yabuno moved his fingers, and *Pathfinder* dissolved into a grainy image of a planet with unfamiliar swirls of brown, blue, and white, revealing an Earth-like planet that was clearly an extreme distance from Earth itself. He gestured toward it as he said, "We've had plenty of years to study Citadel. We keep refining what we know practically every day, although some things haven't really changed.

"Let's consider the positives. The first is that we're pretty damned sure that there're three planets in the star's habitable zone and that Citadel is in the best part of that zone. It's a rocky planet with liquid water and an atmosphere that seems to be the right mix of nitrogen and oxygen. We think that the temperature is within our ranges of adaptability. Gravity may be slightly greater than on Earth, but not by much. We already know that the Citadel year is around three hundred and seventy-five Earth days, so the Citadel year and Earth year are pretty close. The day on Citadel is around twenty-four point three Earth hours, so there wouldn't be too much of a change from the normal human rhythms for day and night. There must be seasons, since Citadel is tilted on its axis about the same as is Earth, with a fairly comparable orbit. We still aren't sure how severely the climate may change from season to season, though. We have indications that Citadel has a magnetic field, which is a good thing if settlers want to avoid having to work with a hell of a lot of shielding."

Yabuno frowned as he pulled up a different image. "Now, let's consider a hell of a negative. There's some nasty radiation in that region that would make it pretty tricky to maneuver any kind of ship to Citadel. While we don't think the radiation affects Citadel itself, we're just not sure whether a ship can even get to the planet. That was, of course, the reason for the name 'Citadel' in the first place, since it would be fairly easy to defend it against invaders. Just control a fairly constricted region, and you control access to the entire system. The region near the planet serves as a fortress that can be used to protect the rest of the system.

"There's no way to know for sure whether Citadel is a golden opportunity or just an opportunity to pursue fool's gold. Although one day we might also strike the jackpot with one or both of Citadel's siblings in that system's habitable zone, there's no point in worrying about those siblings if you can't even get to Citadel. On top of the basic negative is the fact that a probe probably won't give us enough information to figure out how to get to Citadel. We need to be there to figure out any next steps."

Yabuno's frown faded as he concluded, "In short, Sam, even taking into account the negatives we know about so far, Citadel seems like as good an opportunity as we can possibly encounter that's within the reach of our technology."

"What do you think we should do?"

With a dramatic gesture, Yabuno placed *Pathfinder's* image next to Citadel as he said, "We should go there and knock on the door! We haven't been doing all this work only to fold our tent because there might be some tough problems to solve. If Citadel has a magnetic field, then there is a reasonable chance that plate tectonics are keeping things stirred up enough that mining would be very lucrative. Besides, I want to do something different with my life than just sit on my ass and design things."

Austin nodded at the sentiment and said, "Amen, Bret. We need to figure out who will lead this first trip."

Yabuno paused for a moment, before saying quietly, "I know that you'd like to do it, Sam. Thanks to your lifespan, giving up two years to get there and back would mean nothing to you. I can also understand the thrill factor from the possibility of being the first human to set foot on a planet outside our solar system. Hell, it sounds pretty cool to me too! We need to remember that the Citadel Group and this project are about more than just the initial scouting of a star system.

"It isn't a question of whether you could lead this trip—hell, you're the best qualified, hands down! You've been in space before, with technology that was vastly more primitive than what we have today. You have a good understanding of all of the main issues that we've encountered so far, and you know how to lead people. You don't panic in a crisis, and people respect you like no one else. The problem is that one person can't be in charge of this project *and* be in charge during the first trip. Important decisions have to be made at each end, and we have to assume that there won't be any practical means of communication between the two systems for now."

Austin gestured at the images of Citadel as he replied, "Bret, I'm not arrogant enough to believe that I'm the only one or even the best to lead this trip successfully; no one is indispensable. However, because of all the planning that will need to take place, a lot of the critical decisions will have been made before *Pathfinder* leaves our solar system. Someone else can take it over and oversee the project and make any new decisions that need to be made."

Yabuno shook his head, saying, "You'd be away from Earth for a couple of years, Sam. You've seen how it works with large projects; they always need to have major decisions made long after everyone thinks all of the major decisions have been made. You need to be here on Earth as we recruit the people who will be part of the first group of settlers. Also, if you end up lost in space before we even know anything more, it will set things back hugely; it might even kill the project entirely. There's no reason why you can't be the leader of the project *and* the leader of the first group of settlers. In fact, people will pretty much insist on it. After *Pathfinder* returns, we should know enough about the situation that your successor here can handle whatever comes up."

"What happens if the guy that gets there finds out the hard way that there's something about the environment that's lethal to humans that we didn't plan for? I don't want to send a man to a death that could have been avoided if I had been the one there."

Yabuno paused for a moment. After giving Austin a hard stare, which Austin returned easily, Yabuno couldn't help but grin and say, "Sam, we've been friends a hell of a long time. We're doing some bullshit dance around something that you know that I don't. Why don't you clue me in on why you think you'd be such hot stuff out there?"

Austin's face broke into an even bigger grin as he said, "Thank God I still have friends like you who can keep me honest, Bret."

"How about just being glad that you have friends who let you know when you're full of shit, Sam? I'll leave the 'honest' part to others."

"Whatever. Anyway, everyone knows that I've spent the last century and a half since my Apollo Moon mission not aging so much as a day. I still don't know exactly what that damned energy field that showed up did to me. A lot of people also know that I've never been sick since that time."

Yabuno allowed a touch of impatience to creep into his voice as he said, "Old news, Sam. For as long as I've known you during *my* ever-so-normal life-span, and even before then, going all the way back that century and a half, you've always appeared to be in your early thirties, which was your age when you made the moon walk. You're also clearly in excellent shape physically. We all know that you haven't allowed medical science to take a crack at what makes you tick in decades. Although the privacy laws are pretty strict when it comes to medical records, you're probably right that someone would try to clone you to see if the nature of your 'immortality' could be understood and duplicated. This could lead to the end of the human race as we know it," Yabuno concluded with a slight smirk.

Austin's look was even sourer as he said, "Be a smartass if you want, but after seeing what happened when some monsters came up with a genetically engineered New Plague that took out over half the world's population, including forty million in the US, I don't have any illusions about man's capacity for evil. I also don't have any illusions about what some men will do if enough money is at stake."

Yabuno's smirk faded as he said, "OK, point taken. What's the stuff that we don't already know?"

"My body has gradually been functioning at a more efficient level over these decades." Austin's face took on a wry look as he continued, "I can't say that I'm any smarter, but I seem to recover much more quickly from injuries than before. I also seem to have faster reflexes and greater strength. I'm not like a superhero from the old comics, with a cape and my underwear on the outside. I can't lift a car over my head. It's just that in times of extreme stress, especially in what can be a hostile environment in space, I might have an advantage that others wouldn't."

Yabuno couldn't resist adopting a "superhero" pose and asking, "Can you stop a bullet?"

Austin smiled as he said, "Hell no. If you cut me, I'll bleed, so most of the ways a man can die still apply to me."

"Have you considered the possibility that you might start aging normally once you leave this solar system?"

"I've thought about it plenty of times. I just don't think it likely that leaving the solar system would have any impact on what prevents me from aging."

"Why not? For all we know, your current situation could be tied in somehow to the various fields on Earth or the Moon relating to gravity, magnetism, radiation, or something else." There was a look of both wry amusement and concern on Yabuno's face as he said, "Leave the place and you might start looking like the picture of Dorian Gray near the end of the story."

Austin shook his head, saying, "The energy field that enveloped me came from somewhere else. I don't believe it was *of* this solar system at all, so leaving this system won't have any impact on me. Besides, even if I'm wrong, I don't care," he said with a shrug. "I'm not that many years away from the two-century mark. I've already had a far longer life than anyone else is likely to have even with whatever medical science is able to do anytime soon."

Yabuno placed a huge picture of Austin next to the image of Citadel and said, "Getting back to what you've said about why you'd be the best guy to lead the first trip, I don't think it changes anything. The potential advantage that you mention doesn't offset the fact that people consider you to be too valuable to risk losing on the very first long-term test of the *Pathfinder*." Yabuno emphasized his point by making an even more dramatic gesture where the image of Austin dissolved, followed immediately by the dissolution of the Citadel image. Yabuno grinned at Austin, who grinned back, a little sourly.

"Face it, Sam, there's a shitload of stuff that needs to happen if we're going to have everything on schedule by the time *Pathfinder* returns. We need your leadership to make sure that a lot of that stuff happens." Yabuno's face took on a sly look as he continued, "Besides, now that you and Teri have started to spend some quality time together, it'd be pretty hard to spend two years locked up in a prison with no conjugal privileges. I suppose you can ask Teri to star in a special VR program for you. To be fair, you'd want to star in one for her as well."

Austin laughed as he said, "You can be such an asshole, Bret."

Yabuno laughed back, saying, "And your point?"

As they got up to join the other guests, both of them were grinning broadly in that way that men don't want to have to explain to their girlfriends.

CHAPTER TWO

A group of men and women sat throughout the great room in Austin's house, the brain trust and leaders who ran the Citadel Group and kept the Citadel project on track. Any significant issue that was of concern to the project was discussed by them and then passed off to the people who were best equipped to run with it. They were bright, articulate, and at times opinionated. They were in the midst of a sometimes heated discussion about the type of people who would serve as the first wave of settlers on the ships that would be built to follow *Pathfinder* back to Citadel. A woman named Liz Lake led the discussion, using the huge screen as needed.

"I think we're going overboard on the requirements for background checks," Greg Brittel said with a frown. "People sometimes screw up in their lives. Aren't we all about people having second chances?"

"This isn't a rehabilitation activity, Greg," Lake replied. "Yes, people sometimes get into minor trouble when they're young and foolish, and we're not holding that stuff against them. However, people who didn't have the maturity or judgment as adults to do the right thing aren't the people that we want as part of the first group of settlers, even if their offenses happened some years ago. People with histories of substance abuse, domestic violence, poor anger management, and dishonesty, among other issues, are also not good candidates to be settlers. We aren't going to take the chance that the stresses of being settlers might bring these traits out into the open."

Brittel's frown shifted to impatience as he said, "OK, moving on to something else, why the hell are we talking about being so strict on the medical backgrounds of the settlers? It should be enough that they're in good health, since we'll have medical personnel along to take care of stuff that happens."

Lake shook her head in disagreement as she replied, "We have to do a better job of planning than that, Greg. These people aren't going to be there for a school picnic. Barring the discovery of some fundamental game changer to the whole idea of settling Citadel, they'll be there for at least ten years. There are a lot of illnesses that can show up in that time that could be hell for the local medical staff to handle. We're not even talking yet about any nasty surprises that might show up within the Citadel environment."

Lake pointed to image after image as she continued, "This is why we need people who rarely, if ever, get sick, and even then only from minor things, such as colds. They can't have any allergies or sensitivities to other environmental factors. They need to be athletic and used to the outdoors. We have to assume that drug supplies may be compromised or simply be exhausted at some point, so no one can have a chronic condition that requires any kind of medication. Other than some of the usual child-hood illnesses, they can't ever have had serious illnesses, which rules out any kind of cancer or cardiac condition, among other things. In fact, they can't have a family history of certain serious illnesses."

Brittel got up and practically used his fist to brush away the images as he pushed back. "People get sick in space now. Sometimes it takes a while to receive medical treatment." He sat down with hunched shoulders.

Lake ignored the blank screen and the shoulders as she said, "While we hope that everything can be treated successfully on Citadel, we have to assume that there'll be no emergency trips back to Earth because of something that can't be handled locally. Therefore, the people who are there have to be the best candidates capable of withstanding those types of problems in the first place." Lake continued quietly, "We have to be realistic and assume that in spite of our precautions, not everyone will survive the settlement experience, either because of disease, accident, misadventure, system failure, etc. We just want to minimize the numbers of those people who will be affected."

"We might be able to reduce the likelihood of violence if we didn't require that nearly everyone be married and that both spouses participate," Brittel said with black humor.

"We've gone back and forth over the issues of emotional and mental health and the impact of various factors on them, such as marriage," Lake replied. "We recognize that angels don't necessarily make the best pioneers; we need people who will be able to make some tough or even ruthless choices that we'd never have to make on Earth. That said, we also don't want people who are primarily loners. Those people tend to be less interested in creating long-term settlements than in just doing their own thing. We need people who are independent, practical, and also dedicated to making the settlement successful over the long term. Married couples with a good mix of these character traits tend to have the most at stake as far as the success of the settlement is concerned. This is especially true if they have or are planning on having children, since they want to leave a legacy to their kids."

"Those children are more likely than others to have an emotional stake in the success of the community. With couples who don't have children, while they may have significant legacies in mind, those legacies won't necessarily be for the benefit of the settlement. At some point, they will pull up stakes voluntarily or involuntarily and are more likely than couples with children to disrupt the community by trying to leave their stake to someone who might not have any interest in the long-term success of the settlement."

Brittel crossed his arms as he said, "I see that we're willing to make exceptions for some people. How come the rules don't apply to everyone?"

Several people gasped, as Brittel's comments were a not-so-subtle dig at Austin. Everyone was aware that Teri Knight had decided that she wasn't the material from which pioneers were made and had broken up with Austin over the issue. Every set of eyes in the room shifted toward Austin, who spoke in a calm voice. "Is there something you want to say, Greg?"

"It seems to me that the rules about married couples should apply to everyone, or they should be scrapped."

"That's the thing about rules, Greg; they need to make sense in the context of the situation," Austin said. "Your approach would simply look for the rare exception that makes sense for a unique set of facts as justification for saying that the basis for the rule is invalid. The team considered the fact that there are certain roles for which the rule about married couples doesn't make sense. Some of those roles include the medical director and certain medical staff. There are also certain technical roles that need to be filled on the mining side, where the entire community will be benefitting from getting those operations up and running as soon as possible. Another role is the settlement leader."

"I guess you're assuming that you will fulfill that role."

"I'm not going to pretend to be surprised over the notion that I'll fill that role. The fact is that a lot of people have made it clear that they won't support this project without my leading it from Citadel." Austin's eyes had a faint trace of amusement in them as he continued, "I'll leave it to others to decide whether I've had any success as a leader."

Yabuno spoke up immediately and walked to the screen, pulling out images as he said, "Yeah, Greg, let's debate whether Sam has been a successful leader. He was the commander of an Apollo mission and walked on the Moon. He was a four-star navy admiral. Oh yes, he was president of the United States for over forty years, thanks to the people being impressed with him and repealing presidential term limits in the Constitution. While president, he got the country through the New Plague and helped set up international structures after the Bio War that have led to decades of mostly peace on Earth. Any questions?" Yabuno stood by the screen, subtly daring Brittel to try to remove the images.

Brittel didn't take the bait, knowing he had to tread carefully as he said, "I'm not questioning Sam's leadership qualities, Bret. I'm just saying that if we make an exception for him, then we should make an exception for anyone else who wants it."

"How's *your* marriage doing, Greg?" Yabuno shot back. "Is that why you're making such a big deal about the issue? Anything you want to share with us?"

Brittel's face was red with fury, and he tensed as if ready to lash out at Yabuno. Before Brittel could say something, Austin said, "While the rule with these meetings has been that people can engage in robust discussion, we need to consider when we've moved beyond robust discussion to something else. Bret, I'll leave it to you to decide whether your last comments were part of 'robust discussion' or something else. Greg, likewise, if you want to be able to make pointed comments to a member of this team, you need to be willing and able to accept pointed comments when they are directed at you." As Austin had intended, Brittel began to relax. Yabuno, having made his points, wiped the images and returned to his chair without further words.

Austin smiled as he continued, "I think we'll be able to cool things down a bit as we talk with our legal advisor. How are you, J.W.?"

"Old, fat, and ugly," replied a man who had been watching some of the previous give-and-take with a look of amused entertainment. J. W. Preacher III was a man in his early seventies, with dark skin offset by generous sprinklings of white in his full head of hair. His eyes were full of intelligence and, unlike some members of his profession, his smile was warm and genuine. He had about him the air of a man enjoying his life.

With a wicked gleam in his eye, he continued, "I noticed that no one disagreed with any of what I just said." The room burst into chuckles. It was impossible not to like Preacher within a few minutes of having met him. Preacher couldn't resist needling the group a little before getting to the business at hand. "Listening to your brand of 'robust discussion' is the most entertainment I've had all week. I enjoy a conversation where the bullshit is either set aside or understood for what it is. Some of my new clients seem to think that they need to shovel their bullshit at me instead of being honest. In time, they learn that if they want to stay a client of mine, they need to leave the bullshit at home."

Austin grinned as he said, "For those of you who don't already know, this is J. W. Preacher III. He's one of the best lawyers around. With no offense intended to the women in his family, he got at least some of his smarts from his father, grandfather, and great-grandfather, each of whom helped me out with some important legal questions way back in the day. J.W. is here to answer any legal questions you may have."

Preacher's face stayed friendly, but he was all business now as he began, "Thanks, Sam. I'm delighted to meet some of you for the first time and to say hello to the rest of you again. Let's start by understanding who I represent. I represent this venture and not any of you individually. As far as I'm concerned, Sam is the voice for this venture, so I take my orders from him. Sam has tasked me with setting up the legal framework for this venture, including setting up the mechanisms for your making your claims for your holdings on Citadel. I didn't do any of this in a vacuum; Sam spent a lot of time talking with you to figure out what would work and what wouldn't work, then he and I spent a lot of time figuring out how to set up this venture with that feedback in mind."

Preacher moved around the room with a relaxed stride as he continued, "Is the approach we've created perfect? Hell, no. In fact, if I told you it was perfect, you should run from here as fast as possible, because I'd be giving you a load of that bullshit I was talking about a few moments ago. Although we've looked at the rules for establishing mining claims on Mars, for example, there's so much that has never been done before that we are largely in new legal territory. Please understand that no court on Earth or Mars is going to work out any disputes arising from this venture. I've set up a private form of dispute resolution for that purpose.

"Just because I'm representing the venture and not you individually doesn't mean that I won't talk with you about the structures we've set up. In fact, I'd be glad to talk with any of you to make sure you understand how everything works. This is important stuff, and the last thing I want is for you to be a part of this venture without having everything explained to you."

Brittel asked, "Aren't some of these restrictions illegal? I thought you couldn't base things on whether someone was married, for example."

Several people sighed at hearing Brittel trying to rehash the previous argument. Preacher merely smiled and said, "I'll leave it to others to continue the 'robust' discussion on the merits of certain of certain restrictions in place with the venture. As to the legal side of things, the government got out of the business of policing most relationships for signs of politically incorrect motives many years ago."

With a nod to Austin, Preacher continued, "You can thank Sam for having the courage as president to do what should have been done long before. However, it wouldn't really matter whether governments were still in the business of intruding into people's lives to look for politically incorrect activities. This is purely a private matter that isn't subject to the control of any government on Earth or elsewhere." Preacher looked back at Brittel directly as he said, "For that reason, if this venture wanted to limit the settlers to married people who only speak Swahili and are fans of the Cubs, it would have every right to do so. Therefore, the only reason to question these restrictions is on the basis of whether they make sense for the venture."

Brittel asked, "What happens if we don't like the way you've set something up with the venture, such as the scope of our land claims?"

Preacher responded, "The first thing I'd do is to make sure I've explained everything so that you're not forming opinions based on an inaccurate view of things. After I've had that conversation with you, if you still don't like something, you'll need to keep in mind an important fact. Not everyone is going to like everything about this venture. It is unworkable to have everything subject to change because someone doesn't like something about it. Everyone joins the venture under the same rules. If someone doesn't like those rules, then he is welcome to get off the bus and wait at the bus stop for someone else to develop a ship with warp drive that can get to Citadel. Since no one else has done it yet, you'd be in for a pretty long wait. Of course, even if someone else came up with that ship, you might not like that venture's rules either, so you can keep waiting at that bus stop as long as you want.

"One thing you all need to keep in mind, which I'll mention more than once as we talk over the next few weeks and months, is that we're deadly serious about the need to keep the activities of this venture private and confidential. For example, there's a lot of fancy technology that I don't understand that you're developing for this venture. That technology is not for you people to share with others. The easiest way for you to lose your stakes in Citadel is to forget this fact.

"Another point to make, although you didn't quite ask the question, is that this venture needs a decision maker, and Sam is that person. You know that Sam is smart about consulting with people before making decisions. However, sometimes there won't be the luxury of consultation, and someone will need to make a decision right away, whether in space or on Citadel. You've already decided that Sam is the right person for that role."

Preacher smiled as he continued, "Don't worry; we're not trying to set Sam up as a dictator. Eventually, if this venture works out, you'll form your own government, with the rules you think are right.

"This is something that no one has ever done before. Even the settlements on Mars and the Moon were established knowing that Earth was still there as a place to fall back to if necessary. No such luck this time. If things go wrong on Citadel, you'd better be prepared to deal with them there, because Earth is way too far away to help.

"If you want something with everything tied up neatly for you, then you should probably stay on Earth as I plan to do. I have been fortunate indeed to have been married for nearly fifty years to the mother of my six children and to have been blessed with over a dozen grandchildren, with more on the way. For my listening pleasure, I have the best collection of jazz music on the East Coast, which goes well with sipping from a glass of fine wine. It won't be many years before my oldest son, J.W. Preacher IV, takes over my law firm so that I can enjoy what I hope will be a long retirement. If you don't want to sit on your ass and enjoy fine wine and even finer jazz music, if you want to be pioneers, then be pioneers and take some risks! Hopefully the rewards will match those risks. Whatever happens, your lives will never be the same again."

Preacher stopped, grinned, and said, "I've probably spoken much too long already. I'll be glad to answer any individual questions you may have."

Lake smiled as she said, "Are you sure you're a lawyer, J.W.? You sound a lot like a coach reminding us why we're in this game."

Preacher smiled broadly and said, "All part of the job of being a 'counselor.' Seriously, you are embracing something other than playing it safe, which not many people have the courage to do. It is something that is larger than any of you as individuals, and I truly hope the Lord has a special blessing for all of you."

CHAPTER THREE

Pathfinder was poised at the edge of Earth's solar system, ready to take the first real steps toward a new world. Austin thought *Pathfinder* was a beautiful ship. He'd checked it out from stem to stern, both inside and via space walks, and knew it as well as anyone did. From the outside, one could see the twin warp-field generators, which turned out to be the most stable approach to creating a warp field for travel through space. While space was always at a premium on any ship, the bridge was large enough to accommodate a half-dozen people, including the ship's captain and the pilot. Virtually any system aboard the ship could be monitored from the bridge. She'd been checked and rechecked and was ready for the trip.

Austin mused that the same could be said about *Pathfinder's* captain. Although he wasn't an old man, Captain Ortiz had been in space for over twenty years, with experience as a captain for the last ten. The old joke was that he had ice water in his veins when it came to dealing with tough situations. He'd been training with his crew for months, and the confidence they had in each other radiated throughout the ship with a special aura. Austin had been around plenty of crews, both in space and planet-side, so he knew he was looking at a tight crew that worked together well.

Yabuno had been green with envy when Austin had told him that he wasn't going to Citadel as *Pathfinder's* engineer. "Damn it, Sam," he'd said, "there are plenty of people who could handle things here instead of me. You want the best engineer along on this trip."

Austin had had a bemused look on his face as he replied, "That sounds like something I said to someone once. Face it, Bret, you're just as irreplaceable as the technical guiding force within the project as you claim I am as its leader. Pick one of your people for the job." Yabuno walked away grumbling. He came back with a name, and Austin agreed that the woman would be able to handle any problems as well as anyone. Yabuno had to stifle some more grumbling when the candidate accepted the offer with great delight.

Austin knew that the captain needed to be seen by his crew as in charge, so Austin wasn't aboard *Pathfinder* as she ventured to the edge of the solar system. Austin had stayed aboard one of the ships that had accompanied *Pathfinder* as an escort to this point. He faced the display and exchanged some last words with the captain before departure.

"I don't mind saying, Captain, that I'm more than a little envious of you for being the first to take *Pathfinder* to another world. However, that envy is tempered by the fact that *Pathfinder* is in fine hands with an excellent crew and an exceptional leader for her captain."

Ortiz smiled with gratitude as he replied, "Thank you, Sam. I couldn't agree with you more as far as the quality and skill of this crew is concerned. I'm not bullshitting when I say it's a privilege to be the captain of this crew. I appreciate the trust you've placed in me, and I'll make sure you agree that it was warranted."

"Captain, we both know that one of the toughest things that you'll have to do as captain is determine at multiple steps whether the conditions justify continuing with the mission. The thing none of us can do from here is to understand fully what you'll encounter once you reach the Citadel system. I want you to remember that if you determine, in your best judgment, that the risks with proceeding would present an unreasonable danger to the lives of your crew, you have every right to turn around and return to our solar system, with no one questioning that judgment. That's true even if you have to make that decision based on incomplete or unreliable information."

Austin continued, "I've commanded enough missions to know not to second-guess the judgment of a leader like you. I want to make sure you know that as well. The objective is to learn what we can, without placing the safety of the crew at unnecessary risk. *You're* the one who will decide what is unnecessary."

Ortiz smiled as he replied, "I appreciate the sentiments, Sam. Some people would either expect me to be gutless or reckless. I intend to be neither. I don't intend to throw away the lives of my crew, and I hope to God that the risks will allow us to check out the system thoroughly."

Austin smiled and said, "Good luck and Godspeed, Captain Ortiz."

"Thanks, Sam. See you in a couple of years." The image on the display terminated.

Austin received word that *Pathfinder* was ready to begin her journey. The display had gone back to a long picture of the ship as she got into position for the trip. The countdown was called out, and everyone waited to see the proof of her departure. The countdown ran to zero, and *Pathfinder* was gone, with only a small distortion that lasted a few moments to show that she'd been there at all. Austin prayed that they hadn't seen the last of the proud ship or her crew.

CHAPTER FOUR

E ven without any means of communication between *Pathfinder* and Earth, *Pathfinder* had never been out of anyone's thoughts over the past two years. It was understood that there was no reason to be concerned over any failure to return by a specific date, since no one could be sure what the ship's captain and crew would have to investigate while there.

As Yabuno had reminded Austin, there was still a lot of work that could be done in *Pathfinder's* absence. The work of reviewing and selecting the settlers who would join *Pathfinder* and the new transports on the first journey continued.

Austin sighed over the fact that some people had trouble understanding that he meant what he said about the selection of settlers. He thought back to a recent conversation he'd had with an outside group dedicated to deep-space exploration. Afterward, a US Senator who thought of herself as being very important intruded on his time as he was getting ready to leave.

"Senator," Austin began, "we are looking to select the best settlers possible, which means we aren't going to bring some people along for the ride who might not work out."

"I'm sure you are, Sam, but sometimes the best person is someone who can bring something extra to the table, such as the support your project might need in Congress, for example."

Austin kept his smile civil as he replied, "First of all, we don't need anything from Congress, as the Citadel Group functions outside of any government jurisdiction and doesn't need anyone's blessing to do what we are doing. Even if it were otherwise, if we want this project to succeed, there can't be any special considerations for a candidate that are based on wealth, prestige, political connections, or some other factors having nothing to do with being qualified."

The senator's eyes seemed to glaze over slightly as Austin explained the rules, as if she didn't need to worry about them. She said, "I have the perfect candidate for you. He's so outstanding that I know you'll want to send him to the head of the line."

I wonder how many other people think he's anything more than just mediocre? Austin mused to himself as he said, "Senator, we have a strict policy that there are no favorites when it comes to being considered. If you know someone that would be a good candidate, please tell him to apply in the usual manner and go through the screening process."

The senator frowned as she said, "What about members of your Citadel Group? I understand they're taking up all of the available openings."

"That isn't the way it works. The only special favor that the Citadel Group team members receive is to go to the front of the list of people to be considered. I consider this to be reasonable in view of the commitment that these people are already making toward the success of the project. However, that's as far as it goes. If they qualify, then they'd be selected over others. If they don't qualify, then they won't go."

Yabuno was in a meeting with Austin and others discussing the preliminary work on the transports. Yabuno stood in front of a large screen, weaving images into and out of his comments. "We've continued with the preliminary work on the transports, as many of the systems differ from those aboard *Pathfinder* and need to be tested separately. We're getting close to having the first prototype ready for trial runs, much as we did with *Pathfinder*. We sure as hell don't want to go forward without knowing what *Pathfinder* has to report." Yabuno stiffened as a new image showed up on his screen without any warning. There was only one message that could come through without his having pulled it up first.

A new voice said, "*Pathfinder* has returned! Right now, she's at the edge of our solar system. The rest of the trip to the inner solar system will take place under conventional propulsion." The room burst into applause, with everyone having something to say all at once.

Yabuno beamed with excitement and spoke to the image, "That's great news, Casey. We know that using the warp-field generators within the solar system might lead

to some unpleasant results, especially since those generators have had two years of hard work. Can you patch in
any new images of *Pathfinder?*"

A quick movement from Yabuno shoved everything
else on the screen aside, as the new images came into view.

Brittel exclaimed, "It looks just the way it did when
it left!"

Austin had a worried look on his face as he said, "Take
another look, Greg. I see some serious wear on the ship's
exterior. *Pathfinder* has spent much of its time letting
space time warp past it, instead of moving by itself in normal space, so it isn't clear why the wear is so extensive."

Yabuno's look was equally serious as he ventured, "I
wonder how much of it is from radiation?"

Lake took a call on her link. Moments later, her face
drained of color. As everyone in the room fell silent, she
shed a tear and said, "Not everyone came back. The captain and two of the crew are dead. The first officer is in
charge, and they're telling me he looks much older than
he did two years ago."

The mood was somber as the team pieced together
the information from the trip.

Once again, Yabuno stood before the screen,
although his movements seemed less casual than before.
He'd replaced the recent image of *Pathfinder* with one
showing the scout ship within the protection of their
space yard. Everyone moving around the ship was wearing the kind of suits used for serious radiation incidents.

"While we know there's actually a lot of good news
from *Pathfinder's* voyage, we owe it to everyone to focus

first on why three people are dead," he said. "Captain Ortiz's log entries plus the ship's sensors and interviews with the survivors show that the radiation fields were even nastier than anticipated. There was no straight path to Citadel that was safe. They had to spend a couple of months using remote probes and the ship's sensors to map out possible safe paths to Citadel. These routes involved having to make and log precise course changes from time to time. It was painstaking work, made even more difficult by the fact that the radiation made it difficult to interpret the sensor readings.

"They were faced with a difficult choice once they'd completed their readings. They could either trust that they had gotten it right and follow the trail to Citadel that their readings said was there, or they could decide to abandon the effort and return home. The captain and crew agreed together that they hadn't come that far only to turn around without having learned much about the Citadel system. I'll stress what we already know, which is that the rules under which they were operating gave them full discretion to turn around and come back if they believed that the radiation posed too great a risk, with no questions asked.

"We know that the captain and the pilot were on the bridge and the rest of the crew remained within areas that are more heavily shielded. That decision was lethal for the captain and pilot but saved the lives of the rest of the crew, at least for the near term. They had almost gotten the path right, but the readings had been screwed up by the radiation. Their trip to Citadel gave them the final data they needed to figure out the correct path.

Unfortunately, by the time *Pathfinder* reached Citadel, the captain and pilot were already dying."

"Why can't we just add more shielding to the new ships so that we don't have to worry about the radiation?" Brittel asked.

Yabuno shrank the image of Pathfinder and brought up an image of a transport as he replied, "You can see the difference in size. The new ships are *big*, Greg. It isn't practical to try to place huge amounts of shielding on them. Also, it wouldn't matter anyway. While we're trying to improve the next generation of shielding, there isn't really any shielding that we have today that works for very long against that radiation. The rest of the crew would have been dead after another thirty minutes in the radiation field, even staying within the more heavily shielded areas of *Pathfinder*. The medical staff is still checking them out to understand how badly their health has been compromised from the exposure they received. The good news is that we have the data on a safe path to Citadel. Without it, there would be no point in going back there."

Lake asked, "How did they get back here, if the ship was already contaminated?"

"We built a lot of redundancy into *Pathfinder*, Liz," Yabuno replied. "Although they knew they couldn't stay on the bridge, they were able to reroute its functions to engineering. It was a lot more cramped than on the bridge, but at least they were still alive. What's even more amazing is that they went to the planet and did some scouting before returning. They could have turned around after confirming that they'd figured out the safe path, and people would have been happy."

"Can *Pathfinder* even be used again?"

"Yes, she'll have a complete overhaul that'll include extensive decontamination, plus replacement of certain critical components and modules that can't be decontaminated properly. Take a look." Yabuno tapped several spots on the *Pathfinder* image to show what was needed. He continued, "Although Greg's suggestion about extra shielding isn't practical for the new ships, it's a different situation with *Pathfinder*, which is much smaller. In fact, we don't really have any choice. Many of the systems and sensors were degraded substantially as a result of their exposure to the environment in the Citadel system, and *Pathfinder* in particular needs to be able to be used for other tasks there. Therefore, we'll work in more shielding for the bridge and other critical areas. It helps that we know a lot more about the radiation that they encountered, so that we'll do a better job of ruggedizing *Pathfinder*. We'll also upgrade engineering to provide for better control over the ship's functions in the event that the bridge can't be used. When we're done with overhauling *Pathfinder*, she'll be a hell of a lot tougher than she was originally."

"That accounts for two of the dead," Austin said. "What happened to the other one?"

Yabuno brought up an image of an animal that was unlike anything seen on Earth as he said, "He was attacked by one of the more ferocious animals on the planet. In the food chain, we'd consider them to be somewhat akin to the large cats on Earth, although these animals look a lot different from a lion or tiger. They're incredibly fast and expert at hiding until prey comes along. Our guy never had a chance to do anything except blink. The other crew members killed the animal with their weapons. As you can see, the markings on the animal look something like the spots on a cheetah. Since this animal likes to be sneaky and catch its prey off guard, they called it a 'cheater.'"

Austin's face showed grim amusement as he looked around the room and said, "I guess this will remind people why it's mandatory that they be armed. Although we've already screened everyone on the issue, we'd better go back to them to make sure they understand what can happen if they don't take it seriously. If they want to die quickly, they can just walk around like tourists and the fauna will take care of the rest. Anyone who doesn't come to terms with these facts can stay home."

CHAPTER FIVE

Yabuno and Austin were having a sometimes heated private follow-up on the report about *Pathfinder*.

"Don't take this all on you, Sam," Yabuno said. "Captain Ortiz knew what he was doing, and there isn't anything you could have done differently to have turned things around."

Austin's blue eyes were darker as he said, "Are you sure, Bret? My gut keeps telling me that something different could have been done to get better data on the radiation levels, although I can't put my finger on what it might be."

"We've all put our heads together on this one. Ortiz did everything that could have been done and is dead anyway. Shit happens, and you, of all people, know it. What you think is your gut telling you that you could've done something different is really the guilt you feel over not having been the one to die instead of Ortiz."

"You're probably right, and I even understand it intellectually. However, emotionally, I can't help thinking, *Damn it, I should've been there!*"

"Sam, if you'd been there, you'd be dead now and so would the Citadel project. Without you as the public face and heart of this project, we'll never get to Citadel. If it helps, I don't feel any better about the fact that my engineer's health is probably shot to hell, assuming that she even has a future beyond a few months. I know that she was a volunteer, but I selected her and she'll never be the same. While I understand your reaction and respect the hell out of the humanity in you that it shows, if you're going to keep tearing yourself apart over what happened, you need to ask yourself if you're tough enough to be the leader of the settlers. If you're not, then stay the hell home and let someone else do it!" Yabuno got up to leave, and his voice softened as he said, "I happen to believe that Sam Austin is tough enough for just about anything. I hope he does, too." Austin was silent as Yabuno's footsteps faded away.

Liz Lake greeted the news of *Pathfinder's* return with mixed emotions. On the one hand, it was incredible to have confirmation that their technology had been validated and that there was a real world out there to be explored and settled. They would learn from what had worked and what hadn't worked and incorporate that knowledge into the new ships that would take the settlers to Citadel.

On the other hand, Lake knew that her fiancé wouldn't be going with her to Citadel. She thought back on the conversation they had had the previous evening.

"All of the information we have so far from *Pathfinder* shows that settlements are possible, John. Citadel is by no means a 'tame' world, but people who are willing to make a commitment to the place have a good chance of building something amazing. We can build our own world and make our own rules." Lake looked through a window with a smile as she said, "Of course, we won't be able to take a place like this with us. However, the pictures from Citadel are at least as beautiful as the views around here."

"We'd have to give up almost everything we know in order to go to Citadel, Liz," John said.

"Yes and no," Lake replied. "It's true that at first Citadel will have a rural feel to it. There won't be any cities or related infrastructure in place that we take for granted here. However, Citadel wouldn't look like an early nineteenth-century settlement in North America, with the women in long skirts and tending fires in log huts with no windows. Although space will be limited, we'll take along a lot of technology that would amaze the folks from three hundred years ago."

"I don't know if I even understand that place, Liz."

Lake turned to him and asked, "What's wrong, John?"

"I know what I have *here*, Liz. I have a good life, with lots of friends. Going to Citadel would mean giving those things up. Although there'd be some twenty-second century technology present, Citadel wouldn't be a twenty-second century place. I wouldn't know what my life would be like in five years, let alone ten or fifteen years. No matter how you want to describe it, it would be a life filled with a lot more hardships than we have now. Three people died there. Others may die during the trip. More will die once we get there, since we'll be oblivious to almost everything that happens on that planet and the learning curve will be pretty steep. I don't like the notion of dying on a world that I don't know for reasons I don't really understand.

"The other thing I don't have any more is *you*, Liz. It's been terrific to see you so engaged and even energized by this project. The problem is that months ago you became someone else, and I didn't have the courage to face up to it. We've lost *us*."

Lake placed her arm on her fiancé's shoulder and said, "John, we still have time to find *us* again. I can try find a way to step back and not be so consumed by the project. However, one thing that won't change is that I'm going to Citadel. I *need* to go to Citadel. The question is whether you want to go to Citadel, assuming that everything were fine between us again. If you do, then we can work out everything else. If Citadel isn't the future that you have in mind for yourself, for us, then I'm not sure where we go from here."

"*I'm* sure, Liz," John said gently as he removed her hand from his shoulder. "There's no place for us anymore. I've already packed my things. I love you and truly hope you find what you want with Citadel, even though I won't be there to share it with you when you find it. Good-bye." He kissed her on the cheek. In a moment, he was out the door and gone forever from her life.

As she thought back on the previous night, she realized that she'd been unfair to John by not making sure a long time ago that going to Citadel was really something that he wanted as much as she did. If she'd acted sooner, she would have realized that things had actually been over for a long time.

In addition to how she felt about the loss of her relationship, her life was now screwed. Instead of being married within a couple of months as she had expected, she was now facing the strong likelihood that she wouldn't be allowed to go to Citadel. Being married was a key requirement, and she understood why it was in place. She'd still be on the team to get the project completed if she wanted, although she wasn't sure how she felt about it at the moment.

She knew she'd be spending that evening with a close girlfriend having a good cry while finishing off a bottle of wine. She just hoped that her friends wouldn't try to set her up with someone new; it would be pretty damned hard at this point to find someone who would be of interest for the long term. It would be even more unlikely to find someone who was also truly interested in Citadel the way she was.

After having her cry, she decided to stay with the project. She was still part of the most exciting thing she was likely to experience in her life. Word got around about her breakup, of course. While there was a lot of sympathy, there was also a certain distance that started to open up from her colleagues who were going to Citadel. They would be sharing certain experiences and issues that she wouldn't. While she understood why it started to happen, it still sucked that it happened.

Late one afternoon, she and Brittel were the only ones still in the room after the team had been tackling an issue relating to the communications systems among the new ships. Brittel seemed to have something on his mind but was reluctant to talk about it. Lake was debating whether to ask him about it, but she wasn't sure she wanted to have that conversation. While she was having her internal debate, Brittel seemed to have made up his mind. He said, "By the way, Liz, I think it sucks that you can't go to Citadel because you aren't married. I haven't made much of a secret about my feelings about that rule."

Lake replied, "Thanks, Greg. Yes, it sucks that I can't go, but I supported the rationale for the rule when the team adopted it and intellectually I still do. The emotional side is harder to deal with, but I don't have any choice."

Brittel looked down for a moment as he said, "I can understand about not having any choice."

"What do you mean?"

"My wife and I have been drifting apart for a long time, and I don't see becoming pioneers as doing anything to improve the situation. In short, I want to go to Citadel, but I don't want to go with my wife."

"I'm sorry, Greg; I didn't know. If things are truly as bad as you say, how could you possibly be willing to go to Citadel? For that matter, how does your wife feel about it?"

A bittersweet tone crept into Brittel's voice as he replied, "My wife is willing to go to Citadel because it's something that I want to do and because she's young and looking for excitement. She doesn't have a clue about how far apart we've become."

"What are you going to do?"

The tone became downright bitter as he said, "If my wife and I get divorced, I can't go to Citadel. If we stay together and go to Citadel, I know that it'll be miserable and will get worse over time."

"Going to Citadel without the right partner is a terrible idea. It seems to me that you don't have any choice but to see if things can be worked out with her. Citadel should take a backseat to your marriage. If you can work things out, Citadel may still be an option."

A look came into Brittel's eyes that Lake didn't recognize. "There's another option."

Lake was confused and said, "I don't understand."

Brittel moved close to her and took her hands in his as he said, "I want to go to Citadel but not with my wife. You want to go to Citadel but aren't married. I've always been attracted to you, Liz. When I heard about your engagement ending, it seemed to me a sign that we should go to Citadel together, as a couple."

She was shocked at the suggestion and snatched her hands back as she replied, "You've already made a commitment with your wife to go to Citadel. She must have invested a lot of emotion into that decision to go. Doesn't that count for anything?"

Brittel was dismissive as he said, "I'm not going to pretend that there wouldn't be a huge impact on her emotionally. Does it count for anything? Perhaps, but ultimately, I have the right to change my mind about going to Citadel with her, regardless of her feelings and plans. You already said it wouldn't be a good idea to go to Citadel with someone where I'd be miserable, and you're right."

Brittel moved toward her again, although he didn't try to hold her hands as he said, "I want to be clear about what I have in mind, Liz. Even when we've disagreed on something relating to the project, you've always impressed the hell out of me. You're everything that I want in a partner for Citadel. I'm ready to leave my wife and go to Citadel with you as husband and wife."

She realized that she hadn't really known Brittel at all. She felt several emotions running through her at the same time, including sadness and revulsion. Unconsciously, she leaned away from him as she said, "Greg, marriage doesn't work that way for me. When I tell a man that I want to marry him, I have to be in love with him. I don't love you. I truly don't mean to be cruel, but I don't even feel a potential spark of interest that might be worth pursuing. Even when I feel some interest in a man, I have to believe that we would work well as a couple. Although it seems that I don't know you nearly as well as I thought I did, I know you well enough to know that we wouldn't be a good match. We have incompatible views in too many areas."

As the words of rejection registered, Brittel's face began to turn dark. He started to answer, but Lake cut him off with a gentle move of her hand as she continued, "Finally, I couldn't get past your willingness to set aside your wife and your marriage vows for what seem to be selfish reasons. If I were to agree to what you ask, I'd be just as selfish as you regarding your wife. I couldn't live with myself if I were to help treat another person that way." Her eyes were sad as she continued, "Also, I'd have to assume that if you did it once, you might do it again somewhere down the road if you decided that I wasn't what you wanted after all."

Brittel was angry and having trouble coming up with words that wouldn't just repel Lake further. He blurted, "Liz, I think you're making a mistake, both about me and about your future. I'm not just proposing a business arrangement that enables us both to get to Citadel. I'm proposing a partnership that's emotional as well as economic."

Lake shook her head as she replied, "The answer is no, Greg. From what you've said, I'm not sure which of us would be more miserable. I'd be miserable having to stay on Earth, but you'd be miserable going to Citadel with someone that you don't want as your wife. I can still find a life here on Earth, but you're pretty much stuck once you get on the ship. I know what choice I'd make. You might want to think about your choices before it's too late. Good night."

After Lake left, Brittel picked up a paperweight from a desk and threw it against a wall, sending glass fragments flying everywhere. He was in a foul mood. He'd thought that Lake would see reason, but she was too stubborn to see that her ethics and a stupid rule would doom her to staying on Earth. He hadn't been lying about his attraction to her. He wanted very much to make her body belong to him.

He didn't worry much about whether she would tell his wife about their conversation. He could either deny that it ever took place or turn it around so that it was Lake who asked him to leave his wife and go to Citadel with her. He'd kept his wife in the dark about his feelings, so she wouldn't have any reason to believe Lake. He realized that he had no choice but to stay with his wife for now and see what options might show up down the road. He consoled himself over the fact that he would continue to have sex while Lake only had herself.

CHAPTER SIX

The prototype trials were over and construction of the new ships was well underway. Austin had collected the team back at his home to go over the progress of the project and then to have some fun before everyone became consumed by the final push to launch the ships. Lake was giving an update on the people who had been selected as settlers. The huge screen had various images of couples, some familiar and some not.

"We'll be starting the intensive portion of the orientation and training within a couple of months. Since the ships should be ready to go in eight months, that should be enough time for everyone to be ready. We'll continue with training during the flights themselves." She nodded at some of the familiar faces on the screen with a smile as she continued, "This means that for some of you in this room, you'll need to start delegating your work to others on your teams to handle, if you haven't started already. Soon, you'll be in training to learn how to be settlers, so that won't leave much time for a day job."

She smiled wryly as she said, "While having fun is a good thing, make sure your birth control is working, because pregnant women aren't allowed on the ships, regardless of the due date. That also means that women can't get pregnant during the trip. We won't take any chances on the impact on a fetus of warp drive or a sustained space flight. We're still talking about a microgravity environment, remember." She nodded back at the screen and said quietly, "I don't need to post any pictures of what could go wrong." She smiled as she concluded, "What you do after landing on Citadel is your own business."

As Yabuno got up to give a technical briefing, Lake made it a point not to look at Brittel. Despite his proposal to her over a year ago, he was still with his wife. She felt sorry for the wife and wondered if she had done the right thing in not telling her about Brittel's overtures. Lake knew that she might be viewed as having sour grapes over her own situation. She realized that Brittel probably had counted on that fact in approaching her. Since she'd first thought about the issue, several couples hadn't been able to handle the decision on what to do about Citadel and had split up. She wondered if Brittel had approached any of those other women with the same proposal he had made to her. If he had and gotten an acceptance from any of those women, people would know about it soon enough, once couples and larger groups started with the intensive training. She shivered slightly in revulsion over the thought.

The meeting had ended, and the people had gone their separate ways. Most were going to follow up with their teams and then have some fun while they could. As Lake was preparing to contact some of her team, Austin approached her and said, "Liz, can I have a moment of your time?"

"Sure, Sam. What's up?"

"I need a partner for the settler training."

Lake was surprised and asked, "Why, Sam? As the leader of the community, you aren't expected to be a settler."

"I never planned on playing it safe and being on Citadel without getting my hands just as dirty as everyone else's."

"Sam, there's a reason why you were president of the United States for over forty years. You showed outstanding leadership during some extremely tough times. The people on Citadel will need that leadership. No one thinks you need to spend your time as a regular settler when you have so much to offer as their leader."

Austin's blue eyes were intense as he said, "To be blunt, I'm not going to Citadel because I want to be the leader, Liz. I view being the leader as part of the price I have to pay to get the project off the ground. I need to make the commitment of being a settler, because I plan on making Citadel as much my home as it is for anyone else over there. While it'll be different without having someone with me, I want to earn my land grants the same way as everyone else and live in a house that I build on my land." Austin grinned as he said, "I'm not so pure as to reject the extra land grants that I'll receive as the leader. I'll probably earn those grants several times over!"

Lake shook her head slightly as she replied, "I don't have anyone to suggest as a training partner. All of the couples will need to stay together for their training. As we were discussing a while ago, it's been a surprise to find that all of the people filling the other positions have spouses that will be joining them. We really thought there would be some unattached people on this trip. Turns out you're the only one."

"What about *your* being my partner?"

Lake felt an emotional twinge as she said, "Sam, I'm not going to Citadel, remember? Unlike the members of the team that are going, there won't be any handoff of my responsibilities to someone else. I can't oversee the training if I'm acting as a training partner."

Austin persisted, "Don't you have members of your team who could take over for you if necessary?"

"Of course I do; we all do."

"What's the problem, then?"

Lake didn't like where Austin's persistence was taking her. The emotional twinge became a full-blown knife as she answered, "A long time ago, I came to terms with the fact that I'm not going to Citadel. I can handle the feelings that I know I'll have in overseeing the training for everyone else. I don't know if I can handle the feelings that I'd have if I were going through the training itself, only to stop and go back to my day job once the day for departure arrives." Lake wiped a tear from her eye as she turned to leave. "I'm sorry, Sam, I can't do it."

Although Lake had tried to bury herself in her work while at Austin's ranch, Austin had been adamant that she put the work aside and relax. She was delighted to find that Austin had a baby grand piano in an upstairs room. Like most of the rooms in Austin's home, the view outside the window was a beautiful combination of mountains, trees, clouds, and sky visited by wildlife in the air and on the ground.

The piano was tuned perfectly. Lake was a superb pianist and hadn't found much time lately to play. She lost herself in the joy of having hours to play without interruption. One day, after playing for an unknown amount of time, she was surprised to see Austin in the doorway holding two glasses of wine. He smiled as he said, "Your playing is so beautiful that I really regret interrupting, but the air outside is even fresher than inside the house. Why don't we finish this wine and then go out to a spot with a view that will take your mind off everything else? I even have a lunch in a pack."

"That's kind of you, Sam, but I enjoy playing the piano. It's been ages since I had the chance to play for more than a few minutes at a time. Besides, I probably wouldn't be much company anyway."

Austin brushed away her protests with a wry look as he said, "You need to get out of the house for a while. You don't have to talk with a crowd of people who are going to Citadel, if that's what's bothering you. The only one you'll have to talk to will be me."

Lake finally smiled and said, "All right. I suppose you know your own place well enough that we can get away from everyone else for a while."

Over the next few weeks, Lake learned more about the ranch than she had picked up from all of her previous trips combined. Although she'd known about plenty of spots where the scenery was beautiful, Austin showed her places she'd never dreamed existed, with their brilliant colors clashing with and complementing everything else at the same time. She also learned far more about Austin himself. He had let plenty of people see that he was very down-to-earth and willing to poke fun at himself. Most people didn't understand how restless he had become. He had talked about it while they were enjoying a remote area of the ranch.

"I've lived the better part of two lifetimes, Liz. A huge portion of that time has been in service to a country or an ideal, or both. I served in the navy for over a half century. At least *that* was planned. I sure as hell never planned on being president. I would never have even been vice president if my buddy Jack hadn't needed to resign the vice presidency because of his terminal cancer. Although I was well known because of my career in the navy, I didn't want to serve as vice president for the remainder of Jack's term. I even turned President Thomson down when he asked me to step in for Jack. It took Jack's arm-twisting to get me to say yes. That answer was with the understanding that I was done after Jack's term ended and wouldn't be on the ticket for another term. History then played a nasty trick on me when Thomson was assassinated not long after I became vice president. I didn't have much choice about it at that point; the country needed leadership, and I couldn't let the people down.

"While I like to feel that I've made a positive difference for the country and beyond, I also feel like I've seen so many things that we've gotten wrong that we'll probably never be able to get right on Earth. Going to Citadel is a chance to start over and try to get things right." Austin's face took on a rueful look as he continued, "I'm under no illusions that we'd get everything right on Citadel, of course. Any time that people get together to do something, there will be compromises that get in the way of doing the right thing. However, it's worth giving it a try to do better there, and I hope to live long enough to see if we were right."

Austin gestured back toward the house, which was shielded from view by the pristine setting of mountains, trees, and clouds, and said, "While I don't want to abandon this place forever, I need to put some distance between it and me for a while."

Lake realized that she was crying. Austin noticed and asked what was wrong. "I'm not sure this has been such a good idea, Sam. I now have another reason to be sad when the ships leave for Citadel. I'll miss you and think about you every day, even if it's years before I see you again."

Austin said, "One of the things that Suzie did for me was to insist that I live in the present instead of the past. Austin's eyes took on a more intense shade of blue as they focused on Lake's face. "Part of living in the present is being willing to take chances. If you stay behind when I leave for Citadel, I'll miss you as well. I want you to come with me instead."

Lake wiped a tear away as she said, "I appreciate your willingness to take pity on a girl who cries, but I can't go with you. It would always seem that I was doing whatever it took to get to Citadel, which isn't fair to you."

With a tender movement, Austin reached over and wiped away another tear. He replied, "Liz, you tend to be pretty hard on yourself. Even though the commitment to Citadel is to stay for ten years after we arrive, I plan on staying for at least twenty years. I might even stay longer. I want to make it my home and help get the settlement launched the right way. What I don't want to do is spend the next twenty years thinking about the woman I love staying behind on Earth instead of being with me and building a home, a life, and a family together. If that's what you want to do with your life as well, then there's nothing 'mercenary' about your coming with me. Why are you crying again?"

"Sam, I've been in love with you for a long time. I couldn't bring myself to do anything about it because it might screw up your plans for how to deal with going to Citadel. For that matter, I wasn't sure if *we* were seeing each other."

"I haven't been spending time with you just to admire the scenery, Liz," Austin said gently. "I've had similar feelings for you for quite some time." A wicked gleam appeared in his eyes as he smiled and said, "Of course, there's *another* type of scenery I'm sure I'd admire a lot."

The same gleam appeared in her eyes as she said, "The feeling's mutual, Sam. It's a good thing you brought a comfortable blanket along for this picnic, because I don't think I could wait to admire the scenery until we got back to the house."

Austin told everyone that he would be taking care of something for a couple of weeks and wouldn't be available for discussions during that time. He reminded everyone that while they were at his ranch, they should make sure their teams were handling things so that they could relax before things became impossibly busy. Liz had already withdrawn to herself a lot while at the ranch and seemed to have disappeared completely. She and her team had already put together the training and orientation that the settlers would receive. She asked several of her people to be prepared to provide the training and orientation to the settlers.

Finally, it was a week before the training and orientation was to begin and the team had reconvened at their offshore location. The time off had done them a lot of good, and everyone was in a good mood. When Liz got up to talk about the status of the training and orientation, people noted that she seemed to have a healthy glow to her skin, even though no one could remember seeing her outdoors around the ranch for a while.

She finished her update, framed by the huge screen and the images she'd brought up, saying, "I'd like to mention some changes on my team. Angie will be overseeing the training and orientation for the settlers instead of me. In fact, I'll be delegating my regular responsibilities over to her."

Several people looked around in confusion. Some even wondered if Liz was announcing that she was resigning from the project rather than deal with the departure of the settlers. There was more than a little shock and sadness, since everyone had thought that Liz had dealt with the situation very well.

"You're probably wondering what this means," Liz continued. "It means that I'll no longer be available to oversee that role from here." Her face suddenly burst into a smile with enough wattage to blind everyone as she said, "Don't look so sad. I'm not leaving the program. My name is now Liz Austin, and I'm going to Citadel as a settler with my husband, Sam!"

Although the silence in the room was exquisite, it only lasted for a couple of heartbeats before the meaning of the announcement caught up with everyone and loud cheers erupted throughout the room. The women mobbed and hugged Liz and Austin equally, many of them crying with joy. Austin's smile reached well beyond his blue eyes, throughout his face.

No one noticed the dark look in Brittel's eyes or the fact that he didn't offer congratulations to the new couple.

CHAPTER SEVEN

The training had been underway for a couple of months, and in view of Liz's changed status as a settler, Angie was giving an update. She was smiling as she brought up images of various couples and discussed their progress, saying, "I told you a couple of months ago that you'd learn to do things, such as set up your prefab housing, prepare the soil for farming, set up your communications systems, set up sanitation facilities, get your water supplies set up, etc. Most of you are doing reasonably well so far."

She nodded at Austin with a grin and said, "Some seem determined to be able to do practically anything needed to handle their own farming, mining, irrigation, manufacturing, and technology repair and development. Special thanks to Sam for working with others to figure out how to adapt the power supplies and electronics to specialized uses and holding workshops for everyone. The same thanks go to Liz for her multiple insights."

Liz smiled and thought she'd never thrived as much emotionally as she had over the past few months, what with the excitement from the departure that was drawing nearer, plus the training and the passion that she and Austin shared as husband and wife.

Angie continued on a more somber note, "A few couples have been having a lot of difficulty with the training, in part because of a lack of cohesiveness as a team. Since the objective is to make everyone successful, these couples will receive plenty of extra training."

Although keeping his face neutral, Brittel gritted his teeth over the fact that he and his wife were among those who needed extra training. Since he viewed himself as extremely intelligent and therefore capable of understanding just about anything, he assumed that the fault was with his wife, Louise. Not for the first time, he cursed the fact that Liz had turned him down. Liz was clearly smart enough to be a good partner for him. He also envied the obvious physical attraction that Austin and Liz had for each other. He assumed that Austin couldn't see past the physical attraction to understand that Liz was only interested in him for his ability to give her a place among the settlers.

Austin, Yabuno, and Brittel spent a lot of time with the rest of the technical team going over the progress of the ships. They had arranged for *Pathfinder* to set up a number of beacons and relay stations during its original trip to Citadel so that the settler ships would have an easier time of staying on course. It might even be possible to communicate with Earth from Citadel. Both Yabuno and Brittel played with the huge screen.

"To recap what we already know," Yabuno continued, "these beacons can help confirm a ship's location, which is especially important if a ship's warp field fails during a trip. They can also be used to help to recalibrate for any course corrections that might be needed.

"Another objective is to create mini–warp fields that can be used to transmit messages from one beacon to another," Brittel added. "They'd act like relay stations. If a ship is in trouble, then a message could be sent in either direction, or both. Of course, it would still take a while to get assistance to that ship, but our protocols require all ships to have extra supplies so that they can wait a long time for that assistance if needed. It isn't perfect, since it would still take a long time for messages to get to Earth or Citadel and then to get a ship out to provide assistance, but it's better than just writing those people off. This system couldn't be used as a taxi service for people, but messages don't need things, such as life support, food, room for people, infrastructure, etc."

"Where do we stand on the viability of this system?" Austin asked.

Brittel pulled up an image of the trail of beacons. "We've had some success in getting messages to travel between two beacons, although we haven't yet been able to get a beacon to relay a message further down the line," he replied, pushing away the rest of the beacons for emphasis. "In time, we hope to have that problem solved and have a pretty good system in place. Since we always assumed that there would be no ability to communicate with Earth except through messages passed back and forth between ships, this should be a nice bonus once it's up and running. We may even be able to keep refining the system, at least on the computers, while we're heading toward Citadel, even though we won't be able to benefit from it during this trip."

Austin turned to Yabuno and asked, "You've had some interesting insights into what might be possible as we improve upon this system, Bret."

Yabuno pointed to a familiar image as he replied, "We need large, complex warp-field generators for the large, complex ships that we've built. We will, over time, improve upon those field generators and be able to cover distances even faster than we can today. On the other hand, as Greg pointed out, messages don't require any of the things that make ships large and complex. Therefore, the rate of improvement of the speed for transmitting messages may be faster than for improving the speed of ships. We're not there yet, but we think there's a good chance we'll be able to send messages from Earth to Citadel faster than a ship can make the trip." He grinned and added, "Of course, it still won't be instantaneous communication the way you see in science fiction, but who knows what we might be able to do someday?"

Austin said, "Let's talk about the status of the ships."

Yabuno pulled up some real-time images and began, "The exteriors and infrastructure are basically done, although we'll be doing fine-tuning all the way until departure. The warp-field generators have been installed and should be powered up and ready for trials by next week. We think it'll take less time to get everything in flight shape than it did for *Pathfinder* because of what we've learned from *Pathfinder's* trip. This will give us a good chunk of time to get everything calibrated for a long trip. One of the key things we already knew before

Pathfinder is that for extended trips, the initial calibration of the warp-field generators is very important.

"That's just the beginning, though. *Pathfinder* reinforced the hell out of the notion that during the trip, the stresses build up and the field generators become unstable without recalibration. We nearly lost *Pathfinder* several times because of this problem." Yabuno pulled up an image as he said, "Take a look at where the generators were heading from a stress perspective. The only reason we were able to handle the issue before they became too unstable was because we had planned on monitoring them carefully throughout the trip anyway. Most other people wouldn't have been as careful and might have ended up in a lot of trouble. With what we learn about the system over time, we hope to be able to implement a continual recalibration capability."

Austin looked at the entire team and said, "This is great work, guys." He looked at Yabuno pointedly and said, "*This* time, I'm going to do some piloting. You never know when that skill might come in handy."

With a month to go, nearly all of the settlers were ready. Austin met with Liz, Angie, and the rest of their team as they reviewed the status of each of the settler couples. Angie smiled as she said, "You and Liz are testing out as fully qualified, which isn't a surprise. We've benefitted hugely from the suggestions from both of you about how people can tweak what they have to get more out of everything."

"What's the story on the other settlers, Angie?" Austin asked.

"Just about everyone is far enough along that we're confident that they'll be able to handle things on Citadel." Angie frowned as she brought up a familiar image. "The one couple we're concerned about is Greg and Louise. They don't seem to work well as a team. For some reason, Greg has a huge chip on his shoulder when it comes to anything that Louise does. He never stops to consider whether he might be the one with the problem. He seems to have a high opinion of himself and doesn't consider Louise to be his equal. When we test Louise separately, however, she's as smart as Greg and probably better at some of the tasks. Her problem at this point isn't so much a lack of skills as a lack of self-confidence. Greg rarely lets pass a chance to criticize something about her."

Austin studied the image for a moment before asking, "How do you want to address the situation?"

"We have regular feedback on skills assessments anyway. We have another one coming up tomorrow. I'll be a part of that meeting and let them know that they haven't brought their skills to the level needed to have a strong chance of success on Citadel. They've had this feedback before, but it hasn't sunk in. Although we've never sugarcoated the message, I'll have to be fairly brutal at this point, especially with Greg, and let him know that he needs to get his head out of his ass and start acting like a partner if he wants to go to Citadel. I know that we're counting on him to handle a number of issues relating to getting in place the settlement's communications network, but that has to take a backseat to the question of whether the two of them are prepared to survive on Citadel."

"I agree completely," Austin said. "While Greg's skills would be missed, we have enough redundancy in skills among the settlers that we can handle whatever he would have handled. As for as his leadership role for his team, Greg's number two from his team will be going. She's very sharp too and can step into the leader role if needed. In short, I won't support bending the rules for him, especially since that might jeopardize his and Louise's well-being." Austin turned to his wife and asked, "Liz, is there anything you want to add?"

Liz was torn over whether to let them know about Brittel's proposition to her, as it provided a potential explanation for Brittel's behavior. However, it had happened over a year ago and might have only come up because of a rough patch in his marriage. After she had turned him down, he had stayed with his wife. They had gone through the same extensive counseling that the other couples had and had stayed in the program. Until the training had begun, she had had no reason to believe that Brittel and his wife were any less suited for the trip than anyone else. Even now, it could just be that they weren't well suited as a team, with Brittel's ego being the prime reason.

Ultimately, she knew how important going to Citadel was to her and she wasn't ready to be the reason why Brittel wouldn't be cleared to go. Fortunately, there were more impartial people who should be making that call anyway. She said, "I think Angie knows what she's doing and we should listen to her."

Angie's words to Brittel had indeed been as brutal as promised. She didn't take bullshit from anyone and didn't let Brittel try to weasel his way out of accepting responsibility for his marital team's lack of readiness. She let him know that he had a couple of weeks to turn his attitude around or he wouldn't be going to Citadel. When Brittel tried to get her to back down because of his value to the project, she just smiled, pulled out her pocket link, and started to connect to Austin's link. Brittel had no choice but to back down. He wasn't happy that this conversation had taken place in front of Louise, but it was clear that Angie wanted Louise to understand how the team saw the situation.

Overnight, Brittel made a show of turning around his attitude and working with Louise as a team. To his surprise, they did well enough that Angie let them know a couple of weeks later that he and Louise would, indeed, be going to Citadel. Angie strongly advised them to continue to work on their teamwork during the flight, since there wouldn't be time for more training once they reached Citadel. At that point, they had to be ready or they'd fail.

While Brittel was all smiles on the outside, he decided that the time had come to hedge his bets.

CHAPTER EIGHT

Austin and Liz had made a quick trip to *Rancho La Mirada de Oro*, which was the full name of his ranch, to say good-bye to the place for what might be decades. It might even be forever, depending on what happened after they boarded their ship.

They were surprised and delighted to find that Austin's family was waiting for them. His sons and daughters were there, along with plenty of grandkids and great-grandkids. Many of the young children called her "Grandma Liz," which she found didn't make her feel old at all.

Austin's oldest daughter, Ellen, invited them to eat, saying, "The family has a huge spread set up, with some of Dad's favorites, such as juicy steaks topped with roasted broccoli, cauliflower, and red potatoes. The men have great pride in their preparation and barbecuing skills and insist the women spend some time with you while they take care of cleaning up. The women won't say no to that!" After plenty of chuckles, Ellen continued, "Please join us up at the lake after we've eaten, Liz. Dad, you can stay here with the other men until we call for you!"

It wasn't long before Liz found herself at a part of the lake she hadn't visited before. Although a few birds of prey circled high overhead in their lazy patterns, practically touching the clouds, the place was secluded and gave the women a chance to swim and chat in plenty of privacy. Liz wondered about the reason for the privacy. She doubted it was because none of them was wearing anything while swimming in the clear, cold water or after they'd climbed out of the water onto the shore, entranced by the sparkling flickers of sunlight that danced on the water's surface.

As they dried off and relaxed on soft towels while enjoying the warm rays from the sun, Liz looked around and noticed that it seemed to be a requirement that the Austin women were in good physical shape as well as beautiful. Liz couldn't help but admire the fact that Ellen looked to be in her forties, even though she had to be in her sixties at least. A lot of Ellen's appearance was due to the fact that her face was practically unlined. Her hair also had no gray in it. Liz was fairly certain that neither feature was artificial.

"You're probably wondering why we picked such a secluded part of the lake to swim, Liz," Ellen began with a smile. "You've already figured out that we aren't shy about being naked while enjoying a swim, especially where everyone around is family."

Liz smiled back as she said, "I guess I'm the same way when it comes to swimming, so I don't think you're worried about my modesty either."

Ellen continued, "The privacy we have in mind is so we can talk without others interrupting, even if it is with the best of intentions. I mentioned a moment ago how we are around family. I want you to know that you are a part of our family now, and you're a most welcome part at that."

Liz smiled and said, "I appreciate it, Ellen. The only concept I've had of a family was my parents, who've been gone a long time because of a traffic accident. I've never known what it was like to have a large bunch of people that I could call "family." Her eyes became melancholy as she continued, "It can't be easy for you to see your dad with someone else after all the years he and your mom were together, especially since I'm young enough to be your daughter."

Ellen chuckled as she said, "You're being kind, Liz, since I have granddaughters that aren't much younger than you. In one sense, it's always hard when you lose a parent. My mom, Suzie, was just as much the heart and soul of our family as is my dad. The two of them had an amazing bond that still serves as an inspiration for me. I could do a lot worse than to ask myself how either of them would handle a difficult situation." Liz noticed that several of the women nodded in agreement.

"However, the difference is that we've grown up knowing that our dad would outlive our mom. It took quite a long time for the age difference to be especially noticeable, since my mom had amazing 'youth' genes of her own." Ellen gestured toward her hair. "You've probably noticed that I don't have any gray in my hair. While some of it may be due to whatever our dad has passed down to us from his own unique biochemistry, my mom didn't have any gray hair when she was the age I am now. She always was a believer in staying active through exercise and other activities, and it helped keep her going long past when most other people would have just decided to slow down and 'retire.'

"She was also a believer in the notion that people are given a certain time in this world and then it's time to move on. It might have been possible to keep her going a few years longer when she was in extreme old age, but she wouldn't agree to it. She knew that no one is destined to be with my dad forever, and she felt blessed to have had the time she did have. Part of her understood that my dad needed to be able to let go when the time came, and if she tried to cling to something that was only an imitation of life, it wouldn't be fair to my dad."

Ellen's eyes sparkled as she said, "She knew that one day my dad would need to find another young, intelligent, and beautiful woman with whom he could fall in love and share each other's body, soul, and a new life together. I'm delighted for my dad's sake that you're that woman. There's a light that's come back into his eyes that hasn't been there since my mom died. Thank you so much for bringing that light back."

Liz realized that she was on the verge of tears, although she was feeling happy, not sad. "It's funny how things work out. If it hadn't been for the trip to Citadel, we would never have gotten together."

"Then the trip to Citadel is truly a blessing as far as I'm concerned."

Liz spoke more quietly. "You might not think so, Ellen, if you consider that we may not be back here for quite a long time. I'm not being melodramatic in saying that we may even die on another planet and never see anyone here again."

Ellen's smile grew a little sadder as she said, "I've understood that one day my dad would have to take that step, Liz. His life-span is far too unusual for him to be happy staying on this planet forever. I didn't know if it would happen during my lifetime, but I knew it would happen. When I heard that at one point he would be going to Citadel alone, I was sad that it would happen that way. While my dad is perfectly capable of committing himself to such a great project without really worrying about himself, something like that should be shared with a partner, a lover."

A mischievous look danced around the eyes of one of Ellen's daughters as she looked at Liz and asked, "It isn't any of my business, of course, but I wonder if you became lovers while you were here, at the ranch? It would seem so much like an Austin to do something like that."

If Liz had been able to blush, that question, asked while she was stark naked, would have done it. She thought about that first time, looked down, and realized that she didn't have to blush for her body to give her away. She realized from the smiles from the others that they'd seen the same signs.

Ellen's daughter smiled and said, "What did I tell you, Mom? There's something about this place that brings people together. Please don't think that we're putting you on the spot, Liz. Many of us have made love here to the men that we would marry. My husband and I found an equally secluded spot and said we loved each other." The daughter glanced over at Ellen with a sly look and continued, "I've never shared this with my mom, but we made the most passionate love imaginable. There's just something about this place that seems to elevate the senses."

Ellen returned the look with a wry one and said, "Of course we knew what was going to happen before you did, dear. Your husband is a fine man, and the two of you were going to start your lives together." Ellen's eyes took on a sly look of their own as she said, "Your father and I conceived you during one of our own lovemaking sessions out here, so I understand completely how you feel about the place. In fact, your father and I sometimes still find a moment here where we do what we first did many years ago."

With a broad smile, the daughter expressed mock horror at hearing about her mother's sex life. Others shared similar stories about their experiences with their men. Liz smiled as she thought about the fact that she was introduced by the women into the family with a conversation about the significance of the place to their sex lives. In view of what she and Sam had shared there, she couldn't help but be glad for the place. The giggles became louder as each woman told her own story. Pretty soon, the shrieks of laughter could be heard from across the lake. The only ones there to hear them were some squirrels, who stopped to listen for a moment. They didn't understand what was so funny and went about doing something more important, like searching for nuts.

In time, the rest of the family got together for a swim, although the men gave up trying to understand why some of the women kept giggling. Austin had a pretty good idea and knew he was right when he saw Liz joining in with the giggling, especially when she and Ellen looked at each other.

Austin smiled to himself as he thought of the times that he and Suzie had been aware of what was happening around the place when the kids and grandkids had thought no one else knew. Even Ellen probably thought her parents weren't aware of Ellen's passionate interludes around the place with the man who would become her husband. He knew that Ellen, as the oldest daughter, was now the one who would pass on those stories to the later generations.

Once they had all spent time welcoming Liz into the family, they respected the need for the new couple to have some privacy. The family packed up everything and left to rejoin their lives elsewhere, after everyone had exchanged multiple hugs.

After everyone had departed, the couple stood in the house in front of the great window. Austin looked around and said, "I'm not really used to all of this quiet." He took ahold of Liz's hand and said, "We don't have anything in particular to worry about right now, so let's wander around the place."

As the day turned to evening, they returned to the great room and watched the sun set. Liz gasped, "It's like an explosion of pinks, oranges, yellows, grays, purples, and other shades that don't even names." She reached out to Austin, saying, "I want to make love in this light."

They stayed in each other's arms for a long time, not moving in the fading light, before venturing upstairs to the master bedroom. They enjoyed some wine and then tasted each other's lips and made love again.

Austin woke up the next morning to find golden rays drifting in through the window and playing across Liz's breasts, moving gently as she breathed deeply in sleep. She woke up, saw his gaze, and smiled. She pulled his hands to her breasts and invited him to caress her. He drew in closer, and they celebrated the new morning.

Finally, they decided they were hungry and Austin went downstairs to make breakfast. Liz lay back in bed, enjoying the afterglow from their time together. Soon, her husband came back into the room with trays with dishes on them filled with things that smelled delicious.

Liz said, "I don't remember bringing these things with us."

Austin grinned and said, "The family put this together for us before they left yesterday. For some reason, they thought we might like to have breakfast in bed."

They found that they had hearty appetites. As they finished, Austin said, "We'll take a last look around the place before we head out tonight. Now that we're alone, I need to check out some systems that only I have control over. Also, I want to fix the place in my mind one last time. We don't know what the future holds for us as far as getting back here."

Liz smiled and said, "I don't care what the future holds for us as long as we're together."

Austin smiled back and said, "I'd like to get in one last swim at the lake while we're here."

Liz had a mischievous look in her eye as she said, "Sam, if you want to get me naked, you don't have to go all the way to the lake. If you haven't noticed, I'm already naked."

Austin grinned back and said, "I *have* noticed. In fact, I'd like to do something about it right about now. But I want to get you naked at the lake as well!"

Liz smiled as she lay back in bed, brushed her dark hair out of her eyes, and said, "First things, first!"

CHAPTER NINE

L iz and Austin were aboard the ship that would take them to another world. As she looked around, she commented, "It feels like there's a noise that's competing with the normal sounds aboard this ship as it's getting ready to leave the solar system. It isn't quite something that people can hear. Maybe it's the excitement from the moment that's rippling through the ships."

Austin looked back at her and smiled as he said, "I can see that excitement in everyone's faces. Speaking of faces, I'm pretty damned pleased to hear that Bret and his wife, Donna, have been assigned to this ship. I never expected to be that lucky, considering that the team members who have vital skills have been spread among the ships to ensure that the settlement can survive even if some of the ships don't make it." Austin noticed a twinkle in Liz's eye and responded, "I didn't have anything to do with it."

They made their way to the bridge, where Austin, true to his word, took his place behind the controls as the ship's pilot. He grinned and said, "Here we are, everyone lined up behind *Pathfinder*, in a long wagon train traveling across a different kind of prairie." He paused to make another check of the controls as they continued. "We won't use the warp-field generators until we're clear of all of the giant planets in the system. The gravity distortions caused by those planets could wreak hell with the ship's warp fields and our plans of staying on course."

They made their farewells to each of the giant planets in turn and then were far enough out to be able to start their journey for real. Liz said, "I understand that to ensure that we won't be in each other's way, our departure times will be staggered in thirty-minute intervals, with *Pathfinder* leading the way. We'll also need to be spread out instead of bunched together closely. I was hoping that we'd have a better view of each ship's departure."

Austin shook his head as he said, "The distances involved mean that every ship except the one right ahead of us will leave without our being able to see much of anything. Even that one will probably be something of a letdown. You'll see what I mean when *Pathfinder* heads out. Her countdown is almost complete."

They followed the countdown and sensed, rather than saw, *Pathfinder's* departure. Liz was disappointed, asking, "That's all we'll see?" Austin nodded and replied, "There won't be much more to see when the next ship leaves, either." In thirty minutes, the first of the settler ships commenced its journey but was still too far away for Liz to have much of a sense of its departure.

Because their ship was the fourth one in line, they had a great spot to watch the next ship commence its warp flight. After following the countdown to zero, they were a little disappointed to note a mild distortion and then nothing, except that the ship was no longer visible. Austin turned to Liz and said, "Yes, that's all there is."

They were next. Austin and the other crew members had already spent plenty of time going over their checklists to make sure everything was ready, so there was little to do while they waited. Once they confirmed that everything was ready, Austin would release the controls so that the automatic systems would take over, controlled from engineering. There was no way that human minds and reflexes could operate everything in real time that was needed for the warp-field generators to come to life and place them in their special bubble. Finally, the captain made an announcement to the passengers that they were ready to begin their journey to a world around another star. As the countdown reached zero, the warp-field generators were engaged and the screen went blank.

They'd been underway for a short time. The image from the screen on the bridge was mostly dark, with an occasional ripple being the only reminder that they were doing something unique. Liz pointed at the screen and asked, "Is that all we're going to see out there for the next year? I know we won't see anything like images of stars streaking past us, but I'd hoped there be more to it than that!"

Austin grinned and said, "Yeah, I remember movies and TV shows back in the day that showed those streaks of light. Sometimes, they had nice clear images of other spaceships visible while using their warp drives. Often, they could even communicate from ship to ship at the same time. It was all bullshit, of course. How the hell are we supposed to be able to see images that are light-based when space time is moving past us at faster than the speed of light? It's an even bigger problem for any form of communication that's based on something that's slower than the speed of light."

Liz smiled as she asked, "In view of all the stimulating images and communications traffic that will be passing through, are you going to sit in front of that screen for the rest of the trip?"

Austin grinned as he replied, "No, I just wanted to be sure I was good with both maneuvering one of these space yachts through a solar system and handling the transition to the warp-field generators." Austin released the seat belt that kept him in place in spite of the microgravity, got up, and nodded to a woman who moved into his chair as he made his way toward Liz. He reached his wife and said, "I'm back to being a settler for now. Each of these ships has several trained pilots who also have other duties, usually based in engineering. This station has a shitload of sensors and alarms that let you know when anything isn't quite right, which lets the pilot handle other tasks at the same time. There're always other people on duty here as well so that people can look after each other and avoid feelings of isolation. We don't want anyone to go stir crazy and screw up things on the bridge!"

Now that the excitement from the departure was over, they decided to check out their quarters. Like everyone else, they made their way through passageways with a combination of free floating and rebounds off various surfaces, usually bulkheads. As the leader of the expedition, Austin had been assigned a stateroom that was a little larger than the others, in view of his need to meet and work with almost anyone. Still, the accommodations were neither large nor luxurious.

As they entered their quarters, Austin looked around and said, "You know more about the setup in the quarters than I do."

Liz smiled and said, "You still know a lot about the history, of course. You know that because of the space constraints for many ships, sleeping areas are often without any meaningful privacy beyond an area for changing clothes. However, that approach isn't practical for ships that will be in flight for a year with large numbers of married couples." She reached over to pull a flexible cover across the hatch as she continued, "All living quarters have these flexible doors that can be pulled shut over the hatches to provide for privacy."

They decided to make use of their privacy. As they got out of their clothes, Austin noticed that Liz wasn't wearing a bra. Liz smiled and said, "Like most of the women on the ship, once we left Earth, I stopped wearing a bra. A microgravity environment means I don't need any support. My breasts seem fuller as well. Why don't you check them out for yourself?" Austin was happy to oblige.

Liz pointed to an unusual structure in the bulkhead that they unfolded. She giggled as she said, "The mechanics of sex in space can be complicated, as people tend to fly around and not be able to stay together without some assistance. This thing is supposed to provide the assistance. Someone started calling it the 'love machine,' and the name stuck. Although the team provided training on how to use them, they're awkward to use in real gravity and most couples, including us, put off worrying about it until they were on board the ship. These things have been around for a while. Have you ever actually used one?"

"Can't say that I have," Austin replied.

"Haven't you ever had sex in space?"

He chuckled and said, "No, although my history in space goes back to the early years, sex in space wasn't really an option then. For starters, there weren't any women in the space program during the Apollo missions. Even after women started as astronauts in the 1980s, there was no way to even consider having sex in space. A space shuttle had only slightly more privacy than any of the Apollo units. Although I made it up to one of the space stations, it was never at a time when there were any women on board. I've heard stories about some stuff that supposedly happened up there later but never had any reliable confirmation about those stories."

"Weren't there some married couples in space?"

"Yes, but that was pretty rare in the early days. I was married to Jean at the time, and she wasn't about to travel to space. In those days, space travel was a dangerous business, and it didn't make sense for anyone to embrace it without a damned good reason. After I became president, I stayed planet-bound for years. Suzie and I got married during the big break between my tenures as president. Although Suzie and I were together for a long time, she preferred to travel on Earth instead of in space, so we never needed to worry about it. What about you?"

"This'll be my first time, too." She giggled as she said, "It looks like I'll need to be strapped into that thing!

I think you'll need to be strapped in, too! It looks like there are some handholds as well.

They laughed as Austin said, "I guess I'd better take another look at the manual for this thing."

"Read quickly, Sam!" More giggling followed.

The ship settled into a regular routine, with schedules and locations for continuing training posted to everyone's links and computers. For Austin and Liz, it was largely refreshers and reminders. Although Austin and Yabuno were already friends, Austin and Liz became good friends with Yabuno and his wife, Donna. Austin and Liz spent as much time together as possible, but each of them had duties relating to Citadel to handle. The two men spent a lot of time together discussing a range of issues. When they could manage it, they enjoyed having technical discussions.

"Thank God for your resistance suits, Sam. They're light years ahead of the cumbersome things you first developed thirty years ago. It's usually a pain in the ass to keep up with an exercise program during a long trip in space, but you don't have to think about the suits. They've been very gradually increasing to an equivalence of 1.1g, which is just over Citadel's gravity of 1.09g. It hasn't been painful at all." Yabuno smiled as he continued, "I'll let you in on a secret, Sam. I've programmed my suit to take the resistance up to 1.15. I'm planning on feeling a little lighter and stronger when we get to Citadel. I may even push the resistance up to 1.2."

Austin grinned as he said, "I have the same feeling. Mine's set at 1.25."

Yabuno winced as he said, "Don't tell me you're already there! How the hell can you handle it?"

"I did a lot of specialized weight training in the months before we left Earth, then put on the suit the moment we took off and started increasing the resistance right away. I've also been careful to spend all of my required time in the minicentrifuge to keep the bones, muscles, etc., from forgetting about gravity." Austin had a mocking look in his eye as he said, "Liz is about to move up from 1.15 to 1.2. She looks slender, but don't underestimate her. She might beat you at arm wrestling!"

During other sessions, the talk turned to concern about the warp-field generators.

Yabuno ran his hand through his hair as he said, "We did the best we could at the time, Sam, but I'm still worried about the stability of the warp-field generators for these ships. It was tough enough to figure out how to do it with a ship the size of *Pathfinder*; it's a lot tougher to maintain a stable warp field with a ship this large. While there's no question that using the twin generator approach made things more stable than they would have been otherwise, things keep sliding out of balance over time. The problem is that the process isn't predictable enough to program automatic recalibration into the system. Someone still has to monitor the generators constantly and do the recalibration manually."

"It's almost as if we need another bubble to balance out the first one. They would then tend to keep each other stable."

The frown on Yabuno's face faded as he said, "I hadn't thought of it in those terms, but you're right. A second bubble, if we can figure out how to generate it while the first one is in place, could solve our problems. Come to think of it, if we can figure out that part, I have some ideas on how to solve one of our other problems."

Austin's interest was piqued as he said, "I have some ideas on generating the second bubble. Let me think about it for a few days and then send something over to you to check out."

Yabuno looked at his link and exclaimed, "Jesus! I'm going to be late!" His face took on a wolfish look as he said, "Donna was pretty clear that she wanted to use that love machine in our quarters and that I could sleep on the deck if I kept her waiting too long. We still have trouble with those damned straps sometimes!"

Austin couldn't help laughing as he said, "Too much information, Bret!"

CHAPTER TEN

At first, Austin thought he must be dreaming that he was hearing alarms throughout the ship. He then realized that he had been asleep and was still partly asleep for a moment. The moment passed, and he then knew from some of the alarms that he was hearing that something was very wrong. He undid the straps that kept him together with Liz in their berth and was dressed and out on the deck in moments.

He knew that he needed to head toward engineering right away. He pushed off a bulkhead and flew down a passageway much more quickly than was safe, calling ahead for people to stay out of the way. He kept himself on course by using his hands to make gentle contact with other bulkheads as he continued onward. He thought, grimly, that he probably looked like a flying superhero from the comics of his youth. He didn't feel like one, though. He felt a little disoriented, as the passageways seemed to pitch a bit. *That wasn't supposed to happen*, he thought. He hoped he could chalk it up to a lack of sleep and not something else.

He nearly collided hard with Yabuno, who was racing down a different passageway toward the same destination. They moved quickly through the hatch leading to engineering. Now that they were stopped and holding onto a bulkhead, Austin could feel the movement of the ship as well as see it. One look into the face of the chief engineer and the captain told them that they weren't expecting the movement of the ship, either.

"What's happening, Chief?" the captain asked.

"Damned if I know for sure, Captain," the chief replied. "To start with, there's been some damage to the ship's regular systems, which I haven't been able to assess fully yet. The good news is that from what we've learned so far about that damage, we know how to go about fixing it. The bad news is that the hull has been breached around cargo bay 2, although I've no idea how it happened. It doesn't look like a gash so much as being melted and then ripped off while impossibly hot. It isn't hot, though. Fortunately, no one was there at the time, so we're just looking at the loss of some cargo. The really bad news is that we have major problems with the warp-field generators. We've been able to keep things in balance through constant monitoring of the generators, but something happened and our bubble is contorting like hell. I'm hoping Bret and Sam can tell us why that system seems to be crapping out on us when we're in the middle of nowhere.

Yabuno and Austin looked at the screen for the generators and checked out the data from the last twelve hours. They looked at each other and said, "Shit." They turned to the chief and the captain. Yabuno said, "The way the bubble is contorting suggests that it's starting to collapse. The movements of the ship are due to the fact that the edge of the bubble is weak enough in a few places that the force of the passage of space time past the ship is being felt. We think that for a moment, the bubble weakened just a bit more and a small portion of the ship somehow came into contact with space time that's racing past us at faster than the speed of light. The hull wasn't so much melted or ripped as distorted; the physics in play at that moment are unclear. However, none of the possible outcomes is good news for us.

"We're lucky to be alive at all, because the most likely possibility is that if this happens again and we survive the initial contact, we'll probably be clobbered within seconds by something rushing by us. The only thing that saved us is the bubble contorting in a different manner and pulling us back a bit, which is probably when the distorted part of the hull was pulled apart. The other possibility is that we'd simply be torn apart when the bubble collapses in an uncontrolled manner. If you remember any of the images from the early tests of the generators, you know that those failures were pretty nasty. We don't have any choice but to shut down the warp-field generators and try to figure out what to do about the problem."

The chief looked at Yabuno with hard eyes as he said, "With all due respect, Bret, you'd better be fucking sure about that recommendation. We all know that once we shut down the generators, it isn't as simple as turning on a light switch to bring them back online. Also, the longer they stay offline, the longer it will take to get them back online. That's not even taking into account the problem with forming a stable bubble with the hull ripped open. Are you sure we can't nurse things along while we come up with a solution? What if we try to slow down the space-time distortion so that it isn't moving past us fast enough to cause a problem if we come into contact with it?"

"That might be possible under normal circumstances, Chief," Yabuno replied. "The problem is we aren't dealing with normal stuff right now. The instability that we've found in the generators, combined with the nature of how our generators warp space time is such that it's damned near impossible to slow down enough before the bubble collapses. Our bubble is contorting already, and we won't be able to have a controlled collapse of the bubble soon, which means we'd be screwed. We need to take the generators offline now while we can still control the bubble. We might have problems, but I'd take those over what happens otherwise. In short, there isn't another solution that keeps us from being clobbered or torn apart by space time, Chief."

The captain turned to Austin and said, "What are your thoughts, Sam? We're screwed if those generators can't be brought back online. We're still three months out from Citadel with the generators running normally, which might as well be the other side of the galaxy without them. The nearest beacon is years away without the generators, so we can't even send a message letting others know what's happened." His dark humor came through as he continued, "Even *you'd* probably die from old age before you could get back."

Austin replied, "Everything Bret said is true and the longer we spend talking about it, the more likely it is that we'll just be a pile of debris that will dissipate over time."

The captain was quiet for a moment before turning to the chief and saying, "Shut it down, Chief, the way they say to do it. While you're taking care of that, I have to figure out what to say to the passengers."

While the chief and his people worked on repairing the ship's regular systems and patching the hull, Austin and Yabuno confronted the generators.

"There's no way we can just let the generators 'rest' for a while and try to restart them," Yabuno said after some thought. "Now that we know what to look for, we can see that a secondary imbalance has been in place for some time. We didn't see it before because it was masked by the primary imbalance and our work to recalibrate the primary imbalance. Restarting now won't do us any good as long as that secondary imbalance is still there. While we could probably establish a bubble, it would collapse pretty damned quickly and we'd still be stuck right here. That would be the good scenario. The bad scenario would be that there wouldn't be anything recognizable of us left after the collapse of the bubble."

Austin's face revealed his concerns about multiple problems as he said, "As bad as things are for us, what worries me is that this problem may be playing itself out on some of the other ships. Even if we can get this one back in the game, I'm not sure there's enough know-how on the other ships to solve the problem. In fact, I'm kind of surprised that you and I ended up on the same ship."

Yabuno's face screwed itself into a grim smile as he said, "I pulled some strings to end up on the same ship with you, Sam. Each of us does better when we have a sounding board for our ideas, and we've done pretty well together."

Austin's smile was equally grim as he said, "While I appreciate the sentiment, Bret, it also means that some know-how might not have ended up where it could help another ship in this situation. However, I'm not going to worry about it now. We're going to take advantage of our being here to figure out how to get around the secondary imbalance. It seems to me that our discussions about establishing a second bubble to keep the first one in balance could be the answer."

"We'll need to keep the generation of the second bubble separate from the generation of the first bubble," Yabuno said, "to avoid it being affected by what's causing the first bubble's imbalance."

"We could try to generate the first bubble primarily through one of the generators and the second bubble primarily through the second one," Austin said. "Although using two generators to generate a single bubble has been a means of providing better overall stability for the bubble, we'd still be getting the stability we need through the second bubble balancing the first bubble."

"Thank God we have some serious computing capability available on this ship to work this stuff out and refine it as much as possible before we implement it. We'll need it because we're going have to rely on that computing power for a lot of the usual field testing." Yabuno shook his head. "I'd love to be able to do a lot of the more traditional field testing, but that isn't going to happen. Our field testing is going to consist of generating the first bubble and then the second bubble and seeing if everything remains stable. If it works, we'll need to haul ass to Citadel and pray nothing else fails, because these generators weren't designed to generate the bubbles this way. They're going to fail at some point. This approach is just a stopgap to get us to Citadel; it won't work as a long-term solution."

"I agree," Austin said with a nod. "I think for a long-term solution, for starters we'll need to figure out how to partition the generators in virtual form so that each one can work with the other to generate both bubbles for stability. Damned if I can figure out right now how we'll do it, though."

Yabuno's smile was slightly less grim for a moment as he said, "We'll need something to occupy our time when we reach Citadel. After all, we were only planning on spending our time settling a planet. There must be a few extra minutes we can find somewhere!"

Three days later, the ship was back on course for Citadel and life was mostly back to normal. Austin, Yabuno, the chief and the captain continued to keep a nervous watch on the generators for any signs of instability in the bubbles. They were all jumpier than usual because of the possibility that a new form of instability might be developing that they wouldn't recognize in time, much like how the second form of instability had crept up on them.

Although the bubbles seemed to be stable, there were signs of stress developing within the generators. While they'd worked out a plan for dealing with the design problems, they knew there wasn't much of a margin for error.

Yabuno explained the situation privately to the other three. "We'd damned well better show up at Citadel within a few days of when we're supposed to arrive, because the generators will probably be useless much beyond that time. They might not even last that long. Even being a few days short of getting to Citadel could mean we'll end up years away from anything."

A month had passed, and the four of them were discussing where they stood. Yabuno said, "Even though we're still heading toward Citadel, we have another problem to consider. The generators are becoming increasingly fragile and might not even survive being powered down."

The chief frowned and said, "That means we don't dare try to stop to locate a beacon to let people know what had happened, even if we could be certain that the beacons would work. Being unable to stop also means we can't confirm that we're on course. We're flying blind and hoping that our original course calculations are still good and that the stresses from the warp bubbles aren't throwing us off course. If we're wrong, we could end up nowhere near Citadel and without the ability to even use a beacon to call for help."

Although the captain had been direct with the settlers on the situation, Austin and Liz talked about ways to keep the settlers from a constant state of anxiety. "We need to keep the settlers focused on their training," Liz said. "We know that many of the settlers are taking their cues from us, so we need to make a special effort to show our confidence in the warp-field generators and especially in the captain and the chief."

Austin agreed. "I've gone out of my way to check in with everyone from time to time and make sure that they see me relaxed and looking ahead to our time on Citadel."

Liz sighed. "I wish there were a way for us to be able to let everyone know everything will be OK."

"I've been careful never to promise anyone that everything would be fine, Liz. While I truly hope that's the way it'll end, if a problem comes up, I'll need to have the credibility to tell them while I let them know what we're going to do next." Austin shook his head as he continued, "The guy that has it even tougher than we do is the chief; I swear his hair will be white by the time this voyage ends. It isn't much easier for the captain. While Bret and I think about the generators much of the time, the chief and his people have to do it on a twenty-four/seven basis.

"Bret and I have trained him and his people on what to monitor and when to let us know that something isn't right. For the sake of the morale of this ship, we can't have everyone taking note that we're so worried that Bret and I are there with the chief all the time in case something goes wrong. We won't have a viable group of settlers when we reach Citadel if we do that. We need to stay with our routine and trust that we've been doing everything we should be doing."

As Liz glanced in a familiar direction, a look of desire appeared in her eyes as she said, "Speaking of 'routines,' Sam, it seems to me that that includes not letting too much dust collect on the love machine. We've gotten a lot better at using it since that first time."

Liz was already out of her clothes. As she pulled Austin out of his, he smiled and said, "I don't think that damned manual got everything quite right. I think we can probably update it by the time we reach Citadel. If nothing else, an updated manual may help the next wave of settlers make more effective use of it! I think I'll pass on cooperating in making a 'how-to' video, though!"

"You're damned right, my love. Making love with you anywhere is terrific, but I won't share what we do with anyone else. Oh God! No fair doing that while I'm not even finished strapping in yet!" She gasped. "You've definitely gotten the hang of this thing. You'd better get strapped in here with me, lover, before the entire ship hears us."

"The place is soundproofed, Liz."

"It won't be enough!"

The ship was less than twenty-four hours away from Citadel. Yabuno and Donna were squeezed into the Austin stateroom, talking about where they stood with their journey. Yabuno said, "The chief isn't taking any chances; he's watching the generators like a hawk up until the moment we arrive. I'm glad none of the settlers seemed overly worried about the fact that the ship's warp-field generators will never take the ship back to Earth."

"They might feel differently some years down the road," Donna said.

Liz spoke. "Although the settlers have stayed in remarkably good spirits for the past year, even when it wasn't clear whether we'd be able to reach Citadel, everyone is ready to get away from recycled air, ship rations and accommodations, and microgravity." She chuckled as she continued. "Let's face it, not everyone has taken to the love machines."

Donna nodded with a smile and said, "I've seen more than a few couples with that look in their eyes. The moment they can find some privacy when planet-bound, they'll be working their way through some long pent-up lust! I'm not sure how long it will be before they're in a mood to focus on anything else."

Yabuno's voice took on a mock-serious tone as he turned to Donna and asked, "I hope you haven't been sharing with anyone the details of our adventures with the love machine."

Donna laughed as she looked at Liz and then back to Yabuno and said, "While we may have shared some of the moments from the love machines, it was only the funny ones, without the gory details."

Finally, the ship was ready to reenter normal space. After the captain gave the word, the chief initiated the program for collapsing the bubbles. Austin and Yabuno were there in case anything didn't work as planned. Everything went smoothly, and the chief took the generators offline for the final time. Some of the lines that had etched themselves in his face relaxed. Huge smiles sprang up on the others' faces once they saw the chief's worries were behind him.

"Sam, Bret, it's been a pleasure sharing this trip with you," the chief said. "I've been privileged to use truly historic technology developed by two men that don't let setbacks stop them for long."

Yabuno said, "Chief, this ship wouldn't have gotten anywhere without the top-rate care you gave to her. It's been a pleasure to work with you."

"Chief," Austin said, "it would be an honor to serve with you aboard another ship, if that chance should come along."

The captain didn't have time for pleasantries, as he needed to determine their precise location and to find out if any of the other ships was nearby. He wasn't worried about being a few days late; the protocols provided for all of the ships to wait just outside the Citadel system for up to ten days after the arrival of the first ship after *Pathfinder*, so that ships that had to stop for repairs or other reasons could catch up. If at all possible, they wanted to make sure all of the ships could enter the system at the same time and take their places in orbit around Citadel together.

The captain's face broke out in a huge smile as they received an answer to their message. Most of the other ships had already arrived and were glad to hear from them! After receiving information on the location of the other ships, he realized that they were in a cluster around four hours away. He gave orders to the pilot to head the ship toward their colleagues. After the captain made an announcement to the passengers about their arrival and contact with the other ships, the cheers were loud enough to be heard through the ship.

As the ship came within sight of the other ships, the captain called Austin to the bridge. When Austin walked through the hatch, the captain nodded and gave instructions to begin a live broadcast from the bridge throughout the "fleet" as well as within their ship. The face of the captain of *Pathfinder* appeared on the screen. "Sam Austin," he began. "Although we're still waiting for one of our ships to arrive, it is time to confirm that this crossing has been completed. That being the case, on behalf of all of the ships present and yet to arrive, I acknowledge that you are now in formal command of this settlement group. The next steps that we take, including entry into the Citadel system, will be under your leadership and direction."

It was silly, of course, but Liz could have sworn that she heard cheers coming from every ship out there.

SETTLEMENT

CHAPTER ELEVEN

A ustin's first formal videoconference with the team was extended to the captains of the ships, since they would have some immediate duties to handle. Austin started with Brittel, asking, "While we're waiting to enter the Citadel system, what have we learned from the beacons?"

Brittel replied, "So far, no messages have come through from Earth or from Number Nineteen, the missing ship, Sam. This isn't surprising, since there's no way to be sure how long it would take for a message to arrive. We're going to deploy the special beacons and other equipment to let the missing ship know that the rest of us have already arrived. We're also going to establish a communications link with Citadel to let them know as well. All of this will help guide the ship into the system to join the rest of us. From Citadel, they can use the communications system to continue to try to send messages back to Earth and to implement upgrades throughout the system from the entry point back to Earth."

Austin nodded and ordered *Pathfinder* to visit Citadel's radiation field and determine whether their information on the safe path to Citadel was still valid. Her captain nodded, replying, "In view of the extreme danger posed by the field, we brought along upgraded sensors/markers, to help determine when we are cleared to venture throughout the rest of the solar system. They'll also let us know when the safe path changes."

Austin had Yabuno report to the rest of the team on the circumstances in which their own warp-field generators had failed. Yabuno stood in front of the screen, manipulating images as he explained, "Over half of the ships reported having had similar problems. Fortunately, they were able to make it to Citadel before the generators failed completely. Our team will check out the warp-field generators on all of the ships to see where things stand as far as being able to get back to Earth when the time comes. Let's hope that at least some of the ships will be able to make the return trip."

Austin turned to the group and said, "The next full team meeting will take place on the tenth day of the first settler ship's arrival, although many smaller meetings will take place during that time as needed, to get ready for deployment on Citadel once we get past the radiation field. Let's get moving."

"Thanks, everyone, for getting back together," Austin began. "It's now been ten days since the first settler ship arrived. We've plenty of things to cover, but let's get to several items first. Greg, what's the status of the communications link to Earth?"

Brittel replied, "Although everything tells us it's up and running, Sam, we haven't detected any signals that we can confirm to have come from Earth."

"What about anything from the missing settler ship?"

"Nothing's come in at all. As we know, the only way for a ship to figure out its progress toward Citadel during a voyage is to make a stop reasonably close to a beacon, which isn't easy. For all we know, they could be past the last beacon and still be plenty of years away from Citadel if their warp-field generators have failed. At least we have a communications system from here to Citadel that will alert us if and when they arrive."

Austin turned to Yabuno and said, "Bret, I guess that takes us to a discussion about the warp-field generators. Please tell everyone what you've learned from checking out the ships."

Yabuno responded, "We already know that over half of the ships experienced problems with their field generators. Through a miracle or just damned dumb luck, nearly everyone was able to make it here intact. Our ship was one of the unlucky ones in that regard, since our field generators failed on the way. We were lucky to come up with a stopgap that got us the rest of the way here."

"Your ship was pretty lucky to have the brains on board to deal with the problem and get your asses here in one piece," someone murmured. "I'll take that kind of luck any day."

Yabuno grinned his appreciation as he continued, "What we've learned is that there's a fundamental flaw with the design for the generators for the settler ships. While the original design using twin generators has addressed the inherent instability problem relating to maintaining the bubble, there's a secondary source of instability that we didn't see. The problem didn't show

up in the tests that we ran, so our design doesn't address it. It takes a while for the problem to show up, which is why it's such a tough one to solve. In our case, the bubble had a partial failure such that our ship, for just an instant, may have come into contact with warping space time itself. We're lucky the contact was so brief, because all we lost was some hull plating and cargo."

Yabuno continued quietly, "If it had lasted any longer, there would be two ships missing. I think it likely that the missing ship had a similar problem. Whether they're dead or just a lot of years away from anywhere is anyone's guess."

Austin gave Yabuno a direct look as he asked, "What engineering talent was on board that ship, Bret?"

Yabuno's look back at Austin was just as direct as he said, "They had a couple of my best engineers on board. One of them had had a lot to do with the designs for the generators. They had the brainpower on board to solve the problem if it could be solved."

"What are the odds that the problem happened early enough that they could be heading back to Earth?"

Yabuno frowned as he replied, "Every ship that experienced the symptoms was already a lot more than half-way to Citadel, so a return to Earth is highly unlikely. If they're still alive, they're trying to get to Citadel or a beacon, whichever they believe is closer. If they're more than a couple of years away from either, their supplies will have been exhausted before they can reach their destination. We know what happens when that time runs out."

"What if they try to stretch their supplies and other resources?"

"There are limits to how long they can last, even if they can stretch their supplies and other resources to extreme levels." Yabuno's voice became quiet as he said, "Of course, we're assuming that their ship is still in one piece. They may have had the same result we did, only with full-blown contact with warping space time. I'm not sure which would be worse—dying quickly or slowly. I might pick dying quickly.

"I've confirmed that every settler ship has the same problem, even the ones that got here without the generators crapping out. In view of the problems with the design, we don't dare take any ships out to search for the ship that's missing. There's too great a risk that those ships in turn would be lost. Right now, *Pathfinder* is the only ship with a reliable warp-field generator, and we still need her here to help with everything we need to set up in this solar system. Without knowing exactly where to look, *Pathfinder* could be out there for years without finding anything."

Austin said, "At the risk of stating the obvious, Bret, while we hope this settlement is so successful that no one wants to return to Earth, we have to plan on people wanting to be able to return to Earth in ten years. What are your thoughts on how to address the design problem?"

"I don't have any answers right now, but I do have some thoughts on which I want to work. Fortunately—if *fortunately* is the right word—ten years is a long time to address the problem."

Austin turned to the rest of the team and said, "While no one wanted this problem to happen, it's a good reminder of one of the key things that makes this settlement activity so different from all others. We will, as everyone knows, be doing the work to establish communities and make productive use of this planet and the rest of the system for farming, mining, and manufacturing activities, for example. The thing that we'll also be doing, which other settlements almost never do, is establish one or more centers to continue to develop advanced technology.

"We already have practical results from our activities, such as *Pathfinder* and the settler ships, plus some other things that we'll see when we land on Citadel, for example. We'll continue to add to our portfolio over time. Otherwise, inevitably, Earth will pass us up and view us as quaint country bumpkins using ancient technology and methods. Bullshit! *We're* the ones that will show *them* what a group of people as sharp as what we have here can do."

Austin turned to *Pathfinder's* captain and asked, "Captain Reynolds, what can you tell us about the path through the radiation field? Can we still get to Citadel safely?"

Reynolds replied, "So far, the safe path looks a lot like it did when *Pathfinder* was here under deadlier circumstances, Sam, although we'll still need to map out some areas where some shifting has taken place." He held up his hand to silence the cheers that erupted among the team and said, "Let's not get carried away, folks. I just mentioned that the field shifts. The extent to which it shifts depends on various factors within this system, not all of which we understand yet. For example, we think the orbits of the system's giant planets are bringing the field closer to this spot. In a few years, the 'safe' path may be entirely different from what it is now. We'll always need to monitor the field if we want to survive here."

"Are there any indications that the field's position could shift and blanket Citadel itself?" Austin asked.

"Not based on what we've seen. Once we've gotten into the inner part of the solar system and set up everyone on Citadel, we'll wander around and get more advanced readings on the limits of the radiation field. We'll check out the planets and larger asteroids and see if there are any traces of radiation from the field." Reynolds was quiet as he said, "*Pathfinder* didn't have much opportunity to wander around the last time."

"Thanks, Captain," Austin said. "While we still have plenty of items to cover, let's be sure everyone is on board with first steps for tomorrow. We'll line up behind *Pathfinder* in the same order we did when we left Earth and then follow her through the radiation field to Citadel." Austin smiled and added, "If our ships had legs, we'd be stepping in each other's footprints to stay on the right path.

"All captains already have the coordinates where they'll set themselves up in orbit around Citadel. The advance teams will deploy to the ground. Once the all clear has been given, we'll see a lot of organized chaos as the next waves of people start to move. The key thing to keep in mind is to take the time to get things done the right way, the way we've trained to do them."

Austin smiled wryly as he looked around. "Now for something that some of you will think sucks. We have plenty of hours ahead of us between getting through the radiation field and approaching Citadel and getting started on the landings. Part of doing things the right way means that we're all going to take the time to get some rest after we get clear of the radiation field and reach Citadel. Citadel isn't going anywhere, and we'll be less likely to make mistakes from being exhausted. It'll be pretty much nonstop once we start things on Citadel itself, so don't cheat yourselves out of the rest you'll need." Austin let the grumblings continue for a bit and then moved onto other items. They had plenty more to cover before tomorrow.

CHAPTER TWELVE

Austin was back in the pilot's seat for his ship, just as determined to be at the controls as they entered a new solar system as he'd been in leaving the previous one. He reinforced some points for everyone on the bridge. "All of the ships are in place behind *Pathfinder* as she prepares to enter the field," he said. "The ships are much closer together for this part of the trip, since we want to be certain that our 'footsteps' match. We know that communications might suffer due to the high levels of radiation and the fact that the safe path isn't in a straight line. We'll have to stay focused on the ship immediately in front to make sure everything matches up.

"To make things even more interesting, *Pathfinder* will continue to monitor the field and make course corrections depending on its readings. Everyone has to be alert and ready to do more than just watch the preprogrammed course play out. We're screwed if we get it wrong, because a ship losing its way might spell disaster for the ships following."

Pathfinder glided into the field, followed by the first of the settler ships. The next ship followed closely after the first one, and then Austin nudged his ship forward. As the others proceeded behind them, the effect was like a silent wagon train held together by a fragile, invisible cord.

Almost immediately after entering the field, the ship-to-ship communications deteriorated significantly, to the point that it would be risky to rely on anything one ship was saying to another. Visual communications were also affected, but it was still possible to keep the ship ahead in sight.

Austin had the main screen up, with the ship ahead in view and a display with the planned course up as well. There was a back-and-forth commentary between Austin and the rest of the bridge crew as they made sure he received the information he needed. The voices were clear, the sentences were short, and the bullshit chatter was nonexistent.

"Number Two is still on the planned path, Sam. Another course change is coming up in a thousand meters. Decelerate in eight hundred meters to point fifteen. At one thousand meters, elevation will be down three degrees and the turn will be ten degrees starboard."

"Confirm deceleration to point fifteen in eight hundred meters," Austin responded. "Confirm elevation down three degrees at one thousand meters. Confirm turn ten degrees to starboard at one thousand meters."

Austin looked up and saw that the ship ahead of them was just starting to make its turn. He expected to mirror those movements shortly. As the ship approached eight hundred meters, it decelerated to point fifteen. It was practically crawling as it reached one thousand meters and made the course change. Soon, the entire wagon train would be making the same move. Even with the ships traveling close together, at times, the ships near the front of the train would be one, two, or even three or more course changes ahead of the ones near the back. The communications between the ships continued to be far too garbled to understand.

Multiple course changes later, they were well into the radiation field and fully committed to the journey.

Austin's time in space went back to dead reckoning, so he had a more experienced eye than most when it came to course changes.

"We're coming up on several tricky course changes in a short order, Sam," someone called out. Austin watched the ship ahead make another course change. He frowned when he noticed that it didn't match the path that had been plotted. He said, "Confirm that we have a deviation from the path up ahead."

"Deviation is confirmed, Sam."

"What's the chatter like out there? Can we get confirmation that the change was ordered by *Pathfinder*?"

"We can confirm that there was a ton of extra chatter at the time of the course deviation, but we can't tell what it said. We also confirm that there seems to be extra chatter coming at us from Number Two, but we can't read it. For all we know, they could be telling us to follow the new course or to stay on the original one."

"Shit. If there's been a course change and we don't follow it, we're screwed, along with everyone behind us. If they made a mistake and we follow that mistake, we're screwed, along with everyone behind us. Either way, with those other course changes coming up quickly, we'd have a hell of a time getting back on the safe path if we make the wrong choice, assuming we can even find it."

The captain spoke. "Sam, the odds are higher that it was responding to an instruction to make a course change than that they just made a mistake."

"Maybe, Captain, but I got a look at the way they made the course change. No one makes a course change like that on purpose. The maneuvering was wrong. It looked to me like they held the position longer than they should have because of a screw-up or an instrument glitch, then made the change once their instruments started responding again."

"We can't take that chance, Sam. We need to go with the odds and make the change they did. We'll have to do it quickly so that we can see where they're going next."

"I don't agree, Captain. The more I think about what I saw, the more certain I am that they had an instrument failure, possibly leading to a mental lapse while dealing with the failure. If we follow them, we'll venture into the radiation field and keep wandering through it while we try to figure out how to get back onto the safe path. There are too many maneuvers ahead through this stretch for it to be feasible to take that chance. We'd have to get through plenty of radiation just to get back on the path if we're wrong. We need to stay on the original course."

There was dead silence in the room. The captain spoke. "As the captain, the decision is mine to make. Follow the new course, Sam."

"If we were still approaching the Citadel system and your ship was the only one affected, that might be true,

Captain. If you're wrong, then everyone behind us may end up using these ships as coffins."

"I've heard your concerns, Sam, and considered them. This discussion is over. Make the course change now or get out of the pilot's chair and I'll put someone else in who understands who's in charge."

All eyes shifted to Austin as he said, "I guess I'm done with discussing this point, too, Captain, so I'll just tell you how things stand. Entry into the Citadel system itself is under my leadership. The responsibility for the welfare of the people as well as the success of this mission is mine. Therefore, the decision is mine to make. We're going to stay with the original path."

"Someone had better make a decision pretty damned fast," a voice called out.

"I just did," Austin said quietly. "I've also been keeping track of our position and will make the original course change in another five hundred meters." Austin's gaze shifted back toward the displays, and his voice became harder than diamonds as he continued, "Let's get back to focusing on our safe path, people. Anyone who wants to have any other conversation can get the fuck off this bridge. We're decelerating to point fifteen."

Trying to move around in a microgravity environment is hard to pull off with much dignity. The captain decided to preserve his dignity by staying strapped in his seat. No one approached as they saw a quiet fury ripple across his face.

Everyone stopped breathing as the distance closed and they reached the course-change point. Austin called out, "Elevation is increasing to two point four degrees, turning to eight point three degrees port." As the ship made the turn, he said, "What are the radiation levels?"

"They're holding steady, within safe range," someone replied.

After the course change was completed, Austin asked, "If I'm wrong, now that we've completed the turn, there should be radiation spikes all around us. What's happening?"

"Everything is still OK, Sam."

"What's happening with the next ship behind us?"

"They're following the same path we did."

"Good. I see another change on the original path in seven hundred meters. I'm setting up for another increase in elevation by four point seven degrees and a turn fourteen point three degrees to port." Austin's voice increased only slightly in volume as he said, "We still have plenty of course changes on the board, so stay sharp."

Later, as Austin's ship took her final steps past the edge of the radiation field, everyone started smiling again. Austin asked, "Give us a final report on the radiation."

"We didn't have any incidents where we suffered any exposure, Sam. We're clean."

"That's great news. We were lucky to catch a glimpse of Number One as it made a change ahead of us, confirming that the original path was still valid. We'll stay on this course until everyone is out of the field and then stop to assess things with Number Two. She was stumbling around in there a bit before she got back onto the proper course, and I want to know what kind of shape they're in. I think it's time to turn this chair over to another pilot for now." Austin nodded to someone as he got up, and a moment later, his seat had a replacement strapped in. As Austin floated toward the hatch to the passageway, he nodded to the captain and said, "I'd like a moment with you, Captain."

A few silent minutes later, Austin and Captain Adams were sitting alone in Austin's stateroom. Austin looked at Adams with a wry expression and said, "I don't think there's any point in my saying anything until you get off your chest what you want to say, Captain, so go ahead."

The fury hadn't left Adams's face as he said, "Right now, I'm pretty damned pissed at you, Sam. You overruled me on my bridge by making a call that was mine to make as the captain. You know damned well that captains have the final say on running their ships. While you were sitting in the pilot's chair, you reported to me, damn it!"

Austin waited a few heartbeats before speaking. "I hope you've had your say, Captain, because you're probably not going to like what I'm going to say next. You made at least two mistakes on the bridge. The first was trying to overrule an experienced pilot while he was guiding the ship. You're from a generation where you don't really watch what's happening. You rely on what the instruments tell you instead of what your eyes tell you. I've been in space a hell of a lot longer than you and know a maneuver screw-up when I see one.

"The second mistake was trying to make a decision that would have a direct impact on the safety and success of this mission and the people who are a part of it. I've been an admiral on board ships where I went out of my way not to interfere in the internal operations of the ships. Every captain that ever served as my host appreciated the way I handled my role. On the other hand, they knew better than to try to override my call about a maneuver that would have an impact on the other ships in the group. I said it on the bridge, and I'll say it again: the decision on the proper course to take was mine and mine alone. I cut you off at the knees because there wasn't time to deal with your lack of good sense. I'll do it again if necessary.

"As it happens, if I'd abdicated my responsibilities to you, we might well have had a large loss of life and vital resources. The fault would have been mine, not yours, because the responsibility was mine. As it is, it is my responsibility to get an assessment of Number Two and figure out the impact on the mission."

Austin stood up, a sign that the talk was at an end. He said, "I hope you understand that I'm not going to apologize if your feelings were hurt, Captain, because I did the right thing, under the circumstances. I hope you also understand that I believe you to be an excellent captain who has earned the right to command this ship as she heads to Citadel and takes her place in orbit. It's up to you."

Adams was silent for a moment. Although the outright anger had faded from his face, there was still nothing friendly on it as he said, "I guess I'll have to live with that, Sam." Adams turned and left the stateroom.

A call came in from the bridge. "We've made contact with Number Two, Sam. They've taken on more radiation than they should have, but they may have been able to get back to the safe path quickly enough that there won't be any fatalities. They're going through the decontamination protocols for everyone."

"How long before we have any idea about the long-term prospects for them?"

"We don't know yet; the medical staff is working on it."

"What about the impact on their supplies and equipment?"

"Some of their supplies are probably useless. Some of the equipment may have to be discarded as well. They're working on a more definite inventory and assessment. Based on what their internal sensors are telling them about radiation levels, it appears that they were pretty lucky."

"I hope so," Austin said. "Problems with supplies and equipment can be addressed by having the other ships share some of their supplies and equipment. Let's hope that the medical consequences won't be significant."

"Thank God we don't have the same problem with every ship following us, Sam. We'd be screwed right now if we'd followed Number Two, because everyone would be missing supplies. Some of those ships might have gotten even further off course than Number Two, so we might not have had enough people to settle anything."

There was a hint of a relieved smile on Austin's face as he replied, "It's past, so let's worry about what matters going forward. Tell the fleet that it's time to head for Citadel. By the time we get there, I want a plan in place to deal with any supplies and equipment that Number Two may need."

CHAPTER THIRTEEN

The Austins were both up early the next morning, although "morning" was usually an artificial construct aboard a spaceship. As it had worked out, it really *was* early morning on the planet below them. They'd stopped to appreciate the beauty of the moment as the Citadel sun appeared over the planet's horizon and the image was broadcast throughout the ships.

All of their gear was either packed for transport to the surface or stowed away. Liz looked over to where the love machine was once again folded into the bulkhead and smiled. Austin followed her gaze and smiled back at her.

"Do you think you'll miss having to use the love machine, Liz?"

She snuggled up to Austin as she said softly, "Anytime with you is great, lover." She looked at her breasts, sighed, and said, "If I had my choice, though, I guess I'll trade my perkier, fuller breasts for sex with you in regular gravity."

Finally, the homes had been completed and the settlers had moved into their new lives. Austin and Liz stood in front of their new home, admiring the scenery around them. They thought back on the events of the past several weeks.

The day before the departure, Liz, who was in charge, was giving the final briefing. She used the giant screen with ease as she said, "Because of the importance of communications, Greg and his team have already done some advance deployment and testing on the communications satellites while we've been waiting to proceed toward the Citadel system. These satellites will link up everyone on the surface as well as back to the beacons. While some glitches always happen, Greg is confident that communications won't be much of a problem while the advance teams get to work.

"You already know most of this, but it helps to be reminded about some of these details. Every individual homestead site has already been selected, based on the surveys made by *Pathfinder* from the original voyage. We've formed people into teams to deliver the basic materials to the homesteads. These teams are organized by geographic regions, so that the people who have homesteads in a region are the ones on the teams supplying those homesteads with their materials.

"Once a team has delivered everything to the homesteads in its region, the team will start with the basic setup for a homestead. Although a lot of the work will be automated, there will still be plenty of need for old-fashioned work with muscle power. As teams move on to more homesteads, they'll work even more efficiently as they gain practical experience from having worked on the previous homesteads.

"Although the housing isn't luxurious, the units are still nicer than anything that was available to the original settlers on places like Mars and the Moon. The units come with displays for communications, entertainment, and education. Each unit has three bedrooms and a bathroom, plus a kitchen and great room." Liz smiled wryly as she continued, "We figure that couples that don't already have kids will use one or more of their extra bedrooms as offices, at least until children start making their entrances into the world. Afterward, portions of great rooms will probably be sacrificed to become offices and/or play areas while the extra bedrooms are converted into nurseries.

"The modular design of the units makes it possible to plan for additions to be incorporated into the homes in the future. All of the personal gear has been packed into lightweight containers and deposited in the newly constructed homes." Liz smiled as she continued, "Much of the usual time-consuming chore of unpacking everything and storing it somewhere else has been avoided through the use of receptacles in the housing for the storage containers. Certain storage containers will become dressers, cabinets, etc. Although there will still be some unpacking to be done, it will be far less than would have been needed by earlier settlers. In time, people will customize their homes and environments to meet their needs and tastes. Everything will be powered up using the portable Austin Power Cells that are incorporated into every home."

Liz nodded at Brittel as she continued, "Greg and his people have done some interesting things to improve the safety of the settlers. All homes have a monitoring system that allows the settlers to see what's happening outside while they remain in the safety of their homes. There is technology that prevents doors or windows from being opened while a cheater is near the house. A warning will be issued, and the override command has to be issued in order for any door or window to be opened. Warnings will also be issued whenever cheaters show up on any scanners within another hundred meters beyond the edge of the cleared land, although overrides aren't needed for those sightings."

Brittel smiled. "While cheaters are experts at lying in wait patiently and striking victims without warning, they don't know anything about heat signatures or audio monitors. We'll also be doing testing to determine whether particular sound frequencies are especially irritating to the cheaters to persuade them to leave the area."

Liz's face became somber as she continued, "Everyone will carry at least one sidearm at all times, and most people should also carry a knife. The last thing we want is for people to die through carelessness.

"Getting back to the homesteads, other teams will visit each homestead to deliver the basic farming equipment and related structures for the place. Although it will be up to each settler to determine where to do any planting of crops, everyone has been given the coordinates for the locations that are considered optimal for planting for that site.

"Each region will also see the construction of an emergency shelter. For now, the emergency shelters will be used by the team members who need a place to stay while their own homesteads are being deployed. Later, the shelters will be available for their primary purpose, which is to serve as a refuge in the event of natural disasters or other emergencies.

"Although we won't have anything like a true city, a location has been selected to establish various facilities for the settlements, including emergency shelters, storage of critical supplies, medical care, commerce, administrative activities, and space for gatherings. Other infrastructure will be added as needed. Many people have already started calling it the 'Town Square' or just the 'Square.'"

"It didn't take long to start using the medical facilities," Austin mentioned.

Liz nodded as she answered, "That's true. There were a lot of steep learning curves when it came to dealing with animals as ferocious and stealthy as cheaters. Armed lookouts sometimes forgot why they were lookouts and watched or even tried to help with the construction of homesteads. While they were doing that, the cheaters crept up on them and tried their luck."

Austin shook his head as he said, "Fortunately, enough people stayed alert that new graves weren't needed just yet. Some people already have some nasty reminders carved into their hides, though."

Liz smiled as she gestured around and said, "Speaking of cheaters, we're so far away from the Square that the cheaters here might never have seen any humans."

Austin grinned back and said, "It all goes back to what people are willing to do to get what they want. Land parcels weren't much different."

"Some of it was beyond the choice of the settlers, though," Liz replied. "Although there was a formula for assigning most of the land parcels among the settlers, there were several exceptions. The medical staff had to have parcels that were relatively close to the medical facility, so that delays in cases of medical emergencies would be minimized. Also, the group had to acknowledge that you would be entitled to parcels both as a settler and as the settlement leader, so your parcels needed to be next to each other. You were therefore asked to select your parcels directly."

Austin thought back on the dreams he had for the place as he answered, "I wanted to go beyond simply farming our land, so I started out looking for parcels that had a good supply of water, preferably with a lake. I was even willing to use up some of my acreage grants to get a supply of water that began up in a mountain range, in order to ensure that we controlled the water from its source. I also wanted parcels that were likely to have substances that would be worth mining, had a good supply of timber and good pasture for grazing animals, assuming that good candidates could be found among the native species. Since I wasn't planning on giving up on farming, the parcels still needed to be able to support agriculture. I also wanted parcels located where there would be room to expand over time."

Austin gestured back toward the Square as he said, "I knew we'd have to trade off close proximity to the Square and other infrastructure to have these things, but the settlements here will be hugely different from other ones in some significant ways. The extreme isolation that was a fact of life for most settlers in the past will be offset because of the communications system already in place. Everyone will be available via link or video feed, no matter where they're located. We brought huge amounts of resource information with us that anyone can review online."

Liz chuckled as she said, "While many people wondered if it was a good idea to choose land so far from the Square, no one thinks of you as incapable of looking after yourself. However, most of the settlers simply aren't comfortable being so far from what passes for 'civilization' on a frontier world. In fact, no one has a parcel immediately adjacent to ours, meaning that we are truly on the 'frontier.' If anything, the settlers have hoped for land grants as close to the Square as possible. Outlying regions in a settlement nearly always have less safety and security than inner regions. The inner regions will be 'civilized' more quickly than outlying regions and might even become free of key predators in fairly fast order. They will probably benefit first from infrastructure improvements before outlying regions as well.

"While they might not be able to do as much with the smaller land grants that they will receive solely as settlers, the grants are still substantial enough to ensure that people have options on how to use their land. Besides, there wasn't anything sneaky about your intentions, since others are free to do likewise by swapping parcels among themselves. In fact, many couples who became good friends during the voyage have swapped parcels for other reasons as well, such as continuing their friendships as neighbors. Fortunately, there have been enough settlers that are OK with swapping parcels that most of these requests can be accommodated."

Although the couple still had a ways to go before they would consider themselves to be fully established in their new home, they stopped from their move-in to walk outside their house and survey their new domain. They were both armed, of course.

Austin spoke quietly. "We'll have to fight to keep our land. For now, it'll be dangerous every time we step outside our home, what with the way cheaters seem to be everywhere and ready to attack anyone without warning."

He turned in a slow circle, gesturing away from their house as he said, "While clearing away the vegetation around our house for one hundred meters in all directions is a good start, I want to clear the land back three hundred meters from the house, both for safety and to have room for the additional structures I'm going to build. We have plenty of wood, and I've been planning on how to adapt various components into a combination workshop and sawmill."

"That's why you've been so keen on making sure the databases include a slew of schematics and instructions for a lot of things like lasers used by other equipment." Liz smiled.

Austin nodded. "That's right. The lasers will serve as cutting tools until we can figure out ways to obtain replacements. Everyone can do the same with this information, and we'll post the results so that we can learn from what we do." He grinned as he said, "We'll have to work on how we find some of these components. Some people have already started making choices about what they want to do with their land, and more choices will be made over time."

Liz grinned too. "They might not need everything that they have but would need things they don't have. It's a good thing I've already started spearheading setting up some trading groups so that people can work out how to obtain these things. It'll all start out on the barter system. Who knows? We might even start up a currency from this trading someday."

A mountain beckoned in the distance, banded with alternating streaks of green, brown, and yellow and frosted lightly with white at the top. Delicate wisps of clouds brushed the upper areas with subtle colors and shadows. The water that coursed and splashed down wild channels and valleys overcome with dense foliage would never run out. They looked at the mountain in the distance with pride, knowing that it was now *their* mountain.

Austin gestured at their mountain as he turned to Liz and said, "I'm not sure whether I want someday for the lake up there to be safe enough for us to be able to swim in it or for the place to stay wild enough that it never happens."

Liz smiled with a mischievous gleam in her eye as she replied, "I see you're still thinking about places to get me naked, Sam." She looked down at her breasts and then back up at Austin as she continued, "While I had to give up the unusually perkier and fuller breasts that I had in space, I'm looking forward to the benefits that come with being in a normal gravity environment again."

As they walked back into their house toward their bedroom, Liz guided Austin's hands to her chest and asked, "Do you miss the way my breasts looked in space, Sam?"

Austin's eyes contained the same gleam as he replied, "In space or planet-side, they're always a delightful handful!"

"I'm looking forward to getting my hands on you as well, lover! Now that we don't have to use the love machine anymore, my hands are going to be free to do some things that we haven't been able to do for a long time." Liz's eyes widened as she continued, "I see that *your* hands are a lot freer too. They haven't been free to do that since before we were in space. I hope to hell you locked the front door, because God help any cheaters that show up right now!"

Austin was on another scouting trip to identify local resources to use for his projects at their compound. He'd already located some important sources for the fence he'd be building around the place. As he moved through the woods around his property, he kept note of the data that was coming into his visor via his link. Everything they'd learned so far had confirmed that the biggest menace among the planet's predators was, in fact, the cheaters. He'd already located and dispatched four that were hiding in various trees. There was nothing innocent or cuddly about them. If they saw an opportunity to attack a person, they did so quickly and without warning. While none of the settlers had yet died from an attack, it was mostly due to good fortune.

Austin smiled at the fact that there were trees on the planet. Not only were there trees, but plenty of other things that looked remarkably like the shrubs and other undergrowth that one would find in a forest on Earth. The riot of colors that assaulted the senses here was from a different palette, however, and proof that they were on another world. Like on Earth, photosynthesis had evolved on this planet, so there was a huge amount of greenery to serve as a canvas for the rest of the palette.

The colors attracted plenty of things that were the equivalent of insects. They'd already known about the "insects" from the biological samples that had been brought back to Earth by *Pathfinder*. None of the specimens had survived, however, because of the radiation exposure for *Pathfinder*. Even dead specimens revealed some secrets, however.

Everyone used the insect repellent that had been developed back on Earth, which was based on the best assessments of the insects' biology that were available. They found that it seemed to work some of the time but not always with the ones that were the most persistent. Fortunately, not all of the insects had evolved the ability to pierce the hides of humans, although most of them had developed the ability to be annoying. The medical staff continued to work on improving the repellents and sorting out which insects were the most dangerous. Over time, they hoped to catalogue the flora and fauna more thoroughly. At some point, the people on Earth would be very interested in what they were finding.

Suddenly, as Austin moved along, something in the air changed. Even his caution hadn't been enough to spot the cheater that had been hiding up in a tree, in a cavity in the trunk that blocked his view. He looked up to see it diving through the open space, bearing down on him with claws and fangs ready to tear him apart. He knew he wouldn't have time to bring his rifle to bear, so he moved slightly, spoiling the cheater's aim. As a claw brushed by him, he held out his knife under it and let the animal's own momentum help the blade slice through its belly. While the cheater was distracted by the unexpected pain, Austin had his rifle out and dropped the predator with a single shot to the head.

Austin knew he'd been lucky. They'd need to do some upgrades to their equipment so that cheaters couldn't hide behind or within tree cavities. He didn't bother with the carcass; cheater meat was practically inedible, and he wasn't about to try to recover the hide by himself. It would be the ultimate example of stupidity of he were to be taken down by another cheater because he had turned his back on them while skinning this one. It was better to leave the carcass for other cheaters to find, as a warning. In time, they'd learn not to mess with him.

CHAPTER FOURTEEN

Three years later found Austin working on yet another annual report to the settlers. Austin had set aside the report while he and Liz entertained Bret and Donna. Austin marveled out loud over the changes that had taken place over the past three years. Yabuno smiled and said, "For one thing, Sam, that long trip through space hasn't had any negative impact on fertility. Just about every couple has had at least one child by now and some already have two. It didn't take long before our population had shot up to around ten thousand; now it's even higher."

They were distracted for a moment as two small whirlwinds, a boy with dark hair and blue eyes and a girl with blond hair and brown eyes, paused to make contact with them before moving onto something else. Thinking of Matt brought Austin great delight, even if the boy was a handful. He was fearless and ready to investigate anything. Maddie Yabuno was much the same way. "There are times when fearlessness is not a good thing on a frontier world," Austin mused.

"You were right about being overrun with cheaters once the settlers in the parcels nearest the Square made lethally clear what would happen if the cheaters stayed in the neighborhood," Yabuno said. "That made it pretty tough for you, since it meant a lot of them headed here where they thought it was safer." He grinned as he continued, "Bad call on their part; they learned the hard way not to press their luck with you. Funny thing is that often the sounds of children mean that helpless prey are around, but in your case, it means that you show them even less mercy than before. I'm not sure I've ever seen you miss a shot."

Donna pointed toward the structure in the distance and said, "I still can hardly believe that you were able to set up that incredible fence, Sam; I know we still need to be armed whenever we are outside, but we are quite safe so long as we are on this side of it."

Austin chuckled as he said, "Thanks to the cheaters that everyone encouraged to move our way, we only had a tight window of opportunity to clear away the additional terrain near our house before it would be too dangerous to go outside for very long."

"I'm still amazed that you found all of the materials for the fence nearby," Yabuno said.

Austin ticked off the items that he'd located, "I found everything we needed for concrete nearby, and we had a ready-made supply of timber from the 'trees' we wanted to clear away. I figured out how to create a dye from the bark of the trees and mix it with the concrete so that the fence would blend in more with the land instead of look like a prison wall. I even found local materials to provide the explosives to use to clear away stuff. I blasted a large area around our property that left open space between nine hundred and eleven hundred feet out from the house, which was plenty of room to construct a new fence once the debris was hauled in.

"Fortunately, the explosions scared the hell out of the cheaters, so we usually didn't have any unwanted company while working on creating the open space. We weren't the only settlers to adapt our transport into a tractor/bulldozer. By alternating explosions with removing the shattered stumps and trunks with our modified transport, we were able to clear our space before the cheaters could summon the nerve to return. Once the ring was cleared, we made extensive use of the trees that had been cleared to harvest the wood that would become part of the fence, as well as supply the forms for the concrete pillars."

Yabuno sighed as he said, "That's where *we* came in. I remember plenty of evenings where my muscles complained over what we did. No matter how many labor-saving devices we had, there always seemed to be things that required plenty of nonmechanized effort..."

"Damn it, Sam, how the hell many more of these holes do we need? You could fit a small city inside your perimeter!"

Austin brushed one of his tanned arms across his damp forehead and grinned. "I'm not that greedy, Bret. I only want enough room for a village! Only another fifty holes to go, although you're not on the hook for all of them. Liz has it worked out so that what you do here will match up with what we'll be doing at each of your places. We'll get it done a hell of a lot faster for each of us this way. We'll all breathe a little easier when it comes to cheaters around our homes."

Liz watched the men working with Austin in clearing out the twisted remains of the stumps, digging the holes for the posts and muscling into place the forms for the concrete pillars. The sweat ran down their bare chests freely. A year of using the resistance suits set to a higher level than even Citadel's gravity had left them all in really good shape. In spite of their grumblings, they moved easily and smoothly. Liz smiled as she took and posted the images of the men online. From the responses by the women, there was a high degree of approval with the images. She knew she didn't have any complaints when Austin held her in his arms…

"I'm feeling a little warm just thinking about some of those pictures," Donna said with a smile. "You guys looked hot!"

"Didn't Maddie come along about nine months later?" Liz asked.

"So did Matt, and for the same reason, I'll bet!" Donna replied.

Before the fence was completed, Austin had built a sawmill to handle the lumber for the fence. After the fence was completed, Austin reworked the sawmill into a complete workshop, which he usually just called the Mill, in a nod to its origins.

"Building the fence was just a starting point, Sam," Yabuno said. He walked around, pointing out things as he continued, "Once you were able to avoid having to look over your shoulder for clawed death, you built a very comfortable guesthouse, as well as an addition to your original house. Like nearly everyone, you have a garden for the local and imported produce. It doesn't hurt that you can tap into the river that runs nearby and have indoor plumbing."

Austin smiled as he said, "I documented what I've done and posted it via my link so that everyone else would benefit from our successes and failures." He chuckled as he said, "Liz can confirm there were plenty of failures." Liz nodded with wry eyes. Austin continued, "I was also happy to make use of things that others posted as well."

Liz said, "All of these things have been repeated at plenty of other homesteads. It feels like a real community has been forming gradually out of the wilderness. In spite of the distances, the people seem closer than they would have been on Earth. Everyone can communicate with anyone on the planet, or even elsewhere in the solar system. Everyone takes pride in accomplishments, such as the first crop to be harvested in the season or the discovery of something new that makes our lives a little easier.

"I'm convinced that some areas will become full-blown new settlements or even cities of tomorrow," she continued. "While the area around the Square has begun to take on its own identity, several other areas have started to do so as well. While everyone thinks of himself as a member of the Citadel community, some areas have started to identify with common interests or activities, such as farming certain crops, mining, trade, etc. The regional emergency shelters around have helped, since they provide a common area for people to meet, talk, and unwind."

"There still isn't a lot of what would be called 'infrastructure' outside of the Square," Austin noted, "although settlers in some areas are already starting to cooperate on certain common activities, such as building bridges or trails or even roads. Liz helped make a lot of these things happen, through her efforts to get people lined up to help each other to get things done more efficiently than they could on their own. In other cases, we've had to make these things happen on our own, in view of the distances from others."

"It didn't take long to figure out why cheaters like to hide and wait for victims," Donna said. "Some of the animals they like to eat are well worth our time, too."

"It's funny," Bret said, "that in Earth's food chain some of them probably would have been the rough equivalent of deer and some of them would be more like cows, some more like pigs, etc. In addition to scientific names that nobody uses, we've given them nicknames that are sort of based on their appearance and where they would fit in Earth's food chain. The 'cows,' 'pigs,' and 'deer' are all pretty tasty."

Bret looked over at Donna with a gleam in his eye, and she groaned and said, "Don't say it!"

"They don't even taste anything like chicken!"

Austin said, "The local fauna isn't the only food source we had to learn about. A lot of us have devoted significant acreage toward agriculture. We've had to be practical and make compromises."

Yabuno rolled his eyes as he said, "We needed to make compromises because we've made plenty of mistakes and would have starved while learning from those mistakes if we hadn't used the seeds for Earth crops as a fallback. We've sponsored trips all over Citadel to locate plants that look promising for future planting and harvesting. We now have perhaps half of our farming acreage devoted to Citadel crops and the rest dedicated to Earth crops. Within the next couple of seasons, the ratio will probably be more than seventy-five to twenty-five in favor of local crops, even with an overall increase in acreage planted. It won't be long before we have surpluses available for export to Earth."

Donna smiled as she said, "There's one type of 'crop' we haven't mentioned yet." As the others chuckled, she continued, "It seems that practically every human society or culture ends up developing some type of alcoholic beverage. There was no way we were going to be the exception. Some of the equivalents to Earth grains that we've located for farming also are useful in making beer. We've also found some fairly good equivalents to grapes that can be used to make local wines. So far, not enough hardy souls have expressed enough interest in making hard liquor to make it practical.

"As a result, we now have some breweries and vineyards, usually as small operations that are in addition to other farming elsewhere on the same property." Donna nodded at their cups as she continued, "The first home-grown alcohol was beer, due to the fact that it can be brewed fairly quickly. It tastes pretty good, too. We're looking forward to the day when there will be some good wines ready for drinking.

"A key limit on the consumption of alcohols based on grains is that the grains can also be used for food. People are practical enough to prefer to eat for now and worry about alcohol later. We hope in time to have a market on Earth for wines and beers produced by Citadel." Donna looked again at her husband as she said, "Please don't say it!"

"Too late," Yabuno said with a wry look. "It will be the ultimate in imported alcohol!" A chorus of groans followed. He continued on a more serious note, "That won't be the only thing that Earth ends up importing from us, though. We've been ramping up our mining activities, both on the planet and within the system's own asteroid field. The activities started from the first day, as the mining experts set up operations in space to exploit the resources within the asteroid belt while the settlers were deployed to Citadel.

"Once our geologists confirmed that there is tectonic activity on Citadel, we knew that the pot was being stirred, bringing metals and other materials up near the surface where they can be mined." Yabuno nodded at Austin as he said, "Sam isn't the only one with active mining operations. Several of the land parcels have rich lodes running through them. Collectively, the amount of ore extracted has been enough to justify a number of settlers getting together to establish facilities for processing the ore."

Austin spoke up. "These aren't mines from the Old West, either. They're fully automated and can be programmed to produce specified materials. The mines also have advanced sensors to map out and follow major veins. The equipment can even fabricate and install support structures for the mines themselves as lodes and veins are pursued."

Yabuno continued, "Although there are substantial mining operations in space, it's more efficient, for example, to avoid hauling Citadel ore to the processing facilities in space if the ore can be mined in space. Each set of operations has concentrated on certain needs. The space-based operations concentrate on supplying components for the manufacture and upkeep of all of the operations in space, including transports. Over time, we expect that some materials that are in short supply in Earth's solar system will become valuable for trade. We also expect that as our manufacturing operations became more extensive, we'll be able to supply to Earth a lot of finished goods, especially ones that use these scarce materials."

"It seems that practically every day we're learning more about the biology of the planet and what it could do for us," Liz said. "We've already found that sap from a particular plant serves both as a skin moisturizer and as a more effective sunblock than what we brought from Earth. It even has a nice fragrance. We've also been finding that the chemical compositions of various plants have some promising medicinal benefits. This is great news for our medical staff, as we'll need replacements for some of their supplies, which will run out at some point. Eventually, our medical staff hopes that all of the basic pharmaceutical needs on Citadel will be addressed locally."

"It hasn't been all good news on Citadel, of course," Yabuno said. "While we have an effective communications network in place throughout the solar system, I'm still concerned that we haven't been able to get the communications working back to Earth's system. While there are some promising concepts under consideration, none of us, Greg, me, or any of our people has come up with a definitive solution for the problem. For all we know, everything is working fine all the way back to the last beacon at the other end of the line. With the warp-field generator problem still unresolved, we can't take any ships out beyond our system to try to inspect any of the other beacons."

Austin's blue eyes dimmed in sadness as he recalled the deaths that had taken place over the past three years, saying, "It doesn't help that we knew that deaths are a fact of life in a community of settlers. This was especially likely in the early weeks and months of our time on Citadel, when we knew the least about the place. In some ways, the first deaths were probably the hardest. Up until that first death, we could maintain the illusion that it would always be the way it had been and no one need die.

"Although we'd planned as best as possible in anticipating our immunization needs, we were reminded in stark terms that no plan is ever one hundred percent perfect. One day, Keith Thomas was a big, strapping man with keen, friendly eyes and a booming voice. The next day, he was at death's door with an infection that invaded his body and seemed to taunt the doctors as they tried to treat it. His muscles withered away practically overnight."

Liz spoke. "What amazed me was Keith's ability to resist the infection many excruciating days longer than anyone would have thought possible. The doctors had made enough progress that they felt they could save him if he could last another day." She shed a small tear as she continued, "Keith didn't have that day left in him and died a pitiful shadow of the man he'd been. Sadly, his little girl wasn't strong enough to fight the infection and was gone before her father, even though she had come down with symptoms after him. He was too far gone by that time to understand that his girl had died."

Liz shook her head as she said, "It felt to me like such a cruel twist that Keith's wife, Karen, came down with the same infection several days after Keith and was near death herself when Keith died. Somehow, in spite of her grief over the loss of her husband and daughter, she held on for the extra day that her husband had lacked and the doctors were able to tailor the treatment enough that Karen recovered. It was bittersweet comfort that the doctors were able to learn enough from their treatment of the Thomas family that they could modify their immunization treatments and protect the rest of the community from the disease. Since then, no one has suffered from that particular infection. There have been plenty of other diseases to worry about, though."

"As if that wasn't enough," Yabuno said, "while we were still in mourning over the first deaths on Citadel, it was only a couple of weeks later that another one took place. This time, the invasion wasn't in the form of an infection, but from an old danger…"

There had been an increase in the number of cheater sightings, but they didn't worry Louise Brittel. Although their perimeter fence hadn't yet been completed, their scanners would let her know in plenty of time if a cheater was anywhere nearby. She was always armed when she went outside and considered herself to be a good shot. She was in their vegetable garden, working with several native varieties that had turned out to be delicious. She marveled that even someone as picky as Greg was when it came to eating veggies didn't need any encouragement to eat these plants. She was smiling and never saw the shadow that crept nearer and nearer, shifting and stretching into a deadly presence.

Brittel was working on their planted acreage a couple of miles away. Although their links were tied together so that they'd know about any warnings from the scanners, there was nothing but silence for hours. He didn't become worried until he was done for the day and tried to contact Louise, only to receive the same silence. He worried even more when he saw the fresh cheater tracks pointing straight toward the vegetable garden. Although the grisly find provided its own explanation of what had happened to Louise, Brittel was desperate to know why it had happened.

"After checking out the links and the rest of the scanner system, the best Greg could figure was that some type of glitch had screwed up the scanners temporarily," Yabuno concluded with a frown. "That's a way of saying that we'll never know for sure. One thing we know is that she'd never pulled out her weapon. At least the end would have been pretty quick."

"Some people would prefer to go down fighting," Austin said quietly. "Speaking of how people prefer to do things, what happened is a reminder of how different things can be on a settler world. Settlers often find themselves making decisions that might seem rushed or even mercenary to others but make sense in that environment. Greg and Karen were neighbors and had both lost their spouses.

Within three months after presiding over the funerals for Keith and Louise, I officiated at the marriage of Greg and Karen, which was my first since we arrived at Citadel."

Donna had a bittersweet look on her face as she said, "There seemed to be as many tears at the marriage as there had been at the funerals. I guess we all tried to see past the sadness from the losses and focus on the fact that a new family was being formed. I remember talking with Karen over where they were going to live. Karen's husband and child had died on her property and Greg's wife had died on his. The memories were harder for Karen so they moved in together on Greg's property, although she still has her property."

Austin looked around the group with steely blue eyes as he said, "One thing I've taken to heart is the folly of relying too much upon any one approach for protection. Wherever possible, I've used redundant or overlapping backups to our systems. I'll be damned if I'm going to allow a system glitch to deal death to anyone in my family the way it did to Louise."

CHAPTER FIFTEEN

Austin was distracted from his report by a signal from Yabuno. "What's happening, Bret?" he asked.

"We've just received a signal from the array at the entrance to our solar system, Sam. It says there's a ship that's just outside our front door!"

Screw the report! "What the hell is one of our ships doing out there? Come to think of it, that wouldn't be something that you'd tell me about. Why *are* you telling me about it?"

"I'm telling you about it because it doesn't make any sense. None of our ships is scheduled to be out there. The signal shows a ship that looks just like Number Nineteen, which we know is impossible."

Austin stopped for a moment, remembering that death had visited for the settlers even before they'd reached Citadel. He continued more softly, "What if we were wrong about Nineteen? What if there was a way the crew and passengers could have survived?"

Yabuno's eyes closed for a moment as he remembered his lost friends and said, "I wish to hell that by some miracle they could have survived this long, but the only scenarios that we can figure out have a pretty damned low likelihood of happening. None of them is pretty."

Austin's face brightened as he said, "I hope their imaginations were better than ours. Maybe we'll learn something. Do we have any visuals yet from the area?"

"They'll be coming in shortly."

"Send out an emergency message to the team and let them know that some interesting images will be posted in a few minutes. Let's link up and talk."

Austin, Liz, Yabuno, Brittel, and others were in the main communications room at the Square, with others linked in. The team hadn't been together for a while, and people were having some difficulty controlling their feelings as they looked at an image they knew all too well. The feelings spilled over into chatter that made it impossible to carry on a discussion.

"Well, folks," Austin broke in, "I know how you feel, but how about keeping a lid on the bullshit so we can focus on what we know. Bret, can we confirm that that is Nineteen?"

Yabuno replied, "We can't make out the markings from this angle, Sam, but it looks like a perfect match for Nineteen as far as the shape and configuration are concerned."

"That's like saying it's a perfect match for any of the ships that haven't been converted since our arrival. Have we confirmed that none of them is missing?"

"Yes, all of them are confirmed as being on our side of the radiation field."

"Greg, if that's Nineteen, why haven't they sent us a message? They have the codes for access to voice communication with our array."

Brittel shrugged his shoulders as he replied, "Beats me, Sam. The only reason that comes to mind is that their communications system isn't working. It could also be that their data files have been corrupted somehow and they've lost the access codes."

Someone else said, "I don't think it's Nineteen. Look."

All eyes checked out the screen, not quite grasping what the comment meant. Someone then gasped and said, "There's another one!" It was true. Another ship had appeared on the screen, identical to the first one. Considering that they'd only lost one ship, what they were seeing was impossible. Another ship then joined the others. They found themselves staring at three ships at the entrance to the radiation field, each identical to Nineteen.

Austin said, "We know Nineteen can't have multiplied into three ships. The only other possibility is that these ships are from a more recent launch from Earth. If the Citadel Group had gone ahead and built more ships, they'd be able to communicate with us. The fact these ships haven't used the communications codes suggests that they aren't part of our group."

Yabuno replied, "I'd like to know how the hell they managed it, whoever *they* are. When we left Earth four years ago, our ships were the only ones capable of making this trip. Nothing else was on the horizon at the time that suggested that anyone would be ready to make the trip anytime soon. We know better than anyone how lucky we were to make it here."

"What're the chances that someone else could duplicate our designs to this level of detail, Bret? We didn't make a secret of our departure, and I'm sure there must be countless images floating around of our ships as they left the solar system."

Yabuno shook his head as he stood in front of a large screen. He pulled up images of a Citadel ship, along with one of the visitors' ships. "There's no way that could have happened, Sam." He pointed to a place on the visitors' ship and said, "Now that the images have been cleaned up, I can see a structure on these ships that was only added to ours a month before we left Earth. That change was based on some last-minute test results that we didn't share with anyone."

"You're saying they had help?"

"That's a polite way of saying it," Yabuno said darkly. "I'm saying they had to have stolen our designs and data. It almost certainly had to have happened just before we left."

"I get why it couldn't have happened any earlier than just before we left Earth," Austin began. "Why couldn't it have happened after we left?"

"It's clear that someone built these ships precisely as described in the current design file for the ships. The file was scheduled to be updated a couple of days before our departure to provide for a modification to that structure I mentioned. We'd have incorporated the modification into our ships, but we were too close to departure to be comfortable that the job of configuring it would be completed in time."

Yabuno pointed again at the visitors' ship and said, "The structure that we added was a compromise that did an OK job of dealing with the test results and was one that we could get configured in time to avoid delaying the departure. It wasn't a question of whether the modification would work; it was just a question of having to take more time to get it configured than we had available. If the people who stole our files had gotten the updated file, they'd have incorporated the modification into the structure. Because they didn't, we know pretty much when they had to have stolen the file."

"While I'd like to know how they got our designs at this point, the fact is that three of their ships are knocking at our door, or will be once they tweak their systems to contact us or we give them access. We have to figure out what to do about it when that happens."

"Why don't they just come in, if they have our data?" someone asked. "Our files included the correct path to take to get here safely."

Austin's face had a look of grim amusement as he said, "That data would be their death warrant if they were to use it. Remember what it was like for us when we got here? When *Pathfinder* tried to reconfirm the safe path from her first trip here, she learned that the path had already shifted somewhat. We know that things have shifted again in the three years since that point. We only know it because we've kept the field under continuous monitoring with even more powerful sensors that we've developed since our arrival."

Yabuno continued, "We're still not sure if the shifts have been because of the gravity from the outer planets or something else. We *are* sure that anyone following the original path would be traveling in his coffin."

Liz looked at Austin and asked, "What do you think we should do, Sam?"

Austin looked back and said, "I think we need to have a chat with them. Greg, let's give them access to the communications array and give them a call."

"Access has been granted, Sam. At least we'll be able to talk practically in real time, thanks to work we've been doing to accelerate messages from beacon to beacon. You can start at any time."

"Thanks," Austin said, as he turned to face the screen. He continued, "To the unidentified ships at our doorstep, welcome to the Citadel star system. I'm Sam Austin, the leader of the Citadel settlements and operations. Please respond and identify yourselves."

As the seconds ticked away into minutes, everyone kept their eyes focused on the large screen. Finally, after nearly ten minutes had passed, they received word that a response had arrived. Brittel said, "They've acknowledged your message and are requesting a direct video link, Sam. You can talk to the big screen."

A face appeared on the screen. After four years of knowing each adult face on every screen, it was startling to see an unfamiliar one. What was equally startling was seeing the unfamiliar face in such a familiar setting, as the ship's bridge was identical to the bridges on their own settler ships. The face was of a man who appeared to be in his late thirties. The most obvious feature was his attitude. He either wouldn't or couldn't hide his arrogance. He began, "Greetings from Earth,

Austin. My name is Roger Card. I'm the captain of the lead ship and the leader of this expedition." His smile wasn't entirely friendly as he continued, "Hope you're ready for some competition, Austin, because we plan on becoming your neighbors."

Austin smiled as he said, "Welcome to Citadel, Captain Card, and thanks for the heads-up about becoming our neighbors. Before we hand out the keys to the place, why don't you tell us about yourselves? How many of you are there? How the hell did you get here? Is everyone OK? The works."

Card replied, "There are around two hundred of us, spread out among four ships. We got here the same way you did, spending a year doing not much of anything."

Austin asked, "You said your people are spread out among four ships, Captain. I only see three."

Card replied, "We left with four ships. We expect that the fourth one will be along shortly."

Austin spoke gently, "Don't be too sure about that, Captain. We lost one of our ships during the voyage. We'd give anything for it to show up, but that was three years ago. When we first saw your ship, some of us were wondering how the hell our ship had survived."

"I guess we disappointed you."

"I didn't mean it as a complaint," Austin replied. "We're glad that you made it safely. You can understand that we were hoping to see the faces of those we'd given up for dead."

"Yes, I can understand," Card said with a shrug. "What happened to your ship, the one that didn't make it?"

"While we'll probably never be able to confirm what happened, it seems likely that our ship's warp-field generators failed due to a design flaw."

"It seems convenient to blame it on something that didn't stop any of your other ships from getting here OK."

There was some heat in Austin's eyes as he replied, "It nearly stopped the ship I was on from getting here, Captain. Our ship's warp-field generators failed as well. It was only through incredible luck that we were able to get here. The generators for that ship are now useless. The majority of our other ships had similar problems, but not as severe. They were able to get here, but none of those generators would be worth a damn for a return trip to Earth." Austin's voice took on a more barbed tone as he said, "From what we can see, the same would be true for you."

"What do you mean?"

"Captain, I'm sure you're an intelligent man and know that I don't have a reputation for tolerating bullshit. Your ships are exact copies of ours. We know that we didn't hand out the designs for ours, so the only way you could have gotten them is without our permission. There are less polite terms for what that means, but you can fill in the blanks. That means, among other things, that there's no way that you'll be able to return to Earth in your ships, because your warp-field generators have the same design flaw that ours have." Austin's smile became less pleasant as he continued, "You haven't picked a very good way to introduce yourselves, Captain, and you're going to have to work damned hard at earning our trust, under the circumstances."

"We don't see it that way, Austin. Citadel proper is a big planet, and if you mind your business on your half, we'll mind our business on our half."

There were a few gasps, followed by dead silence that lasted for a full minute. Austin said slowly, "You'll need to explain that last comment, Captain."

"There's nothing to explain," Card replied. "We're helping ourselves to half of the planet. There isn't any limit on the size of a claim. We're just more ambitious than you are."

Austin's eyes became a cold blue as he said, "I guess I'll use the word after all, Captain. You're a bunch of thieves. You've stolen our knowledge, which took an incredible amount of time, effort, and resources to create, and then you have the balls to use it to come here and claim half our planet with what, a hundred and fifty people? I hope I'm wrong in assuming that your fourth ship is lost, but I need to be realistic. We now have over ten thousand people here, and we're not that greedy!"

A look of dismissal crossed Card's face as he replied, "I won't argue with you over how we got the designs, Austin. You can sue us on Earth if you want, although you'll need to be there to do it." His smirk became even more insufferable as he continued, "I guess your design flaw means that the statute of limitations will have expired before you can get your asses back to Earth to sue us. As far as claiming big chunks of the planet, we have every right to do it and we have the means of enforcing our claims."

"What do you mean?"

"One of the reasons why we have a lot fewer people on our ships than you did on yours is that we had to make room for some heavy weaponry. Too bad your ships don't have any." The smile on Card's face was unpleasant as he continued, "As you've said, we've seen the designs!"

"All this planning and greed, and you're forgetting something pretty damned important."

A look of impatience flared across Card's face as he said, "Do you really think that you're the only ones who can figure out how to get through a radiation field, Austin? We have the files with the original pathway that *Pathfinder* developed, and we can make any minor adjustments that may need to be made."

It was Austin's turn to show some impatience. "Those files are years out of date and aren't worth a damn at this point, Captain. The adjustments are anything but minor and are a lot harder to work out than you realize. You may think it's safe to enter the field, but you'll find out that it's a dead end without our updates. Even *we* haven't yet figured out how to predict the changes to the field, and we've been trying for three years."

The look of impatience swelled back into arrogance as Card replied, "I've studied you for years, Austin. No matter what you may think of us, I don't believe for a moment that you'd let us die in that field, especially if you really believe that we can't return home. Your humanity won't let you condemn us to death."

"We'll welcome neighbors, but we won't welcome invaders and thieves. If you want to enter this system, you'll have to persuade us that you'll be the former."

"What do you propose?"

"Before you enter this system, you will transmit the designs for your ships, especially any changes that you've made to our designs. You will also transmit to us all master access codes for your systems. You'll dismantle and eject into space all of your weapons other than personal side-arms. That means all ship-based weapons must go. You'll also need to agree to a much more modest set of land claims. Finally, you'll need to agree to our jurisdiction over your affairs, in the same manner as applies to everyone else on this planet. These terms are not negotiable."

Card's smirk was more of a sneer as he said, "You must think we're a bunch of idiots, Austin, to agree to those terms. We'd be at your mercy."

Austin smiled tightly as he replied, "That's no different than for anyone else that's here, Captain. Your problem is that you assume that everyone else is like you. When we did the screenings for this journey, we were careful to exclude people like you. Thieves and cheats don't make good settlers. We chose people with a different sort of toughness." Austin's face hardened as he said, "Last chance, Captain. Do you accept our terms?"

Card replied, "I have a better idea, Austin. You'd be better off giving us the updated files, because if you don't, then when we finally get through, we won't be in as much of a mood to accept *you* as *our* neighbors. *You're* the one that better accept terms, because we won't offer them again."

Card saw the grim look on Austin's face that showed neither fear nor pity, and he flinched as Austin said the words, "Do you really think so?" Austin continued, quietly, "In my time, Card, I've dealt with people who were much nastier than anything you'll ever be, no matter how far into the sewer you dive. I've killed terrorists and murderers with my bare hands. I've faced down monsters who wanted to destroy Earth. You're a fool to even think of having me as an enemy, let alone the good people of this settlement.

"You have one hour to disarm yourselves as instructed; after that, you can go to hell for all we care. If you've never seen radiation poisoning, it's a lousy way to die. The radiation here is strong enough to send you to hell pretty damned fast." At a motion from Austin, the screen went blank.

The room was quiet for a few moments, as the reality of the situation sank in. Liz moved toward him, lending support without crowding. Finally, he looked around and asked, "Thoughts, folks? There are probably some here who thought I was too harsh in giving them an ultimatum, but I've dealt with too many snakes over the years to be willing to place your safety in jeopardy."

Although Yabuno wasn't smiling, there was a dark humor in his eyes as he said, "Hell, Sam, I thought you weren't harsh enough! I'd have told them to turn around the way they came and take a chance on getting back in one piece. I don't think I could ever trust them, even if they did everything you asked. It's too much to ask of us to be on the lookout for fellow settlers at the same time as we're on the lookout for cheaters. Right now, I'm not sure which would be worse to have around."

Austin smiled sadly, as he said, "I don't disagree with anything you said, Bret; however, I had to try to find a way for them. I've seen what it's like to be trapped in space with no options but to die slowly or die quickly. Besides, they might find that we're a lot more resilient than they think, assuming that they can get through the radiation field intact."

Even the dark humor faded from Yabuno's voice as he said, "I'm glad that I'm not the leader of this community. I don't know how you figure out the right way to balance the needs of this community with a situation like this."

"I'm not sure I know how to do it any better than anyone else. I've just had more practice at it."

"There's movement, Sam," Brittel called out.

"What kind of movement, Greg?"

"Nothing like what you told them to do. They're heading toward the 'entrance' to the radiation field."

"How many ships?"

"All of them."

Austin frowned. "They're fools to send everyone in now, before they even know if it can be done."

"They may not be sure that the others can follow them other than by walking in the footprints of the guy in front," Brittel replied. "That's how we did it the first time."

"God help them, even though they're thieves," Austin murmured softly to himself. He raised his voice as he continued, "Unless they have the most incredible luck, we should have enough time to prepare for their arrival if they somehow get through. This is one contingency plan I'd hoped we'd never need, but let's start things rolling. Greg, let us know once they're in the field."

It wasn't long before Brittel confirmed, "They're in the radiation field, Sam. They're sending out probes to figure out where the path has changed."

"That won't help them once they get further into the field," Yabuno said. "They'll need both patience in using the probes and the skill to figure out how to interpret the fucked-up images that'll come back from the probes. Also, they don't have their own *Pathfinder* to help to figure out things." Yabuno's face revealed a tight smile as he said, "That's an interesting thought."

"What's interesting, Bret?" asked Austin.

"Nothing for anyone to worry about for now, but something for me to think about for later," Yabuno said.

Thirty minutes later, Austin asked for a status on the visitors' ships.

"They're doing all right so far," Brittel reported.

"That's just finishing up the easy part," Yabuno replied. "It'll be like turning a corner; all of a sudden, even the way you came in is gone. They're at their point of no return, and they don't even know it."

"They've made their move 'around the corner' and have stopped. They're sending out even more probes. I don't think they know which way to turn." Brittel looked over to Austin and said, "We could transmit the updated path."

Austin's face was hard as he said, "It's a lot tougher now for them to do what they need to do. If they open their hatches to dump their weapons, their shielding will be compromised. Besides, the radiation is intense enough that any files we would send to them might be corrupted. That would be true for anything that they might send to us as well."

"So we just watch them die?"

Austin sighed and said, "No, I'm willing to help them, if they're willing to take some risk with opening their hatches just long enough to dump their weapons. Make a call, Greg."

After a few moments, Brittel said, "I have contact, although the quality could be better, Sam. You can talk to the big screen."

Card's image showed up on the screen, although there were occasional freezes and jumps to the images. The sound wasn't any better. Card smiled as he said, "I knew you wouldn't let us down, Austin. I take it you're ready to give us the updated safe path?"

"The conditions still stand, Captain. You'll have to take some risk of radiation exposure by opening your hatches where you are to jettison your weapons, but it probably won't be significant if you move quickly."

Card's face flashed with anger as he replied, "Don't hand me that bullshit, Austin! We both know that you're going to give us the safe path data. We can talk about everything else after we get through safely."

Austin's gaze was steady as he answered, "You're not hearing me, Captain. I'm the leader of this community, and the safety of the people in this community is my responsibility. *Your* safety isn't. Don't push your luck; I'm doing you a favor by being willing to let you in at all, considering the circumstances. Your responsibility is for the safety of your people. You've already placed that safety in jeopardy by trying to enter this system at all without knowing what the hell you're doing. You've made things worse by bringing in all of your ships together. Don't throw away the lives of your people trying to bluff me."

Card's look was defiant as he said, "Fuck you, Austin! You found the way in. *We* can do it too!"

"Clearly, you can't. You don't even know which way to turn next. It took us time to map everything out, and that was with *Pathfinder*, which has much better shielding than your ships. As it was, we nearly lost one of our ships when we used the updated safe path the first time."

Card knew he was beaten. The defiance drained from his face as he said, "OK, Austin, you win. Transmit the safe path as soon as we've dumped our weapons."

Austin shook his head. "It's more than that, Captain. There's information you need to transmit, including designs and master codes for your systems. Even more important is that you need to agree to all of my terms, including the fact that your land grants won't be any larger than ours and will be subject to the same restrictions. You will also be subject to our authority. What's your answer?"

"We accept your terms, Austin."

"Good. You know what to do next. You'll hear from us after you've done your part." At a signal from Austin, the big screen went back to the image of the ships.

The minutes passed, with nothing visible on the screen to indicate that Austin's terms were being met. Finally, after nearly sixty minutes, Brittel pointed at the screen and said, "It looks like they're opening their hatches."

"Zoom in on those images, Greg," Austin said. "Let's see what they're tossing over the side."

Although the images blurred for a moment, they cleared up and people were able to watch some heavy-duty weapons floating freely in space.

Yabuno whistled as he said, "No wonder Card thought he had the leverage! Those cannons could have blasted the hell out of us. I wonder if that's everything?"

"That's why I insisted on getting their designs," Austin said. "Let's keep track of everything that's being jettisoned and match it up against what their designs tell us they should have."

"They could be playing games with their designs, Sam," Yabuno said. "They've had an hour to revise them any way they want."

"I know, but the master codes are a different story. We can use them to tell us if the designs have been altered."

"Card is trying to reach us, Sam," Brittel said. "I'll put it on the big screen."

There were new lines in Card's face as he said, "OK, Austin, we've dumped our weapons."

"You'd better be sure that all of your weapons have been dumped, Captain. I damned well won't be pleased if I find out otherwise. That goes for the rest of what you're supposed to send us."

Card's face showed another flash of anger, although it faded quickly into resignation as he said, "You've seen everything there is to see, Austin. We're ready to transmit the codes and designs."

"Go ahead, Captain."

As the image from Card faded, Brittel called out, "We're getting something!"

Austin said, "Bret, check everything out with Greg."

Brittel was startled and said, "I can check it out, Sam."

"I know you can, Greg, but I want multiple sets of eyes on what they send. We have to be certain that they're being straight with us."

Brittel stared at the display for what seemed like the kind of time it took for toast to pop up. He said, "It looks like they're starting with their designs, Sam."

"Are they complete?"

Yabuno spoke up. "At first glance, I don't think so. I don't know yet whether that's because the radiation is corrupting them during transmission or because they're trying to hold anything back. I've already set up a comparison run with our own designs. At a high level, we should know pretty quickly if the files are at least complete."

They waited while it seemed that enough time passed for toast to pop up twice. Yabuno's face looked anything but satisfied as he glanced up from his display and said, "I think they held some stuff back and are counting on the fact that there will be corruption to hide what they've done. They probably figure that the file with the safe path will have the information they need, even if they have to clean up the file somewhat first. Either way, what they've sent us is useless."

Austin's face was somber as he said, "That means they're still playing games with us."

"We'll know for sure once they send the master codes. If they don't work, then they're screwed."

Brittel called out, "The master codes are coming through."

Austin thought for a moment and said, "I want to send an instruction that won't place them in any danger but will make it clear that the codes work. Greg, use the master codes to instruct the ships to generate a distress call. The distress call system has redundancies built in, so that even if the system takes a hit from, for example, radiation, it'll still work. Even if the call itself is somewhat garbled, at least we'll have the confirmation we need."

"I've sent the instruction, Sam."

Minutes passed without any change. Austin asked, "Is there any way to clean up or boost the signal before sending it?"

"We've already done it. If they don't respond to what we've sent, then there isn't anything else to do."

Austin's face was sad as he said, "I guess there isn't anything left but to tell them where things stand. Greg, put me through to the captain."

Card's face appeared on the screen. One look at Austin's face and he had his answer. "I take it that it didn't work, Austin."

"The design files you sent to us showed signs of deletions, which tells us that you're still trying to hide something. We tried to use the master codes to send a simple instruction to your ships, without success. There's no way for us to verify that you sent us everything you were supposed to send."

"The files must have been corrupted during transmission, Austin."

"I don't think so. While the radiation has had some impact, it shouldn't have been enough to corrupt the files to this extent."

"Give us another chance, Austin. Maybe we overlooked something or we can clean up any corruption to the files."

"You've been screwing with us. I warned you about the danger of not sending everything you were supposed to send. At this point, I don't care whether you were just testing us or bargaining for time or doing something else. You're on your own, Captain."

Card took a long, hard look at Austin before the transmission ended.

Austin mused to himself, "They've put themselves into this mess, and now it's up to them to get themselves out of it."

"They're on the move again," Brittel reported. "Shit. They're deviating from the safe path. If they don't back-track right away, they'll never find it." Brittel's voice tightened as he said, "They're circling around, trying to find it, but they're off course. The radiation levels are rising fast. They don't have long before the levels become lethal. It'll be even worse if they keep moving in the same direction. They're probably past straight file corruption by now and moving into across-the-board system degradation."

There were plenty of white knuckles in the communications room as people noted the passing of many minutes while the ships seemed to stumble around in desperation and with no idea where to turn next. Brittel stiffened as he said, "They're trying to go back out to the entrance to the field in a straight line, before the radiation kills them."

"Won't do them much good," Yabuno said. "Look at the hell they have to pass through to get out in that direction. They might as well try to dive through sulfuric acid without a protective suit."

"The signals show that their systems are definitely degraded," Brittel said.

"How much radiation…" Austin asked.

Brittel just shook his head as he said, "Too much, and they still aren't back out of the system. They're already dead; their bodies just haven't finished with the dying part yet."

Austin spoke quietly. "Greg, can you establish a link with their ships?"

Brittel was puzzled and said, "Sure, Sam, but giving them the safe path wouldn't do them any good now. With the shape their systems are in, they probably couldn't maneuver through the path now. With the shape their bodies are in, they couldn't try it anyway."

"I don't want to call them to give them the safe path. They're still fellow humans, and I'd like to give them a chance to send us any final words, in case we're ever in a position to transmit them back to Earth. Set up the link."

"It's up, Sam. Go ahead."

Austin's voice increased to fill the screen in front of them, even though they weren't sure their words were getting through. "Captain Card, our instruments have told us what you must already know, which is that you and the others on board your three ships have received a lethal dose of radiation. There is no path available to get you out of danger in time to make any difference in the outcome. That being said, you and your colleagues are still fellow humans, and as such, we will try to transmit to Earth any messages you may have for anyone back home. There's no guarantee that we'll be able to get any messages back to Earth, but we'll send them once we're able to communicate with them. While the quality of any transmissions back and forth is probably poor at this time, we will do whatever we can to clean up any messages you may want to send. Please respond to let us know that you received this message."

Minutes passed without any indication that anyone had heard the message, let alone tried to send a response. Finally, Brittel reported, "We have a response, Sam. It's in pretty rough shape, though, both the audio and the video. I'm not sure how much we'll be able to clear it up. Here it is."

The man they'd seen on the screen before had vanished completely. His smirk was replaced with the strain from trying to keep functioning for as long as possible. Card was facing the screen, barely able to stay upright in his chair. The video image was mostly frozen, with occasional jumps from one spot to another, although the sound was slightly better.

"The...transmission sucks, Austin...your communications...expected more...supposed to be...for us...there's not...point in...help...needed...around...said our goodbyes when we left...always knew it might be a one-way trip."

"Are there any special arrangements you'd like us to make?"

A few minutes later, they strained to understand the response. "...instructing ship...halt outside your star system. The others...tied in...navigation system...will follow...if systems...still working. At least can say...almost made it to Citadel...do whatever...our effects. Ship's controls...released. Tow her or blast...pieces. No need for a radioactive carcass...I'm not noble...must be getting soft."

The last image they saw was of Card slumped over his chair. He no longer struggled to say or do anything. After a while, the image ended, either because the system had failed or possibly due to there being no further activity for a certain interval. A long-range image of the ships appeared.

No one spoke for some time after the transmission ended. Austin turned to Yabuno and said quietly, "Would you arrange for some remote-controlled thrusters to intercept those ships after they've halted on the far side of the radiation field, Bret? The mining folks should be able to lend us their setup for their own remote operations. Let them know it needs to happen right away, in case the ships are unable to stop. Let's keep everything at a safe distance for now. If possible, use the remotes to gain entry to the ships' systems and files and download the files for review. I'd rather keep our people safe on their own ships than ask them to venture onto those death ships, even with protective suits. There may be some answers aboard those ships, and we're going to find them."

"Do you suppose Card was serious about releasing his ships' systems to us?"

Austin looked at the image of the ships on the screen as he answered, "Yes, Greg, I think he was. I've spoken before to men in space who knew they were dying and wanted to get past any bullshit before they checked out for good. Card was in that place. While he wasn't exactly apologizing for his past actions, he was trying to make things right by keeping the ships out of our system but making them ready for recovery. While I won't condone or forget anything he and the others on those ships did and planned to do, I'll also remember how Card chose to go out."

"The thrusters and control ships are underway, Sam," Yabuno said.

"Good. Let's see what the next twenty-four hours bring as far as what the hell these people were doing is concerned."

CHAPTER SIXTEEN

A t Austin's insistence, the team met together, without anyone linking in remotely. It was extremely rare that the entire team was in the same room together, and people assumed that Austin wanted to emphasize to everyone the seriousness of the situation. Yabuno stood before a screen and manipulated images as he spoke to the others, "As best as we could tell, Card released his systems as promised. The problem is that some of the systems had degraded to the point where getting access and running things remotely was pretty damned hard."

"What did you learn about their ship design?"

Yabuno brought up some images that looked familiar but weren't quite as he continued, "They were definitely trying to hold stuff back from us, and for good reason. As we suspected, Sam, they stole our designs and changed them to accommodate their weapons systems. They had some pretty serious stuff on those ships, not all of which had been jettisoned. It's no wonder that they only had room for a small fraction of the number of settlers that we had on our ships."

"What were they planning on doing once they got into orbit around Citadel?"

"They were going to claim half the planet as Card said, then try to muscle us out from our portion. They wanted to take everything that wasn't nailed down, to get an advantage over everyone else when it came to the resources in this system. They didn't give a damn about long-term settlements or the values that are behind our settlements."

"Were they planning on sending any other ships?"

"No, they seemed to think that they could do what they wanted with the ships they had. Anyway, they didn't build any other ships."

"What were you able to learn about the condition of their warp-field generators?"

The images Yabuno brought up were similar to what their own warp-field generators had looked like three years earlier. "As you can see, they were lucky to make it here. There's no way that any of their ships would have been able to make a trip back to Earth. From the data we recovered, plus our own experiences, it's a good guess that their fourth ship ended up the same way as our ship Nineteen.

"One thing that worked for us was that we had a lot of our technical talent with us on the trip here. We were able to figure out how to get around the problem because a lot of us understood the technology. Their people were just copying our technology without really understanding how it works in detail. From what we saw about the skills of the crews for these ships, they had far less understanding of advanced technology than our crews did. That's not to say that they weren't intelligent; with luck, they might have been able to make it work once they got to Citadel, especially since there was already a human presence here that had done a lot of the hard work in showing how to set things up. It *did* mean that they wouldn't have had the ability to recover from what nearly stopped our ship." Yabuno paused again for a moment as he remembered his own people who hadn't made it to Citadel.

Austin said, "I'm not particularly interested in anything of theirs, but I'll ask the question anyway. What, if anything, of theirs can we salvage and use?"

"There's pretty much nothing of value that can be salvaged, Sam, beyond the files that we've already downloaded; the contamination is too extensive."

Liz spoke. "It wouldn't matter to me if there were something worth salvaging anyway. We aren't grave robbers. We should respect the fact that those ships are their tombs and treat them accordingly."

"I only asked the question because sometimes settlers don't have the luxury of turning down the use of certain available resources." Austin faced the rest of the group as he continued, "As far as I'm concerned, Liz is right; those ships are tombs, to be treated with respect. At the proper time, we'll perform a service for them and record it in case we have an opportunity to make contact with their families. It'll have to be via remote control, since we don't want to try to touch any of the bodies."

"What do you want to do with their ships?"

"We can't bring them into our solar system to park somewhere, and I don't see any reason to contaminate deep space with highly radioactive tombs. I think the best thing to do is send them, along with their crews, straight into Citadel's sun, from the side facing away from our planet.

"On the other hand, especially in view of their objectives and the fact that they were thieves, the files are ours to do with as we please. This brings us back to the basic question, which is who gave the designs to these people?"

Yabuno spoke. "As everyone knows, Sam insisted that everyone on the team be here in person, but he didn't say that it was because I requested that it be this way. I'll start out by telling you what I found.

"At first, it was hard to get a handle on where the thieves got the designs. It wasn't until I thought about the fact that they didn't have their own *Pathfinder* that things started to click for me." He brought up an image of *Pathfinder* for emphasis.

"What's so special about their not having their own *Pathfinder?*" Brittel asked. "They only had four ships. They might not have had the resources to build another *Pathfinder.*"

"Not likely," Yabuno replied. "Remember the conversation we had years ago about shielding? Because of their design, there wasn't much that could be done to improve the shielding for the settler ships. On the other hand, there was a lot that could be done to improve the shielding for *Pathfinder*. Having their own *Pathfinder* would have increased their chances of success hugely, because *Pathfinder* became tough enough to handle much higher amounts of radiation than the other ships. They could have sent their *Pathfinder* through the radiation field separately to map out a safe path. These people were greedy, not stupid. If they didn't have their own *Pathfinder*, it's because they didn't have access to the updated designs. This tells me that they couldn't have simply broken into our systems and stolen our designs, because they would have taken the updated *Pathfinder* designs."

"Why couldn't someone have used an external system to transmit the files?" Liz asked.

"External systems were unable to handle the speeds and file sizes that we needed. Also, external systems were inherently unsecure, so people weren't allowed to use them while the project was underway. We got a lucky break in being able to narrow down the window of time to within a couple of weeks. This meant that we knew the time frame to use in looking for the transmission of a huge file."

"People were sending and receiving huge files regularly at the time, Bret," Brittel said.

Yabuno shook his head. "That's not quite correct, Greg. As you'll recall, we had a security lockdown during that period. Since the only files that large were technical files, they couldn't be sent without an OK from me. Since *Pathfinder's* design had already been completed, no one had any reason to transmit it anywhere, so it was locked away, with multiple passwords and other security in place for protection. We were still doing the last-minute modifications to the settler ships, so some people had to be able to have access to the entire file for their design. All of the 'OKs' that I issued at the time for the designs have been accounted for."

"I don't understand your point," Brittel said with a frown.

"I didn't know it then, but there was a transmission at that time that wasn't tracked officially. The file size is exactly the size needed for the complete design for the transports."

Austin's voice had darker undertones as he asked, "Who gave them the designs?"

"While I can't give an answer for his motivations, Greg gave them the designs."

Brittel's face was an angry red as he said, "You're full of shit, Bret! I don't know what game you're playing, but my transmission logs show that I didn't send anything larger than regular files during that time."

Yabuno looked unimpressed, saying, "You're a communications guy, Greg. You know how to play your own games with transmission logs."

Brittel pushed back. "So I'm a bad guy because you can't figure out how our designs got out and need to blame someone just because he has communications skills?" His eyes narrowed as he continued, "With that kind of reasoning, maybe we should be looking at *you* more closely!"

With a touch of sarcasm, Yabuno said, "Your phony outrage doesn't work, Greg, thanks to something I did years ago that I never thought I'd need to revisit. I inserted a mirroring protocol into our transmission system that copied everything being sent from certain locations, regardless of whether it was logged or tracked. While you were extremely careful to hide your tracks, you didn't know to look for my little surprise."

Brittel was startled and then recovered, saying, "I don't know what you mean by a 'mirror,' but anything you've mentioned can be faked. You could be saying all of this to divert people's attention from *your* being the traitor."

Yabuno smiled without humor as he replied, "I'm glad we agree on what to call you, Greg. I was telling the truth when I said we'd downloaded everything from Card's ships that we were going to be able to download." His gaze turned cold as he continued, "However, I didn't share everything about what we'd learned from those downloads. Although it was *your* team that ran the analyses of Card's transmissions, they came to *me* once they'd heard the expanded version of what Card had to say, which included some interesting words about *you*. At my request, they reported back to you that they hadn't been able to get anything useful from the transmission that we hadn't already heard. You can listen to Card's own words as they damn you."

Yabuno manipulated an image on the screen. A few seconds later, they heard Card's voice. Although the sound quality wasn't always good, they were able to understand much more than they had before. Card's voice began, "We didn't think we'd be in this mess, since we bought your communications guy…expected more from him, like the updated safe path. He's supposed to be an asset for us…he sent us the designs for your ships… not much point in promising him more land after we take over if he won't help out when he's needed. Watch your backs around this guy."

While Brittel found that every other set of eyes in the room glared at him with emotions ranging from mere coldness to outright hate, he flinched as Austin's eyes bored into his with a cold blue fire. Although Austin spoke quietly, there was no mistaking the extreme danger that Brittel faced. "I can confirm the authenticity of the message with your team, Greg. Do I need to?"

Brittel shook his head, saying, "Card was hallucinating from extreme radiation exposure, Sam. I just happened to be someone he mentioned while he was hallucinating. It could have been anyone."

"Card was lucid, Greg, and knew he was dying. Is everything that Bret told us true? Did you sell out the friends and colleagues that you've known for years?"

Brittel was silent.

The pain of betrayal coursed over Austin's face as he asked, "Why, Greg? You've always been a friend and a key member of the team. You seemed to have believed in the dream as much as any of us. You were married to a wonderful woman, God rest her soul, who shared the same dream. You have a hell of a land grant, plus the brains to make a go of it. Why would you place all of that in jeopardy?"

Liz spoke. "I think I know why, Sam."

Austin was startled by her voice as he turned to her and asked, "What do you mean, Liz?"

Liz continued, "It's all coming together for me now. Once I explain it to you, it will mean there's even more bad news. It starts with the fact that Greg didn't really love Louise."

"You're lying, Liz," Brittel said.

Austin turned to Brittel and said, "Greg, I was born in an era where it was a hell of a lot more fashionable for a man to defend his wife from aspersions on her honor. If you interrupt Liz again, I'll show you how men of my day dealt with men like you." Austin turned back to his wife and said, "Please go on, Liz."

She continued, "Everyone remembers back when my fiancé and I ended our engagement. We all know that it meant that I wasn't going to Citadel. It wasn't long after that that Greg approached me in private and let me know that he wanted to go to Citadel but not with Louise. In order to meet the rule about being married, he told me that he was willing to leave Louise and go to Citadel with me as husband and wife." Liz shivered with revulsion as she said, "He said that he'd always been attracted to me and thought it would be a good match."

"Obviously, you didn't take him up on his offer," Austin said.

"I told him that it didn't work that way with me. I had to be in love with the man I would marry and I wasn't at all interested in him. I was also appalled at what it would mean for Louise."

"You didn't say anything to anyone about it."

"Greg never mentioned it again and stayed with Louise. I assumed that he had worked through whatever issues he had with her. They also went through the same counseling that other couples did, and they were still with the program."

Austin was still puzzled. "What does any of this have to do with why he would sell us out?"

"Near the end of the training, prior to liftoff, you'll remember that Greg and Louise weren't working well together as a team. It was clear that *he* was the main problem, and he was told to get his act together or forget about going to Citadel. The timing checks out with when Bret said the design had to have been stolen." She didn't bother to hide her revulsion as she continued, "I think Greg made an arrangement to ensure that he'd get to Citadel one way or another, or at least profit from

Citadel. As it happened, he was able to set aside his ego enough that they completed their training and qualified to go to Citadel, but he couldn't be sure at the time that it would work out. Selling us out was an insurance policy."

Austin's face darkened as he said, "I don't like where this story is going. There's more, isn't there?"

"Yes, Sam." She nodded. "If Greg was willing to get rid of Louise once, without any consideration for the impact on her, there's every reason to believe that he'd be willing to do it again, especially if there was some way to benefit from it. Karen Thomas was a widow with a land grant that is literally next door to his land grant. With Louise out of the picture, he could pursue Karen and suggest that they do what plenty of settlers in similar situations have done. It couldn't be a divorce, because it would have been pretty ugly if he'd divorced Louise just to be with Karen. He might have ended up with just half of his original land grant and nothing from Karen, plus the disapproval of the community. I feel for Karen, because I can't believe she knew anything about what Greg was doing."

Brittel spoke. "Sam, just because you don't like me anymore doesn't make me a murderer. Louise's death was just an accident, just like Keith Thomas's."

Austin replied, "I'd really like to believe you, Greg, because if you had anything to do with Louise's death, we'll have something even nastier to sort out than we already do." Austin turned to Yabuno and said, "Bret, take a team and tear Greg's equipment apart and anything else if necessary to figure out what really happened. Don't accept anything that you can't verify with your own eyes and equipment." Austin turned back to Brittel with narrowed eyes and asked, "Anything else you want to say, Greg?"

Brittel had a look of wounded innocence on his face as he replied, "It was Liz that approached me to leave Louise, not the other way around. It's no secret that she was dumped by her fiancé because he didn't want to go to Citadel. She was desperate to get to Citadel, with no chance to do it unless she could find someone willing to marry her. *I'm* the one that told *her* no, that I wouldn't even consider leaving Louise for her. As far as our having a rough time with the training, some people are better at it than others. I'm not proud of the fact that most of our problems were because of me, but once I was told to get my attitude changed, we did fine." Brittel's voice took on a dismissive tone as he continued, "Liz seems to be the only one that somehow 'knows' that Louise and I weren't in love, when everyone else would tell you just the opposite."

Brittel held his hands up and apart in a gesture of reasonableness as he said, "We all know how dangerous a frontier can be. In spite of our best precautions, Karen's husband and child died from something native to the area. Likewise, in spite of our best precautions, Louise died from something native to the area. She either ignored any warnings or, more likely, didn't receive any because of a glitch in the system. Unfortunately, I was in our fields a couple of miles away at the time and couldn't help her when she needed it the most.

"As far as Karen and I are concerned, I don't have to explain to any of you how two people can find comfort and strength together when dealing with their losses and decide to make a new beginning together. It's different from what each of us had with our first spouses, but with each day, our own bond grows." Brittel looked sharply at Liz as he said, "I suppose now you'll say something negative about *that* relationship."

Brittel looked back at Austin as he continued, "As far as *you're* concerned, Sam, you shouldn't even be involved at this point. You have a conflict of interest, because you feel honor-bound to take your wife's word over anyone else's word, even if there's no evidence to back up her story. It also doesn't place Liz in a good light if it appears that after striking out with me, she bided her time and found someone else to marry in order to get to Citadel. You were really the only person it could have been, since you were the only unmarried person that was going to Citadel."

With a skeptical look, Austin asked, "What reason would Liz have to bring it up now?"

"Liz and I both agree that we had a conversation on the subject of getting married and going to Citadel, although we disagree on the particulars of that conversation. It appears that she never mentioned that conversation to you. This is probably her best chance to tell the story in the best light possible for her, although she'll still have to admit she kept it a secret from you. You can't expect people to believe that you could keep your role as a husband separate from your role as the leader of this community."

Liz had always understood that the day might arise when Greg would try to twist around their conversation, but she was stunned at the effective way that he made it seem that she was an opportunist who had been searching for someone to marry so that she could get her ticket to Citadel. She didn't know if their marriage had taken a major blow because of Brittel's desperate efforts to save his hide.

Austin spoke. "Here's what I think is going on, Greg. You know that there will be grave consequences for your having sold us out. *Treason* isn't too strong a word for what you've done. However, you're not sure how grave those consequences will be. It's another matter if you are found to have killed Louise. There would be plenty of people lining up to supply the rope to hang you if you killed her.

"You've been trying to tell a story to the effect that Liz has been living a lie, has been greedy, opportunistic, etc. The problem is that we already know someone who has been living that kind of lie and is greedy, opportunistic, etc. We know you sold us out while presenting a facade of being a good man and pillar of the community, which is one of the worst kinds of lies in a place like this. The fact that Liz didn't share with me a conversation where you made a revolting offer to her in no way lessens her in my eyes. It happened long before we became involved, and people are entitled to keep past events in the past. I'd guess that there are plenty of women in this community who could provide their own stories of having been on the receiving end of revolting propositions from men."

Austin shook his head as he continued, "Frankly, your own actions have served to impeach your credibility on this claim. You'd have done better to just deny that it happened at all. With apologies to Shakespeare, the web you've created is becoming ever more tangled.

"Your effort to try to distract us by suggesting that I shouldn't be involved was stupid," Austin said wryly. "I'm actually your best hope to see that justice is done, because even though we know you're a liar and a traitor, I'm honest enough to say that doesn't mean you killed Louise. I'm not certain that others would feel the same way. Bret and his people will do their best to get to the bottom of what happened. Once they do, we'll decide what to do with you."

With a cold gaze, Austin said, "Until then, I have the authority to have you placed into secure confinement, which will take place immediately. You are suspended from all of your activities on behalf of the community. Your land grants that you shared with Louise are frozen. You will be allowed to have private conversations with your wife but not with others."

Brittel said, "Although we aren't set up for it, I want a legal representative, Sam. I want that person to be present whenever any of my affairs is investigated in order to ensure that my rights are respected."

Austin's eyes burned through Brittel with their cold blue fire as he responded, "Just where the hell do you think you are, Greg? You're on a frontier world, where people should be able to look each other in the face and know that they can trust each other's word. We already know you've committed treason and gotten into bed with people who planned on taking away our rights and maybe even our lives. When we set things up on Citadel, we made a conscious decision not to create a system where lawyers would end up running everything. Although there are protocols for these matters set forth in the organizing documents for the community, I have a fair amount of leeway in implementing them.

"This is a good thing for you, since I've been the president of the United States and have written amendments to the US Constitution to ensure that the rights of the people are respected and preserved. As far as your request for a lawyer is concerned, you can ask someone to speak on your behalf when the time comes, but you will not interfere with the investigation in any way. I urge you to cooperate fully with the investigation, Greg, because it will go harder for you otherwise."

"I have nothing further to say, Sam, except that you're making a mistake."

Austin shook his head as he replied, "I've made plenty of mistakes. Now I have to clean up one of them."

CHAPTER SEVENTEEN

The room had no luxuries but was comfortable. Brittel had been given a new set of clothes to wear. All of his electronic tools had been taken away, and he didn't have any computer access. A video feed was available, but was limited to the large entertainment library they had brought from Earth. There were plenty of stories in fiction where the evil genius was able to make a connection with practically any system and therefore manipulate anything he wanted, usually to terrible effect, even when the person was in a cell. Thanks to Yabuno, however, reality prevailed and Brittel was cut off from the rest of the community.

A clear partition separated the room from an adjoining room, where Karen had seated herself moments earlier. The partition was immensely strong and easily prevented them from touching each other.

"What the hell is this about, Greg?" Karen asked. "When Sam called me, he said you had sold us out to those thieves, that you were a traitor. Now, they think you killed Louise. What have you done?"

"They're trying to make me a scapegoat for what happened with the three ships that came from Earth."

"Why would they want to do that?"

"Sam is pissed off that Liz tried to talk me into leaving Louise so that she could get to Citadel."

Karen was stunned. "*What?*"

With a hint of outrage in his voice, he replied, "Liz has tried to turn things around to say that I was the one who approached her. She's claimed that I wanted to leave Louise and go to Citadel with her. This is bullshit. *She* was the one that wasn't married, not me. I had no reason or desire to leave Louise, and even if I did, I'd never be able to trust anyone who wanted to make that kind of bargain. Sam's honor is offended by what he's found out about his wife, and he has to try to regain his honor by using that story as a reason why I'd sell out the community. That story also makes it seem like I'd have a reason to kill Louise, when everyone knows her death was an accident."

Karen was confused, saying, "That doesn't sound like Sam. It doesn't sound like Liz, either."

"So you're saying you believe their story?" Brittel challenged.

"No, I'm not saying that," she replied quickly. "What can I do to help?"

"This is a fucked-up system we have here," Brittel said in an exasperated tone. "They don't have lawyers the way they do on Earth. Find someone to speak on my behalf. We need to make the point that they can't just frame someone because of the need to protect Sam's honor."

"All right, Greg. I'll do what I can." It wasn't until after she had left that Karen realized that neither of them had said, "I love you," to the other.

Austin and Yabuno were meeting at Austin's home to discuss Yabuno's findings. Yabuno was irritated and said, "Brittel's covered his tracks pretty carefully over having screwed with his alarms, Sam. I know in general terms what he must have done, but I can't find the proof yet. He's been trying his damnedest to use Karen to stir up a phony sense of outrage over the accusations against him. I feel for Karen; she doesn't realize that she's his dupe, or she just can't face the possibility of having made a horrible mistake in marrying him."

"What's your sense of how everyone else is reacting to Brittel's story?"

"I'd say the overwhelming majority of the people know Brittel is blowing smoke in trying to save his sorry ass," Yabuno replied. "Fortunately, it was Brittel's own people who recovered from the thieves the most damning direct information against him. That said, there are always going to be a few people who have trouble believing that one of their own could be a traitor or murderer."

"I'm going to have to hold a hearing on the accusations, Bret. Do you think I should step aside, to avoid the appearance of a conflict of interest?"

The irritation increased as he answered, "No, Sam, I don't. Brittel has tried to manufacture the conflict-of-interest story to get you out of the way. He'll then try to engage in character assassination on both you and Liz, while pretending to be on some crusade to import into our society the worst aspects of the legal system from Earth, where lawyers can engage in demagoguery and other tricks to avoid getting at the truth. I've always thought that leaving that kind of crap behind was one of the best reasons for wanting to come to Citadel. I don't want to let a piece of shit like Brittel weasel that crap into our society. If you step aside, it might happen. Is that what you want for Citadel?"

Austin shook his head, saying, "The fact remains that Liz is a witness to a possible motive for Brittel wanting to get rid of Louise, Bret."

Yabuno smiled as he said, "There's your answer, Sam. You need to learn not to take on so much at once."

The proceedings took place at the main facility at the Square, with a video feed to every link in the community. Virtually everyone on Citadel was watching, fascinated and disturbed over the first thing approaching a trial on the planet since their arrival.

Austin sat at his desk and declared the proceedings to have commenced. Before he could say anything further, Brittel interrupted, "Sam, before these proceedings continue, I want an opportunity to make an opening statement."

Austin frowned and said, "Greg, we've adopted a different approach on Citadel for legal proceedings from what's been used on Earth. However, I'm willing to give you a few minutes to speak before we proceed."

"Thank you." Brittel turned to face the camera directly as he continued, "As most people know, I've been accused of having 'sold out' the people of this community and of having killed my late wife, Louise. A key part of these accusations centers around an outrageous claim made by Liz Austin for which there is no evidence. A reasonable interpretation of the facts would conclude that Sam's honor has been damaged by the actions of his wife and that my rights are to be sacrificed in order to somehow restore that lost honor." A sense of outrage crept into his voice as he continued, "I must also point out that my rights have not been defended during this matter, as I have had no representation by legal counsel.

"I demand that I be allowed to name my own legal counsel with full power to conduct my own investigation, with the power to compel witnesses to testify and the power to issue my own conclusions regarding the matters in question. Further, it is improper that Liz be a key witness while Sam presides over this proceeding. The fact that Sam insists on presiding over this proceeding is confirmation that he not only should be removed from this proceeding but from his role as the leader of this community. I demand that this matter be addressed before this proceeding continues."

Austin realized that although he had the support of the great majority of the people of Citadel, how he acted next might have a profound impact on his future relationship with those people. He began, "Greg, I guess we need to set the record straight about a few things. The first is that we do not use lawyers on Citadel to do what we can do for ourselves. When you were first placed in secure confinement, you were told that you could ask someone to speak for you."

There was a subtle quality of derision in Austin's voice as he continued, "Since no one is speaking at this proceeding on your behalf, it seems that you either didn't ask anyone, or no one was willing to do so. You appear to have a grandiose view of yourself, to believe that you can appoint a lawyer to conduct your own investigation and basically claim that black isn't white or vice versa. The other possibility is that you're pretty cynical to believe that making a grandstanding speech will persuade the people here to agree to go back to a system that wasn't always about getting at the truth.

"Finally, regardless of your motivations, there appears to be some confusion on your part regarding the subject of this proceeding. The only matter that will be covered today is the accusation of your having committed treason against this community. I understand that Bret will be presenting his findings, which will not include any testimony from my wife, Liz. Therefore, there is no conflict of interest relating to my presiding. The accusations against you as they relate to the death of your first wife, Louise, will be addressed upon the conclusion of that investigation." Austin's eyes hardened as he continued, "Now, shut up and pay attention."

Brittel was in shock as it sank in what was happening. His efforts to sabotage the proceedings and save his hide had backfired. He had overlooked the fact that the solution to the issue he raised was to hold a hearing that focused only on the accusations relating to treason. Liz's story wasn't needed to prove that Brittel was a traitor. While the story might help to provide a motive for Brittel's actions, a motive wasn't necessary in order to prove treason. Human nature being what it was, various people were probably already drawing their own conclusions. The case against him for treason was proceeding, and he was effectively being tried for the death of his wife without having the benefit of being able to challenge the accusations.

Yabuno laid out his findings in detail, and the results were damning for Brittel. When Brittel tried to challenge the technology and interpretations relating to the evidence, Yabuno deflected his objections easily, usually resulting in placing the knife in even deeper. The timing of Brittel's actions, plus information from the files of the three ships, plus the final words from Captain Card made it brutally clear that Brittel had indeed sold them out.

As Austin had already pointed out, Citadel had a fundamentally different approach to proceedings. Hearings were conducted by the presiding official, who was Austin. Hearings were focused on getting at the facts, rather than on two sides each trying to distort the facts to fit their respective theories or objectives. Citadel did not have a formal jury system. Input was provided by a panel of advisors that was chosen randomly. The panel of advisors had been meeting to consider the facts and had returned to the hearing room.

Austin asked the panel of advisors for its assessment of Yabuno's findings. The foreman spoke. "The panel agrees with the findings presented by Bret Yabuno. The panel further agrees that the actions by Greg Brittel constitute treason against this community and should be punished accordingly."

Austin thanked the panel for its work and said, "One of the more pressing issues that we've faced is whether the concept of treason can be applied to our community. This takes us to the question of whether our community is a political entity that comprises more than just a set of mutually beneficial commercial interests. There are other issues to consider, such as the ability to exercise control over a defined area, control one's borders, etc. As most people know from their history lessons, we had to consider these very issues as they related to the Mars settlements. Eventually, we concluded that the Mars settlements had evolved into a 'state' that the community of nations on Earth recognized. While we haven't received any such formal recognition as a 'state' from Earth, that recognition isn't required; I believe that such an entity exists on Citadel.

"It is one of the prerogatives of all states that they have the right to protect themselves from attacks by outsiders as well as insiders, without having to seek permission from others to do so. We have reviewed ample evidence that the group that sought to attack our state was such an outsider. Sadly, we have also reviewed ample evidence that Greg Brittel was such an insider.

"Although our organizing documents recognize that extreme punishments may be appropriate on Citadel, Citadel hasn't felt the need before now to enact a formal criminal code. That doesn't mean that crimes can be committed without punishment. It does mean that it would be useful for us to look to the practices of other states for guidance on appropriate punishment in this matter. It is long settled that treason is one of the highest crimes that can be committed against a state, which is why treason is considered a capital crime by most states.

I've confirmed many death sentences in my years as president of the United States, so I'm fully aware of the great responsibility that comes with the power of issuing a death sentence. I will therefore postpone sentencing until tomorrow, to ensure that proper reflection has been made in this matter."

Karen Brittel appeared in the room suddenly and said, "Sam, I'd like to speak for a moment, if I may."

With great courtesy and gentleness, Austin replied, "Please take all the time you need, Karen."

Karen faced Brittel directly as she began, "Greg, when you first told me about the accusations against you, they didn't make sense and I agreed to help speak out on your behalf. I guess I needed to help you, because if what they were saying was true, I made a terrible mistake in agreeing to marry you. Every time I spoke on your behalf, people pointed out that Sam and Liz weren't like the people that you made them out to be, and I didn't have any answer for them."

She frowned as she said, "The more I thought about it, the more I realized that it couldn't simply be a terrible mistake. Either you were right, or they were right. It seemed that everything was at a dead end when they couldn't tie you directly to any sabotage of the alarm unit at your home. I didn't want to leave it there, because there would have always been the question in everyone's minds. I didn't know how to resolve the dilemma. I then realized that there was something that hadn't been checked out before."

Karen pulled out of her tote bag an item that Austin, Yabuno, and Brittel recognized immediately. It was an alarm unit that was identical to the one that every home on Citadel had. Brittel turned deathly white as Karen continued, "This is the alarm unit that I removed today from the home I shared with my late husband. Neither Keith nor I had ever touched it since it was installed originally, but it's clear that someone has opened it since then. Greg, we both know that you're the only other person who has had access to that unit since it was installed, since I gave the pass codes to you after we were married. No one else has them."

Karen turned to Yabuno and handed the unit to him along with the pass codes and said, "Bret, in bringing this unit to you, I've disabled the security for my own home, which we know is a terrible risk to take. I need to know whether Greg had anything to do with the death of Louise. Please tell me this will give you the answer."

As Yabuno ran his diagnostics on the unit, Karen turned back to Brittel and said, "Is there anything you want to tell me, Greg? I gave you the most precious vow a person can give another, the marriage vow. You gave me the same vow. You owe me a straight answer."

Brittel stared back at her without a word. He blinked and looked away.

Yabuno looked up from the unit and spoke to Brittel. "Now that I know what to look for, I can confirm that this is your original unit, Greg, so I already know what you did. It's time for you to answer her. It's bad enough that you've been spreading your bullshit story. According to your story, everyone has either made a mistake or you're a scapegoat because Sam is pissed that his honor has been damaged by Liz or our system here sucks because we don't have lawyers to hide behind when we want to get away with lying. You sank even lower when you asked your wife to spread your lies. For the last time, give her a fucking answer! Did you screw with this unit so that Louise would die?"

Brittel could barely look at Karen as he said, "Yes."

Karen ran from the room, sobbing.

The room was deathly quiet for a full minute.

Austin said, "I guess we'll deal with sentencing for a different crime tomorrow."

The hearing chamber was deserted, except for Austin, Liz, and Yabuno. Although they were feeling the strain of the last several days, they also felt that a great weight had been lifted from them.

Liz gave Yabuno a hug as she said, "Bret, it was so kind of you and Donna to take Karen into your home."

"Donna called me to insist on it before I could even suggest it," Yabuno said with a smile. "Karen shouldn't be alone right now, and Donna is one of the best people to have around when you need to talk. She also knows how to leave people alone when that's what they need."

Austin turned to Yabuno and asked, "What did you learn from the alarm unit?"

With an angry look that was directed at himself as much as Brittel, Yabuno said, "Greg had managed to swap the ID code for each unit, making it appear that the one at his home was the one that had been there when Louise was killed. That fooled me because there aren't any extras around and all of them had been accounted for. I'd have dug deeper if I'd realized that he had access to another unit. Anyway, I found the 'glitches' that he inserted into the unit. Once you put those types of glitches into a unit, it's hard to fix them without leaving traces of what you've done. Since he had to have a working unit at Karen's house, he didn't have any choice but to repair it and hope someone like me wouldn't check it out."

"Why didn't he just destroy the original unit and give everyone a story about not trusting it?" Liz asked. "Oh, right. We don't destroy anything if we can recycle it."

"That's right," Yabuno replied. "Just about everything in that unit can be recycled. It would have been more suspicious for him to destroy perfectly good components, even with some bullshit story about not trusting them anymore. The show he made of checking out the unit after Louise's death proved that the components themselves were fine. Even after recycling, I'd have been able to track down the components and reassemble the unit and figure out what he'd done. He was stuck with the unit and the story he told about it. Swapping it to hide it was his only option."

Liz looked at Austin and said, "I suppose it wouldn't be proper to ask what sentence you intend to impose on Greg tomorrow."

Austin chuckled and replied, "I don't really care whether it is 'proper' to ask. One of the things I hope we avoid on Citadel is worrying too much about what is 'proper' instead of what is 'right.' I'm sure I can trust you two to hold off on telling people that Greg is going to die by hanging."

"You've made the point before about hanging. To this day, capital sentences from military tribunals and convictions for crimes against humanity include hanging. You're the one who pushed for hanging." Liz smiled as she continued, "If you think I'm going to raise an objection to hanging, you're mistaken. I believe you once said that hanging is appropriate for murdering cowards, bullies, and traitors, and Greg is at least two of those things."

Yabuno said, "One thing I noticed you didn't resolve today was the fact that when Greg sold us out, our community didn't yet exist. Doesn't a 'state' have to exist in order for treason to be committed against it?"

"It's a reasonable question," Austin agreed. "Greg could have argued that all he did was commit commercial espionage and we could sue him for damages. The problem for him was that the organizing documents we all signed made it clear that something more than a commercial enterprise was created. Although a court on Earth might not agree, we aren't on Earth, so *our* view is what matters."

Austin's voice hardened as he said, "Besides, although I'd never let the thieves off the hook for their actions, Greg also bears responsibility for the deaths of the crews of the four ships. If he hadn't been a greedy bastard, they'd never have had the chance to make it here. In some ways, he reminds me of the scientists that took the money to develop the New Plague that wiped out billions of lives over a century ago. None of them gave a damn about the impact of their actions on the lives of others.

"However, those are arguments over whether Greg's actions constituted treason. There's still the question of the appropriate punishment in this case. Because of the question over the timing of Greg's actions and when Citadel became a 'state,' I'm not sure that this is the case where we impose a death sentence for treason. Fortunately, I don't have to set a precedent as far as punishment is concerned, because Greg will be executed for the murder of Louise anyway. This preserves our options to impose capital punishment for treason for future cases without having to address questions of whether we acted justly in this case." With a relieved look, Austin concluded, "I don't want our 'state' to start with that kind of question mark on its character."

CHAPTER EIGHTEEN

Austin informed the public the next day that he was postponing issuing a sentence in connection with the treason case. He didn't need to say that the sentence was being postponed because it was unnecessary. He also informed the public that he was imposing on Brittel a sentence of death by hanging for the murder of Louise Brittel. Because of the public nature of Brittel's confession of his involvement with the killing of Louise, plus the technical confirmation of his actions with the alarm unit, he didn't bother trying to appeal the sentence. He knew that the most that would happen would be that he might see one more sunrise on Citadel while an appeal was considered.

The Square became the temporary home to a gallows, which lent a nineteenth-century feel to the place. Brittel was given until the next morning to prepare for his sentence to be carried out. The community took on another aspect of earlier societies, in that the murderer in their midst was shunned by nearly everyone. Since he was already in secure confinement, the practical effect was that none of his friends or colleagues visited him.

Not everyone believed in shunning, however. The community included people who were members of the clergy in various denominations. In spite of the nature of Brittel's actions and the feelings those actions aroused, they offered to visit and pray with him throughout the night. Although he allowed one of them to stay, he refused to engage in any prayers. Karen refused to visit him and refused all of his attempts at communication. He wrote a letter, which he asked the pastor to deliver to Karen. She refused to accept the letter, so the pastor kept it for another time.

The new morning was beautiful, which made it seem impossible that an execution could take place that day. Brittel squinted from the brilliant sunshine that half blinded him as he moved toward the gallows. For centuries, people had embraced mass communication, and it was understood that the execution was of central importance to the community. No one thought of it as entertainment, as the settlers had managed to leave that sickness behind on Earth. The screening process for settlers had included steps to avoid establishing a subset of society that had a morbid fascination with murderers and others who committed violent offenses against society. The execution was something much more solemn; it was a reaffirmation of the fact that actions had consequences and crimes were transgressions against society and were punished by society. People were also reminded that life was far too precious on Citadel for murder to be permitted or even excused.

On a frontier society like Citadel, execution was the only practical solution to murder. There wasn't anything like a traditional prison. There was also no support for the notion that society should provide the resources to support a murderer to live a comfortable life in prison even though life was denied to his victim. Also, by executing a murderer, society would ensure that no other murders would be added to that person's ledger.

Brittel walked up the few steps to the top of the platform. In a tradition that went back centuries, he was asked if he had any last words. He shook his head. He seemed to have used up all of his passions in his earlier attempts to plead his case, as his eyes had little in the way of animation left in them. His hands were tied behind his back, and a black hood was placed over his head. A noose was placed around his neck and pulled snug without choking him. His remaining lifetime consisted of less than a minute as he was left alone on the platform. In a departure from tradition, the trap door had been rigged so that Brittel's own weight would trigger the release within a few seconds after setting foot on the door. For safety reasons, if the weight was off by more than a few pounds, the door wouldn't open. Because of these changes, there would be no need for an executioner. Technology had been his instrument of murder, so it was fitting that it would now be the instrument of his execution.

A few seconds later, it was over. Brittel's neck had been snapped cleanly from the fall, and his body danced briefly; then, it was still. A doctor examined his body and pronounced him dead, and the remains were taken away, to be buried in an unmarked location. Although there was a long tradition of burying spouses next to each other, there was no support for defiling Louise's grave by burying Brittel next to her. While the memory of his crimes would never fade from the community, an unmarked grave in an unreported location would at least remove from the community a direct reminder of his physical presence.

The gallows was broken back down into its original parts, and very quickly, there was no sign that an execution had ever taken place. People wandered away and got on with their lives. The Square returned from the past to the present in appearance. The sun was shining even more brightly than before.

CHAPTER NINETEEN

A month after Brittel's execution, Austin was still amazed and pleased by something that had taken place recently. He expressed his thoughts to Yabuno. "Practically overnight, I found myself swamped with messages in support of my contention during Brittel's hearing that Citadel was now a 'state' or 'nation.' Brittel's actions, along with the actions of Card and his people, had struck a nerve with a lot of people."

Yabuno nodded, saying, "Did it ever! The town hall meeting you called a couple of weeks ago must have been watched by just about everyone in this solar system. I've never seen such a large crowd in the Square."

Austin grinned and said, "I wasn't quite sure what would happen after I made a few opening remarks…"

Austin called the meeting to order, saying, "I want to thank everyone for participating in this town meeting. There's been quite a lot of commentary from people over what the recent events involving the people from Earth and the help they were given by Greg Brittel means for Citadel.

I'll start off by sharing a few of my thoughts and then asking for your thoughts.

"When we first started our efforts to reach Citadel years ago, it was largely a commercial venture. This left us free to set up whatever rules we wanted. However, what we have learned from recent events is that when people take certain harmful actions against a commercial venture, that isn't the same as taking harmful actions against a country. If we are just a commercial venture, it isn't clear if we have any recourse other than to file a lawsuit against those people, perhaps in a court far away where our rights won't be respected.

"I think we are more than just a commercial venture at this point. We've given this place our labor and hopes to make a home that we've sworn to defend. In fact, we *have* defended it against would-be invaders. Perhaps we'll need to do it again. I think it is time for a reset in our relationship with other nations, so that everyone understands what it means to act against us in this distant solar system." Austin stopped and smiled as he said, "I've probably spoken too long. Let's hear what others have to say. Let's start with you, Gina."

A woman nodded to Austin and looked around at her neighbors before saying, "My name is Gina Albretti. I think what Greg Brittel tried to do to us *was* treason. I'm not really interested in fancy arguments for diplomats to use about when something special came into existence that other nations would recognize as being a new nation. Brittel knew he was supposed to be working with us to set up a community, and he sold us out. Just because some time elapsed between when he sold us out and when the scum he did business with tried to take over doesn't mean he breached a contract, with no hard feelings. He had to know what that asshole Card and his people were planning to do to us, and he didn't care. If he wanted the benefit of claiming that what he did didn't count as treason, he could have confessed to it long before and taken his lumps."

She stepped up to the giant screen and called up a picture of Citadel as she continued, "We're on our own, people! If we want to protect ourselves from a repeat of dealing with people like Card, we need to let everyone know who and what we are. Whatever we want to call what *Brittel* did, we need to call it *treason* if it happens again. While Sam had a difficult decision to make over how to deal with Brittel's treason, if we are clear on calling it treason, there won't be any question going forward over how to deal with it. It also makes it clear what we should call actions against us by people from outside Citadel. Those actions are war!"

There was a great deal of commentary going back and forth, which quieted as Austin motioned that he wanted to give someone else a chance to speak. "Mark, since you're married to Gina, let's hear from you before moving on to someone not named 'Albretti.'"

The man smiled as he said, "Thanks, Sam. The other point that should be made is that I don't see how we can make our settlement work if someone else can come along and claim a huge chunk of Citadel. They wouldn't be subject to our rules and might not believe in any of the things that we do. Making a settlement work is tough enough as it is. Why should we have to compromise our values because someone else wants to set up shop nearby?"

"I need to play devil's advocate, Mark," Austin said. "What if someone wants to set up shop on the other side of Citadel? Even assuming that our population will increase hugely over time and continue with the type of land grants we've had so far, Citadel has a huge amount of land. It could take a long time before our paths crossed."

Albretti smiled as he replied, "That's a good question, Sam. In addition to the concerns I just mentioned, there's a fundamental one that hasn't been addressed yet. If someone else owns a piece of Citadel, then that someone has a right of access to our solar system. A key part of our security is based on the fact that no one gets in here without our blessing. Once someone else has a set of keys, then someone else gets to make decisions on how things are done in this solar system, including security on and off Citadel." He shrugged skeptically as he asked, "How many people here think that's a good idea?"

"There were some pretty heated comments," Yabuno remembered.

Austin smiled and said, "Yes, but we got to a place where I was pretty proud of our people. They decided that they *were* a people and that this place was worth fighting to defend! They made it clear that unauthorized colonists need not apply for real estate here."

"I guess your hand has now been strengthened as far as dealing with anyone else who tries to set up a settlement without our blessing."

Austin's blue eyes had fire in them as he replied, "You're damned right! As far as I'm concerned, I have as much right to tell people to go away as does the president of the United States to anyone that wants to enter the US."

Yabuno's eyes were worried as he said, "While we're prepared to tell them they can't enter our solar system, if they don't have a way to get back to Earth, where do we tell them to go?"

The fire in Austin's eyes dimmed as he answered, "I hope that no one else is such a damned fool as to try to reach Citadel without even knowing if our expedition was successful. If anything, it would be even more foolish to come without knowing if Card made it safely. Having the authority to tell people to get lost is one thing, but I hope I never have to decide to do it where it might mean condemning people to death. We're going to be stuck with some lousy choices until we can solve some of our major technical issues!"

CONTACT

CHAPTER TWENTY

Months later, things had settled back to normal on Citadel. As Austin got up to answer his link, he noticed that it was just past 2:30 in the morning. He looked over his shoulder at Liz and remembered that she would be in full view of the screen in their bedroom. It had been a warm evening, and the covers were thrown back. She wasn't wearing anything. Austin enjoyed the view of her body as it was outlined by the faint light and then remembered that he wasn't wearing anything either. After putting on a pair of shorts, he went into his study and answered his link.

It was Yabuno, who said, "Sorry to wake you, Sam, but I had to call you right away!"

"At least you said you're sorry," Austin muttered to himself and then continued more loudly, "What's so important, Bret?"

"We've had not just one breakthrough, but break-throughs on multiple fronts!" His voice trembled with excitement as he continued, "We've finally solved the problem with the warp-field generators! Not only that, but we've also figured out how to create a practical arti-ficial gravity field at the same time. On top of that, the team has figured out how to solve the communication problem with Earth, so we can let them know what's been going on here and to get their asses to work building new ships. I'll give you a few details, and then we can talk some more later."

Two hours later, Austin walked back into their bed-room. Liz stirred partly awake as he came in and asked, "What is it, Sam? Why are you up?"

"Some days are even better than others, my love," he said. He pulled the covers the rest of the way off her body and kissed her firmly. Without another word, she was fully awake and pulling him out of his shorts. With a playful, husky tone in her voice, she said, "Make sure the door is closed, Sam. There's a price to be paid for waking me up in the middle of the night, and you're going to pay it." She gasped as he started paying the price and said, "Oh, God! You pay that price so well, and you damn well better do it repeatedly!"

"Gladly!" He chuckled.

Later that day, after the price had been fully paid, Austin was back on his link with Yabuno and the rest of the team discussing the new technology breakthroughs.

Austin asked, "How long will it be before we can get a working prototype for the new warp-field generators?"

Yabuno replied, "Instead of giving you a series of interim estimates, I'll go a step further and say we can have a new ship with the warp-field generators opera-tional and ready for field tests in around four months."

"Stop bullshitting me, Bret!"

Yabuno shook his head, saying, "I'm not bullshitting, Sam. I've been working on this approach for the past year, and as I've been working through the problem, my notes have been taking on the look of a formal design anyway. Give me another week to work with my team to finish developing the formal design from my notes, and we can get started. The approach to the ship's artificial gravity is related to the approach for the new generators, so I'll do the same thing with my team to put together a design for it."

Austin asked, "How sure are we that our manufacturing operations are ready to build something with this level of complexity?"

"We set them up the moment we arrived at Citadel, and they've been undergoing almost constant refinement since then. We've been able to do everything from fabricating major replacement components for the transports to building new transports themselves. It's true that we haven't been constructing warp-field generator components for anything except *Pathfinder*, but we know how to build what we need for the new generation of ships."

"What impact will the new design have on the transit time from here to Earth?"

"It should cut the time at least in half," Yabuno said with a smile. "It might even get down to a quarter of the time. If it doesn't, it shouldn't be long before further refinements get it there."

The excitement started to show in Austin's voice as he asked, "When will we be able to send communications to Earth?"

Melody Lambert, who had taken over Brittel's responsibilities, replied, "We'll probably be ready in a month."

"How much time will it take to send a message to Earth?"

"Around a month, give or take a week," she said. "Within a year, we should be able to get it down even further."

"How the hell can we do it?" someone wondered.

"We've discussed this before," Lambert replied patiently. "If we structure messages the right way, they have no mass to worry about. Each message is its own microbubble, which can travel much more effectively than the larger bubbles we have to create for manned travel." She grinned as she said, "Someday, if we're able to throw some interesting quantum mechanics concepts into the mix, we might even have virtually immediate conversations."

The discussions continued for quite some time. As they did, Austin mused on the fact that the team was very much a social organization, as well as the organization that made sure things got done on Citadel. Austin worried about the changes to the social aspect of the team if the project he was about to discuss came to pass.

"Now that we're done with everything that can be covered for now, I'd like to mention something that's been on my mind for some time, even more so since the business with Brittel and the town hall meeting a couple of weeks later. We've taken the position that we are now a state, and rightly so, in my view. I think it's time for us to establish a more formal structure of government for our state."

There was pushback from the others, including Yabuno, who said, "We've been doing fine so far, Sam, so why the interest in making a change?"

"I've become ever more aware that most of the authority for running things is held by just a few people. For obvious reasons, I'm even more aware of the fact that I have huge final authority over things that perhaps I shouldn't have. I presided over a hearing that determined that someone had committed treason." Austin had an uncomfortable look on his face as he asked, "Should I have been able to do that?"

Supported by a chorus of chuckles, Yabuno replied, "You've always been good about consulting with others as needed, Sam. Most people are interested in getting on with their lives and leaving other things to the team to handle."

"I know that. What I want to know is when is it time for over eleven thousand people to have more of a say over what happens in their lives?"

"That's just it, Sam," Yabuno said with a nod of his head. "They *do* have a say over what happens in their lives. They have a say by just going ahead and doing it. No one asks permission for well over ninety-five percent of what happens around here. You've been terrific about not butting into the private affairs of people, and they appreciate it. They trust that when they need to be consulted about something, you'll make sure that it happens."

"That may be fine for now, but what happens if, for example, I were to be eaten by a cheater?"

There was a lot of laughter in the room as someone replied, "You need to give us a more likely example than that, Sam. You're a hell of a lot more dangerous than any cheater. Every time they've tangled with you, there've been more dead cheaters."

Austin chuckled back as he said, "OK, so cheaters haven't done too well when they've crossed me. There're plenty of other ways a person can die here, some of which we just haven't found yet."

Yabuno replied, "We take your point, Sam, but I don't think this is the right time to have this conversation. We're about to devote our energies toward implementing three major pieces of technology that will have a huge impact on our lives here and our relationship with our friends back on Earth. It isn't fair to ask us to distract ourselves at this time. While I can't speak for anyone else, I'm willing to give the matter serious thought once we've gotten our new technologies up and running. What about the rest of you?"

After listening to multiple voices in agreement, Austin realized he needed to back off for a while. He wasn't going to let it go indefinitely, however.

CHAPTER TWENTY ONE

It was another beautiful morning, and Austin sat in his study, enjoying the view through the windows. True to Yabuno's estimate, it was a month since their meeting and the communications array would be brought online later in the day. Austin was looking forward to sending the first message to Earth and had been thinking for quite some time about what he'd say. He was enjoying some rare quiet time because Matt was spending a couple of days with some of their friends and their children, so he and Liz had the house to themselves for a while.

He'd been at work on his message for days and had spent the last couple of hours on the last part of it when Liz came into the study. She had just gotten out of the shower and was drying her hair with a towel. Because Matt wasn't around, her towel wasn't wrapped around anything other than her hair. She had what Austin called her "Mona Lisa" smile, which was when she had an enigmatic look on her face.

"What's going on, Mona Lisa?" he asked with a smile.

"Remember when I made you pay the price for waking me up a month ago?"

Austin grinned and said, "I can truly say I've never had so much pleasure paying the price for anything."

"It turns out that you did more than pay me. You put in a deposit on a baby! We'll get the deposit back with interest in less than nine months."

In a moment, Austin had Liz in his arms as he kissed her both tenderly and passionately. As her towel dropped from her hair to the floor, she said quietly, "I hope you can set aside that message for a while, because I want to celebrate with you." By the time they got back to the bedroom, Liz gasped and said, "Oh, God! You celebrate just as well as you paid the price for waking me up! I want you to celebrate repeatedly!"

Austin merely chuckled in reply.

Later that day, with the celebrations concluded, Austin was back in his study, looking into his link. He began, "Greetings to my friends and colleagues on Earth, Mars and the rest of your solar system. For anyone who doesn't know me, this is Sam Austin, the leader of the Citadel settlements. It's been a hell of a lot longer than we had hoped before we'd be able to get a message through to you. I'm pleased to report that all but one of our ships arrived safely. I'm sorry to tell you that our ship number nineteen never arrived at Citadel. Unless, by some miracle, that ship managed to return to Earth, it and the people aboard are presumed lost in space. I was glad to have had a chance to know them; they were good souls, and we would have been proud to include them among our neighbors and colleagues.

"One of the blessings that we've received is landing on a beautiful world. While it would never be mistaken for the beauty that is Earth, it isn't hard to appreciate the beauty that we have here. I've included with this message a sample of the many images we've taken of our home. This place is not only beautiful but bountiful. Although we've made plenty of mistakes and will doubtless have plenty more lessons to learn, we've already had successful plantings of various local crops that are terrific sources of food and other materials we need. While these plantings haven't been sufficient by themselves to meet all of our needs, the combination of these crops along with what we brought from Earth for planting has been sufficient to sustain us. We are hopeful that within the next season or so, plantings of local crops will not only sustain us but result in an abundance that we can share with our friends on Earth.

"In addition, this world and the other bodies in this solar system have an abundance of minerals and other precious materials, and we have developed an advanced system of mining to take advantage of these resources. We also made sure to bring along an advanced set of skills relating to manufacturing, so we are able to manufacture and fabricate practically everything we need.

"We have also continued to work to maintain the skills that we have in many advanced fields. We aren't merely a nineteenth-century society that has some nice twenty-second-century comforts; we are a twenty-second-century society that is continuing to advance and grow scientifically and technologically. We'll be letting you know about some of our advancements at the right time.

"Among the many blessings we have received are the births of many children, who are doing very well here. I am delighted to count my son, Matt, among these children. We now number well over eleven thousand people, with our numbers growing practically every day.

"It's important not to leave the impression that this is an easy place in which to live, however. We're still learning to adapt to this planet's climate and ecosystem, which can be harsh even for those who pay attention to its moods. There are various wild animals and microorganisms that are quite deadly and have claimed lives. No man or woman goes anywhere without being armed and with good reason. This ecosystem is unforgiving when it comes to carelessness on our part in protecting ourselves. Citadel is not a place for the faint of heart. All in all, however, this world is now our home and we have grown into a true society."

Austin's gaze became less friendly as he continued, "This brings us to a disturbing chapter in our lives. I'm sure that there are people there who are curious as to whether a group of four ships that departed from Earth some time back made it to Citadel. I will report first that three of those ships made it to the entrance to our system, although they didn't make it into our system. The fourth ship never arrived and is presumed lost in space. These ships were comprised of people who had stolen our technology and know-how that we spent years developing. How do we know? We know because they admitted it.

"We also know that they were helped in their theft of our technology and know-how by Greg Brittel, who was one of our own. Brittel put his greed and self-interest ahead of the good of our community. The thieves didn't give a damn about our goals or values. They planned on claiming half of our planet immediately and forcing us out of our own holdings with the weapons they had brought with them. They sought to enter our system without the use of our files on an updated safe path through the radiation field that surrounds this solar system.

"All they had to do was to abandon their weapons and submit themselves to our authority, and we would have shared our files with them and tried to find a way to make things work. In view of their plans, that was a bargain they weren't willing to make. In their arrogance, they sought to enter our system anyway, trusting to a level of skill they didn't have to somehow see them through the radiation field. Unfortunately for them, their arrogance was no substitute for our files, and without those files, the outcome was deadly for them. It didn't take long for them to die from extreme radiation poisoning. They never saw a sunrise on our planet.

"They were still fellow humans, so we gave them a burial in space, with their ships being their coffins. For reasons of safety, due to the extreme radiation contamination, their ships were directed via remote control into Citadel's sun as their final resting place. We recorded the proceedings for anyone who had a loved one aboard one of the ships. We will send that recording separately."

"I'm sure you've been hoping for a signal from us that it was safe to send over additional groups of settlers.

Unfortunately, even if we'd been able to communicate with you earlier, we would have had to tell you not to send anyone. We discovered a major design flaw with our warp-field generators, which we believe was the reason for ship Nineteen not making it to Citadel. My own ship nearly didn't make it here, either, and none of our original ships is capable of returning to Earth with their generators.

"The good news is that we can announce some of those technological advancements I mentioned earlier. Bret Yabuno and the rest of his team have solved the problem with the warp-field generators and are constructing a new ship that will be equipped with the new generators. Within a few months of your receiving this message, we hope that this new ship will be operational and capable of returning to Earth. What's at least as exciting is we believe that this new ship will be equipped with a practical artificial gravity!"

Austin grinned broadly as he continued, "Imagine the benefit of being able to travel here without wearing the resistance suits I invented many years ago. We are enclosing a separate message to the Citadel Group with a series of encrypted files with the information necessary for our people to construct these ships in your solar system, as well as other insights we have developed from our time here. I can confirm that the criteria that we established for the selection of settlers for Citadel were well considered and should continue to be used for future potential settlers."

Austin's face now took on a more forceful appearance as he continued, "In view of the rampant greed, along with a complete lack of respect for the values that underlie our approach to colonization, that was demonstrated by people who thought they could make our home into something that it is not, I must now share with the people of Earth some facts of life as they relate to Citadel. Citadel is now closed to any colonization by anyone other than our people.

"While there will be those that question whether we have the right to claim an entire world for ourselves, we have already seen what happens when the wrong people decide that they can just take away what belongs to others. The fact remains that we are the ones who devoted years of our lives to facing and overcoming all of the daunting problems connected with traveling to another world. We are the ones who have taken the risks to get here and build new lives. We are the ones who will defend this place with our lives if necessary.

"There is another reason why we claim to have jurisdiction of Citadel to the exclusion of others. We have come to realize that we are more than a collection of disparate individuals, each seeking to gain some form of wealth for himself without a thought for either his neighbors or the community. While each person is free to pursue his life's dreams, he also recognizes that he owes something to others and acts accordingly. This means that we are now a state, with everything that that name implies, and we insist upon recognition as such. I have enclosed a formal declaration to that effect, which has been approved by the people here. While we're working out the details, including what we will call our state, we'll probably always answer to 'Citadel.'"

A warm smile returned to Austin's face as he said, "This is not meant as an unfriendly gesture toward Earth. It couldn't be, since Earth is where I was born, where everyone here was born, except for some of the children. I have been blessed to have many friends on Earth and hope that that will never change. It is the world I have served for close to two centuries. It is the world I hope to visit again.

"We're excited at what the future holds for both worlds. We have excellent prospects for a great deal of trade, especially over time as we are able to ramp up our production. We have access to quantities of precious materials that are only available in much reduced quantities on Earth, and we will be able to provide increasing amounts of native food and other materials that are under cultivation. We've already made some important contributions to medicine from our access to native flora and fauna, and we'll be glad to share those contributions with you. In short, we will both benefit hugely from this cooperative relationship.

"Once again, we call upon our organization to resume the work of screening, selecting, and training settlers for their lives on Citadel. You will now have means to build the ships that can take you here, and we look forward to welcoming our new settlers with open arms."

CHAPTER TWENTY TWO

A lthough Austin had been back in space multiple times during the nearly four years that they'd been on Citadel, this time was special. He, Yabuno, and others were taking a closer look at the new ship that was coming to life in the space yard. They could see another ship in the distance in another space bay that was also coming to life, although it was further away from completion than this one. Austin mused over the fact that it seemed to be the nature of these projects that although it appeared that several portions of the ship's exterior were not yet completed, it was difficult to tell at a glance how close the ship was to completion. Completion of the ship and certification for trials was supposedly only two weeks away, which seemed impossible. If Austin hadn't seen it happen plenty of times before, he wouldn't have believed in the miracles that would have to take place to close everything up.

Curly Stephens, who was in charge of the yard, was making much the same point as she brushed out of her face a strand of the wavy red hair that had given her her nickname. "I've heard it from others, Bret. 'How the hell is Curly going to pull this one off?' The answer is that we're already nearly done with everything. Most of the ship is completely up and running. We've even tested out all of the environmental stuff for all but the last few places that are still open to space. Thanks to your people, we've already tested out some of the last of the critical systems elsewhere, such as the warp-field generators, so that we can reduce the amount of troubleshooting when we integrate them into the ship and bring them online. We still need some elbow room, so it's a lot easier to have easy access to some key areas up until practically the last moment. Once we close up everything, it'll be a hell of a lot harder to do anything major to the ship."

Yabuno smiled and said, "I've seen what your people can do even with ships that don't have huge entry points for service. They're are like surgeons who can operate through tiny incisions and do amazing things."

Stephens grinned as she said, "We've had some pretty damned intense discussions over how to put these ships together, haven't we? We appreciate the fact that you paid a lot of attention to our suggestions. While I can't promise any miracles, we should be able to do some amazing things pretty damned quickly thanks to your design."

Austin spoke. "It's terrific that these ships can be converted from passenger to cargo and back to passenger status a lot faster than before. We'll be in much better shape to bring settlers here and then send trade goods back to Earth and then start the whole thing over. That's the reason we've taken to calling them 'transports' instead of 'settler ships'; they can carry anything!"

Austin peered into the distance as he continued, "If I didn't know better, I'd say you've taken *Pathfinder* completely apart and are starting over. I'm glad, in a way, that you're building a replacement for *Pathfinder* from scratch and leaving the original ship alone for now. I know that we'll have to come up with a new name for the new ship, but for now, I guess we'll keep calling it the new *Pathfinder*. I'm looking forward to seeing the new *Pathfinder* start her trials in a few months. It's funny that the new, improved *Pathfinder* will take as much time to build as a brand-new transport."

Yabuno said, "As you know, there've been some major design issues to handle. First, we're upgrading the warp-field generators from what *Pathfinder* uses now, and it's a design that has some key differences from the one we're using for the transports. Because of those differences, the design for this ship's artificial gravity will be somewhat different as well.

"Second, we're ruggedizing *Pathfinder* so she'll be even better at handling trips through the radiation field. We're under no illusions regarding whether we'll ever be able to incorporate enough shielding into the design to make it possible to get through the radiation field without using a safe path. However, we believe that what we're doing is providing a greater margin of safety for the crew when checking out that path.

"Third, we keep learning how to improve our ships, and this is a good time to incorporate those improvements into the ship. We might not embark on such an extensive set of upgrades again for several years, so we need to make sure that everything works together as planned. If we don't get it done right the first time, the new *Pathfinder* might end up as an expensive piece of junk.

"For obvious reasons, we didn't want to simply dismantle the original *Pathfinder* in order to upgrade her while this work is going on. You never know when we'll need a ship with a dependable warp-field generator, and the original *Pathfinder* has the only one we trust. Once we've gotten everything nailed down with these new ships, it'll be the right time to do the same for *Pathfinder*."

Stephens mused, mostly to herself, "Some people are so damned sentimental that they'd rather leave *Pathfinder* as she is and put her in a museum where she'll never be useful again. I'd rather do what I can to keep *Pathfinder* useful so she'll be doing the things she was meant to do. Besides, we don't have any time or use for museums yet. Maybe by the time I'm old and tired, we'll open up a museum for stuff. We'll probably put me in it!"

Stephens waved toward the empty bays as she said, "Take a look around, people, because it won't look like this again for quite a while. Once the new transport checks out, these bays will all be full; we'll be building plenty of them and hauling bodies and goods back and forth like you've never seen!"

Austin looked around, smiled, and said, "There're a lot worse things to have to do than to plan for the future success of Citadel. Damn, it's good to be back!"

CHAPTER TWENTY THREE

Austin was in his study when he received a message over his link. "What is it, Bret?" he asked.

Yabuno couldn't keep the combination of anger and disappointment from his expression as he responded, "A reply to your original message has just arrived, Sam. The president of the United States has responded to our claim that Citadel is now a state."

Austin's face took on a wry expression as he asked, "Why do I have the impression that the reply was not to your liking?"

"They told us to go fuck ourselves. They used diplomatic language to say it, but that was the message."

"Why don't you forward the message over so I can listen to the cheery news?"

"It's already there. Have fun listening to Her Majesty."

In spite of the news, Austin couldn't help but smile as he listened to several more choice words from Yabuno in describing his opinion of the message.

He called up the message and listened as the president's face filled his screen. She began, "Greetings to everyone on Citadel, with an especially warm greeting for you, Sam."

Austin didn't worry about the rest of the message until the president got to the part about Citadel being recognized as a state.

"I'd like to move on to a more difficult topic. We can appreciate the sense of community that you have undoubtedly forged through your common experiences, which include dealing with those who would do violence to the values underlying your community. However, that sense of community does not transform a group of people into a state, with the same rights as, for example, the United States of America. Sam, as the leader of your community, you have an obligation to avoid stirring up fantasies within your community that are completely inconsistent with reality. While we might be willing to review the individual land grants that you have claimed for yourselves and decide if they are sufficiently reasonable in scope that we would recognize them as valid, we cannot go beyond that point to consider a small community on a distant planet as being equal in status to any of the countries on Earth.

"While some of you may want to argue that Mars is a better model, I'll point out that Mars wasn't recognized as a sovereign state until many years after the first settlements were established. I'll also point out that Mars had a much greater population than Citadel and accepted a certain amount of oversight from Earth. If, at some point many years from now, Earth were prepared to recognize the sovereignty of Citadel, a similar arrangement would probably be required."

Austin didn't care about the closing remarks, either. After a while, he looked up to see that Bret was trying to reach him on his link.

"What did you think about Her Majesty's message?" Yabuno asked in an acerbic tone.

"Courtney has always had trouble accepting that things aren't the way they were years ago. She's determined to throw around her weight as the president of the United States instead of learning how to be an effective leader. For starters, she still hasn't come to terms with the fact that the Citadel Group is independent of any Earth government. To her way of thinking, this would be a chance to clip the Citadel Group's wings and reassert her own authority."

"Don't you mean reassert the authority of the United States?"

With a rueful shake of Austin's head, he replied, "In her mind, the two are the same. It's amazing that this issue has resurfaced decades after it was resolved during my tenure as president. I understood way back then that the attitude of people like Courtney was shortsighted. There's no way to put the genie back in the bottle once groups push beyond the confines of Earth into space. When that happens, there's no way for Earth governments to have any effective control over what those groups do in space, especially once you get away from bodies that orbit Earth."

Austin's thoughts took him back decades as he continued, "Mars was a special situation, because of the efforts by some rogue elements on Mars to threaten Earth with annihilation. I should know, since I gave the orders to take out that threat. Earth needed to have some measure of say over some of Mars's actions in order to ensure that another threat like that one couldn't happen."

"Jesus, Sam, Citadel isn't even remotely a threat to Earth," Yabuno snorted. "Harrington is full of shit if she thinks otherwise. The distances alone would make it virtually impossible for Citadel to do anything that would threaten Earth's well-being."

"The extreme distance has even more significance than just a lack of a realistic threat, Bret. Under the thinking of people like Courtney, Earth can claim some form of jurisdiction over what happens anywhere in the cosmos. This kind of thinking isn't just delusional; it is probably dangerous as well. There may be intelligent life out there that is more advanced than ours, even if we've found nothing yet to support that notion. How would Earth feel if another race were to come along and claim the right to do whatever it wanted to Earth just because they felt it was their business and they had more advanced abilities to back up their claims?"

As Yabuno's eyes widened in alarm at the thought, Austin continued, "That's the problem with that attitude. If you demand it for yourself, then you have to accept that others may feel the same way. In fact, under those circumstances, you have to accept that others have the right to do whatever they want to do to you if they visit your system. The only practical means of protecting one's right to avoid interference in one's own system is to recognize that others have a similar right for their systems. That means that Earth has to recognize that what happens in Citadel is none of Earth's business. If it doesn't, then heaven help them if someone else comes along who believes that what happens in Earth's system is their business and they have more advanced technology than Earth to back it up."

Yabuno replied, "I hope we never have to put any of those points to the test. For now, it means that people like Harrington are unable to see what hypocrites they are on the subject. They might not even be honest enough to admit that what they claim is merely a somewhat paternalistic approach is really a 'might makes right' approach. The problem with that approach is that it always seems more appealing when you think you have more 'might' than anyone else. It only sucks when you find out the hard way that you're wrong."

Austin said, "She also misunderstands certain actions by US presidents that go back to before my tenure as president. It is considered legitimate for US presidents to speak up when others take actions that conflict with the norms that are accepted by the international community. These norms include respect for the rule of law, respect for human rights, threats to the peace or safety of other nations, etc."

Yabuno grinned. "You expressed your views pretty forcefully on more than a few occasions, Sam."

"Those were unusual circumstances," Austin replied with a chuckle. "They included dealing with the Bio War and the aftermath where we had to rebuild various nations that had to replace ones that had ceased to exist. Courtney doesn't understand that the additional influence that the US president still has from that time arose because people had confidence in my judgment. She doesn't get the connection between her own lack of judgment and her reduced influence."

"She also has a lot of nerve to suggest how things would work out years from now," Yabuno said. "She'll be long retired and without any say in the matter."

"I think both of you have it wrong," Austin replied. "I don't think she'll be retired at all when this matter is resolved."

"What do you mean?" Yabuno frowned. "I don't see Harrington changing her mind about Citadel, especially now that she's made a formal pronouncement on the subject. I guess it could happen that some form of de facto sovereignty could happen that gets us a lot of what we want, even without formal recognition."

Austin shook his head, saying, "I'm not talking about de facto recognition, Bret. While there would be value to de facto recognition, it still wouldn't be the same thing as formal recognition. Courtney and her successors would always be in the position of snubbing us and acting as if they had leverage over us in everything relating to the relationships between the two systems. I'll be damned if I'm going to start out with that kind of relationship with Earth."

The fire returned to Austin's eyes as he said, "While I'm not certain just how it will happen, before Courtney leaves office, Citadel will be recognized as a sovereign state. It will happen without any compromises on our part, either. We have certain advantages from an economic and techno-logical standpoint, and we shouldn't be afraid to use them to get what we want. I want to make sure that I can look her in the face when she has to accept that reality!"

CHAPTER TWENTY FOUR

Austin had been grumbling ever since he'd lost his bet with Yabuno and had to stay behind on Citadel while the trials were underway for the new transport. While neither of them was allowed on board the transport during the trials, Yabuno had been aboard *Pathfinder* as she guided the new transport through the radiation field to the "entrance" to their solar system. *Pathfinder* provided Yabuno with the best seat in the house as the new transport took off from their solar system for the first serious test of the new warp-field generators. Hours later, when the transport returned and her captain presented his report of the trip, it wasn't clear whether the crew or Yabuno's team had the biggest grins.

The trials consisted of more than one trip, so it was now Austin's turn to relax aboard *Pathfinder* as they waited for the new transport to return. The transport had departed from the opposite side of their solar system, as part of a challenge of seeing how well the new ship could navigate along something other than the communications beacons.

While there hadn't been any move to assign names to the earlier ships other than *Pathfinder*, Donna Yabuno had suggested naming this one the *Keith Thomas*, an idea that turned out to be hugely popular. Since Thomas hadn't had any surviving children, it seemed an appropriate way to ensure that his name would continue for posterity. Instead of being known as one of the early settlers who died on Citadel, his name would be synonymous with the first class of transports that could finally make the journey to and from Citadel safely. Karen Thomas had been touched by the gesture and given her heartfelt approval. There were tears in her eyes when she smashed the bottle of champagne across the bow for the traditional launch of the new ship. *Come to think of it, there were tears in a lot of eyes at that moment,* Austin thought.

Austin thought back on a conversation he and Liz had had recently on the implications of finally having ships that could bring additional settlers to Citadel. "In a few years, our population could be in the tens of thousands, if not a hundred thousand," she said. "One of the things I've been thinking about is how we're going to accommodate that much growth. We may end up with regional clusters that are based on the needs of particular regions." She looked down at her belly and smiled as she thought about the contributions they were making toward that growth.

"It's always been clear that the community has to have growth in order to stay healthy and survive," she continued. "This has been reflected in the people who were selected as settlers; most of them had made it clear that they intended to have more than one or two children. Fortunately, the planet has far more in the way of land and other resources than we'd need to sustain that growth, with the asteroids able to supply anything that Citadel itself couldn't."

Austin smiled and said, "One thing that we have in abundance is experience."

"Thank God!" Liz laughed. "For starters, the newer settlers will have parcels that are next to the parcels that the originals settlers have. Thanks to the technology and experience available from the original settlers, they'll benefit from the fact that things are already more 'civilized' on one side of their parcels."

"They'll still need to be cautious when traveling," Austin said with a wry look. "It'll still be quite a while before cheaters stop prowling the area. At some point, though, they'll reach a critical mass and find that many things are simply much easier to do than before."

Liz gestured toward the wilderness as she said, "The process will repeat itself plenty of times as new settlements are formed at greater distances from the Square in land that will be tamed and transformed all over again into new cities."

Austin thought, not for the first time since his conversation with the team months ago, that a planet with that kind of growth and population would need to have a more formal government in place. He raised the subject again with Liz, saying, "Regardless of the confidence that the settlers have in me and my judgment, I won't be the leader forever." With a twinkle in his eye, he continued, "The day will come when it'll be time for me to leave that role, either because I'm tired of it or because they're tired of me!

"I want to be sure that when that day happens, there is a government in place that does something that most governments don't do. It would be a government that reflects a commonly held set of values and also actually meets the needs of the people. Most governments, regardless of their lofty proclamations, function on the premise that they exist to guide or even coerce the people into doing what the government wants them to do. There are usually some self-appointed elite groups of people who feel that they should be the ones making those decisions, regardless of what the people want."

"You've already made a huge difference when it comes to getting away from 'political correctness,' Sam."

Austin nodded as he said, "I like to think so. Even though I led that fight decades ago, too many people in authority still act as if everything that people do has to be filtered through a PC lens for approval."

Liz chuckled as she said, "That's what I mean, Sam. We've done our best to ensure that the settlers don't have that filter. I've heard plenty of conversations on Citadel where people make clear what they think of the PC police when they come calling." Her blue eyes were bright as she said, "I've heard conversations that are pretty 'robust' and show a depth of character that is pretty positive for the community's future."

Austin nodded back at Liz as a smile came over his face. He said, "I hope that this will be the first community to finally rid itself of this filter and go back to people having the right to say and do what they think without the government claiming to have control over those thoughts and actions."

Austin's thoughts returned to the present when he heard Gina Albretti, one of the people with 'robust' views on Citadel as a state and the one responsible for certifying the *Keith Thomas* as ready for service, speak. "That's strange," she said with a frown. "Our communications array is telling me that there's a ship at the entrance to our system. If that's the *Keith Thomas*, she's way the hell off course. If that's any of our other ships, I'll have the hide of her captain for violating protocols when we're running these trials."

Austin asked, "This is way too early for the *Keith Thomas* to be back, Gina. Could it be a ship from Earth?"

"I don't see how, Sam. Our own people at the Citadel Group couldn't possibly be far enough along with their own construction to have a ship built and launched before our first one is up and running. The rest of Earth knows that there isn't any viable alternative to our design available, so I doubt that anyone would be stupid enough to try to get here with a ship based on the old warp-field generators. Besides, we made it clear that we hold the keys to this system. No one gets in without our data on getting through the radiation field."

"Can we get an ID for the ship?"

"No one's responding to our queries."

"Let's get confirmation on the locations of the other ships."

"I'm already checking on it." Her frown was mixed with puzzlement as she said, "Every ship is accounted for. That means it has to be the *Keith Thomas*. Maybe something is screwed up with her communications system."

"That suggests damage of some kind. Let's get a visual assessment."

Albretti's eyes grew larger than dinner plates as she gasped, "Sweet Jesus and Mother Mary! That sure as hell isn't the *Keith Thomas!*"

It sure as hell wasn't. The ship looked nothing like anything that had ever launched from Earth. It was a nightmare of tangled curves and lines, with a color that was indeterminate. Sometimes, it was brown, and sometimes, it just faded into the black background of space itself. It was hard to tell whether some dark colors were just shadows or structures. It seemed to absorb whatever light was available, so that it was difficult, if not impossible, to get a good sense of its outline. Human concepts of form, function, or style were nowhere to be found on that ship.

"How big is that ship, Gina?" Austin asked.

"I'm not sure. The light seems to blur or fade or shift somehow when I try to get a direct reading. The best guess I can give right now is that it must be at least ten times the size of the *Keith Thomas*. It could be a lot bigger."

"Why is it just sitting there?" someone asked.

"Two reasons," Gina said. "First, they're probably curious about our communications array. They'd have to know that it means there's intelligent life here, probably in this solar system. The second is that their ship is way too big to be able to get through the radiation field, even if somehow they knew the safe path and tried to stay on it." She smiled as she said, "We still hold the keys to this place, Sam."

"I wouldn't take bets on it, Gina. Take a look!"

As they watched the large screen, they noticed a shape separating itself from the body of the ship. Watching it was unsettling, as it wasn't simply a smaller scout ship being launched. It was an integral part of the main ship that looked as if it were setting itself up as a separate entity. As it withdrew, various lines and connections pulled apart, in a kind of organic process until the smaller shape was finally free of the ship. The smaller shape began to move under its own power toward the entrance to the system.

"How big is the smaller ship?" Austin asked.

"It's still hard to tell, Sam, but I'd say it's at least three times the size of the *Keith Thomas*. It'd be a tight fit in a few spots, but it could probably make it through the radiation field. They'd still need the keys, though," she said with a tight smile.

"They seem to be doing OK so far. In fact, they're going exactly where we'd go. Make sure Citadel knows what's going on."

"They got the alert the same time we did."

"Get Bret and the rest of the team on the link, Gina. We'd better talk while we have some time."

"They're already waiting, Sam. Go ahead."

Austin wondered if his face showed the same combination of excitement and concern he saw on the faces looking back at him from the screen. He began, "I guess everyone knows that an alien ship has dropped anchor just outside our system. In this case, alien sure as hell doesn't mean a ship from Earth. We're not sure about the size, but it's at least ten times bigger than the *Keith Thomas*. For obvious reasons, a ship of that size could never enter our system directly, due to the radiation field. You all have on your screens the image of what probably passes for a scout ship for them. Even though it's at least three times the size of the *Keith Thomas*, it seems to be working its way through the radiation field without any difficulties so far."

"What do we know about them, Sam?" Liz asked.

"Not much," he said with a shrug. "Nothing that looks like that ship ever came from Earth. We know that the nearest star to this system is too far away for anyone to be able to make a visit using conventional technology for propulsion. This means that wherever they're from, they had to have gotten here with some form of faster-than-light travel technology. Even if we could build a ship that large, we couldn't build a warp-field generator that could get it anywhere. We have to assume that the rest of their technology is just as advanced."

Albretti said, "The good news is that they must have physical limitations, since they aren't willing to send their mother ship through the radiation field."

"Have they responded to our hails?" Austin asked.

She shook her head, saying, "We've been broadcasting everything that our protocols have called for, but they either don't recognize it as communication or they don't care enough about it to try to respond. Since they're advanced enough to know our signals aren't just background noise, it's probably the latter. I suppose it's possible that our forms of communication are so different that there isn't any point in their trying to respond." Her face showed some worry as she continued, "I hope that's it, because if they just don't care about responding, then I'm not sure what that says about how they feel about us as beings."

She looked back at the display and called out, "They're on the safe path and passing through the field a lot faster than we would."

"What do you want us to do, Sam?" Yabuno asked.

"There isn't much that you can do, except make sure all emergency planning is being carried out. Everything nonessential should be put on hold for now. Get everyone into the emergency shelters and make sure everything can be handled from there. Keep all transports away from Citadel until we know it's safe for them. We never developed Citadel as a fortress, despite the name, and we're largely at their mercy. I hope to God they have some."

Austin's smile was tight as he said, "I never really appreciated until now what it would mean to have a visit from an alien race. We have no idea whether they're nice folks or whether they're ready to snuff us out. We can't quite take a hostile posture, because that might lead to a tragic result. On the other hand, we don't want to be a foolish group of sheep that's wiped out because we didn't take sensible precautions."

"What are you going to do, Sam?" Liz asked.

"I'd like to be there with you, but until we know the score, I don't want to take *Pathfinder* any closer to the mother ship. We don't have any weapons, and it wouldn't take any effort for that ship to swat us like a fly. Our being way on the other side of the system may mean that they don't know we're here, and I'd like to keep it that way if possible. Also, the *Keith Thomas* will be back at some point, and someone will need to let them know what's happening. Get Alan Turner ready to review anything they might transmit to us. He's amazing when it comes to interpreting symbols. If anything happens, try to keep broadcasting for as long as you think it's OK to do it. We'll try to do the same."

"Don't do it if it'll place you in any danger, Sam."

Austin's smile was hardly visible as he said, "We didn't come all this way to be stopped by the possibility of danger, my love." Austin looked at the rest of the team as he said, "We'd better stop chattering for now so that you folks can get everything done you need to with not nearly enough time to do it." For just a moment, he looked back at Liz and said, "I love you, Liz. I'll see you again soon."

"I love you too, Sam. I'll hold you to that promise."

The people on *Pathfinder* continued to watch the progress of the alien scout ship through the radiation field. It was clear that the ship had much better sensors than they did, because it only slowed down when it needed to complete a turn. Still, the ship was careful not to stray into the radiation, which suggested that there were limits to its shielding too.

The *Keith Thomas's* current trials included extensive testing of its warp-field generators, so it wasn't due back for at least another ten hours. Austin hoped they wouldn't have to worry about what the mother ship might do with the appearance of a much larger ship than what it may have detected so far. The *Keith Thomas* might well be viewed as committing a hostile act if it appeared out of nowhere and moved toward the mother ship.

As Albretti let them know that the scout ship had cleared the radiation field, she alerted them to a course change. "They're now heading directly for Citadel. Wait, that's not quite right." She looked back over her shoulder at Austin as she said, "They're heading toward the yard. I hope to God they just want to check out our technology for building ships and other stuff and have a laugh at how childish it is compared to what they can do."

"How long until they reach the yard, Gina?" Austin asked.

"A little over two hours at their present speed."

"What's the status of the yard?"

"Almost everyone is gone," she replied.

Austin frowned. "What do you mean by 'almost'?"

She brought up images of the ships in the yard, saying, "First, there are several crews that are handling the scheduled maintenance for three transports. They say they're almost done with two of them and can leave pretty much anytime. The third one needs a lot more work before it's going anywhere. It isn't powered up right now. There are also a few people working on the new *Pathfinder*. They can't leave without going through a proper shutdown."

Austin made his decisions quickly. "For the people who are doing the work on the transports, tell them to get the two ships that are operational out of there now and not to come back until we tell them it's OK. For the third ship, tell them to leave it and go now. For the people who are working on the new *Pathfinder*, tell them to wrap it up and get the hell out of there. We'll build a new bay for them if anything happens to this one."

"They say there'd be a lot of contamination if they don't do it right."

Austin's eyes were full of fire as he said, "Damn it, tell Curly I said 'fuck the contamination and get their asses out of there *now*!' I don't want *anyone* there when our visitor arrives. If she isn't clear on any of my directions, tell her I want to talk with her."

"Yes, sir," she said.

Stephens said much the same a moment later.

Austin had Albretti modify the image from the yard into a split screen, so that they could keep an eye on the yard and watch the approach of their visitor. After two hours passed with no sign of the scout ship, a small dot appeared on the screen and became larger with each second. They started to see some features but had the same problem getting a reliable view of the ship because of its contours and colors.

The first bay was empty, with the next two bays occupied. The visitor came to within five thousand meters of the first bay and then stopped. The ship had something like a probe that started to show a dull glow. Suddenly, the bay was consumed with electrical overloads, with multiple fires breaking out. The image from the bay failed almost immediately, and they had to rely on images from the other bays.

"Looks like some kind of EMP attack," Austin said.

"Yes," Albretti replied. "It's as powerful as something from a nuclear weapon, even though they're generating it through something else. Look!"

They watched in shock as the structure of the bay began to fail, twisting into something grotesque and unrecognizable. The scout ship moved toward the next bay, with the new *Pathfinder* abandoned and helpless to resist. After getting into position, the scout ship's probe once again gave off a dull glow, and even more spectacular fireworks burst from the bay and *Pathfinder,* sending angry splashes from across the rainbow in every direction.

As various materials within *Pathfinder* became super-heated, they exploded, rupturing her hull and ripping apart the bay itself. The scene was no less one of horror just because they couldn't hear any of the carnage.

After *Pathfinder* was no more than a ruined hulk, the scout ship moved on. It approached the bay with the transport and showed that its EMP weapon could easily destroy a ship much bigger than *Pathfinder*. Once again, ship and bay were fused together and blasted apart under the relentless onslaught. When the scout ship was done, there was little left that resembled either a bay or a ship.

The scout ship repeated the scene with each of the remaining bays. It seemed that after so much destruction, it would be time for the aliens to pause and reflect on what they had wrought. Reflection didn't seem to be in their nature, since the ship moved directly toward Citadel. They ignored the shards of twisted materials that continued to glow and burn from the hellish combination of metals and synthetics that was all that was left of the bays and their occupants.

Even the background noises aboard the original *Pathfinder* seemed to have faded into the silence as everyone absorbed the shock of what they'd just seen. Albretti turned to Austin and said quietly, "I don't think we need Alan for any translations, Sam. Their message has been pretty damned clear."

Austin knew there was perhaps four hours before the scout ship reached Citadel and began to destroy its infrastructure. He didn't believe for a moment that the EMP device was the only weapon the ship planned on using against the settlers. Once Citadel's technology was fried, there were probably other weapons available to hunt down and destroy every human on the planet. After Citadel was back to its original nonhuman population, it wouldn't take long to destroy any stragglers and the rest of the settlers' operations in the system.

Austin had seen enough. He had an idea of how to take on the scout ship, but it was a one-way ticket for those who would take the challenge; there'd be no return trip or miraculous turn of events that would save them.

The ship somehow became even quieter as Austin turned to face everyone, with blue eyes full of cold, grim fire. The tone in his voice matched his face as he said, "I don't know about the rest of you, but I'm not going to sit around on my ass while our families and friends are being slaughtered like their lives don't have any meaning."

Albretti replied, "What do you have in mind, Sam?"

"I'm going to take a page from history and take *Pathfinder* to the mining operations. I'm going to upgrade an asteroid projector into a rail gun to fire some asteroids into that ship's hull. I'm betting that even a ship a hell of a lot more advanced than ours will get the worst of it when it takes a direct hit from something with the speed and energy from those hunks of rock."

"I'm with you as far as wanting to do something," Albretti said, "but how would we get around the mother ship? It would take hours just to get there, and we already know what they're likely to do if they see us. Even if we were to try to use the warp-field generators to get to the entrance, we'd still face the mother ship. I don't know how we'd evade it, but even if we did, we couldn't take a chance on using the generators within the system. At best, we'd still be hours behind the scout ship. There wouldn't be much left on Citadel by that time."

Austin looked hard into her eyes as he said, "That's why we have to consider another option. The only way this could work is if *Pathfinder* goes straight toward the mining operations from here."

Looks of surprise rippled across faces as Austin's comments sank in. Albretti's eyes widened as she answered, "That would take us right through the radiation field. We don't even know if *Pathfinder* would survive the trip." She left out what they all knew, which was that as bad as it would be for *Pathfinder*, the ship would be in better shape than they would. It wasn't even clear how long they'd be able to function before succumbing to the radiation poisoning.

Austin nodded solemnly, saying, "That's right, Gina. I don't need to spell it out that this is a one-way trip, not just for *Pathfinder*, but for anyone who goes along. We don't even know for sure that anyone could survive long enough to be of any use. Everyone has families to think about, and it's up to each of us to decide how to do what's right for our families. Nothing will be said about anyone who wants to sit it out. We have lifeboats, and it may be possible to get to the *Keith Thomas* when she returns, if she survives. Depending on what happens on Citadel, your best bet may be to take the *Keith Thomas* back to Earth and let everyone know what's happened. She's done well in her trials, and it's reasonable to assume that she'd be able to return to Earth safely."

His face had a tight smile as he continued, "I've already decided that I'm going. I could really use some of you to help, but I don't need all of you to make it work.

This stinks, but you only have one minute to decide what you're going to do. Our people on Citadel may need any extra minutes more than we do. We have work to do, so I'm heading over to engineering, where I'll be running things. No one needs to hang around the bridge any-more. Join me in engineering or get on a lifeboat with my fervent wish that you, and hopefully your families, live a long life. Regardless of your choices, it's been an honor to work with each of you." He turned and left the room.

Albretti set the controls for the ship to head for the mining operations at high speed, with a timed delay of two minutes before engaging. She said to the group, "You have one minute to make up your minds, then another minute to get into a lifeboat. *Pathfinder* heads out in two minutes, rain or shine. Good luck." She turned and headed toward engineering.

When she arrived in engineering, she found Austin already at work, setting up equipment they'd need to remove an asteroid projector and upgrade it into a rail gun. He looked up, saw it was Albretti, and frowned. "Gina," he said, "get on a lifeboat. You have a baby who's four months old. She needs you more than I do."

Albretti walked over and faced him off from twelve inches away as she said, "I'm doing this so that Sofia will have a chance at living. Besides, you're going and you have a baby on the way who won't ever see his father. You're doing this for the same reason, so shut up and tell me what you need me to do."

The coldness in his eyes eased for a moment as he gave her a small nod and said, "OK, I need someone who can adapt *Pathfinder's* navigation system into something that can handle firing control solutions for a rail gun and have it launch these rocks. It has to be 'smart' enough to work out spread patterns in case the alien ship tries to evade the rocks. Set it up so that it can take components from the mining operations in case *Pathfinder's* systems are too degraded to do the job. *Pathfinder* still has to be maneuvered from this system. I need it in under four hours, and it has to be something that only needs one person to operate."

Her eyes looked into Austin's sad, blue eyes as she said, "I understand, Sam."

The two of them looked up to see a crowd entering engineering as people asked for their assignments. In spite of the situation, the cold in Austin's eyes melted away for a moment. When *Pathfinder* departed for the mining operations, she had all of her lifeboats on board.

CHAPTER TWENTY FIVE

B y having *Pathfinder* travel at maximum velocity, they were reducing the amount of time in the radiation field, although Austin knew it wouldn't be nearly enough to change the outcome for any of them. Because everyone had stayed on *Pathfinder*, Austin was able to have people conserve their energy somewhat by working in short shifts, waiting a brief time, and then taking over for someone else. There wasn't much point in having people sit around in reserve, since their energy would start to fade pretty soon anyway. Better to use them while they could still contribute to the effort. He suggested that they record any last messages they wanted during those breaks. Although he was in charge of everything, he took the time to contact Citadel to let them know what they were going to do.

It didn't make things any easier to hear the reactions to the message. "Sam, you can't do this!" Liz pleaded. "There has to be another way!"

"There isn't any choice," he replied. "You've all seen what they did to the yard. Citadel would be back in the

nineteenth century or earlier after they completed their
EMP attacks. We have to assume that they have other
weapons at hand that will finish the job and wipe everyone out there. They can then take their time and finish
the job through the rest of our solar system. The mother
ship is the cork on the bottle, so there's no place in this
system to hide for long."

"Can't any of the transports do this?"

He shook his head, saying, "No one is in the correct
position to get either to the mining operations or Citadel
quickly enough. *Pathfinder* is a faster ship anyway."

"You can at least save yourselves, Sam," Yabuno said,
his eyes pleading. "Wait for the *Keith Thomas* to return
and then get your asses back to Earth. Start over somewhere else. The new technology works; make it work
somewhere else."

Austin's eyes were melancholy as he replied, "The
Citadel Group has the new technology, too, Bret. They
can make it work somewhere else, if it comes to that. As
far as bailing out is concerned, we didn't come this far to
build our homes and a new community, only to sit back
and watch our loved ones be slaughtered. I gave everyone
the option you mentioned of waiting on a lifeboat for the
Keith Thomas. They turned me down. We left a beacon for
the *Keith Thomas* explaining what was happening.

Austin's eyes turned a grim shade of blue as he said,
"We thought some vultures from Earth were our greatest threat, but we were wrong. If we don't do something
about it, we'll never be safe anywhere, maybe not even on
Earth. I told Earth that we would defend Citadel with our
lives, if necessary, and I meant every word. We're not sure

we can get to Citadel in time as it is; a lot of it depends on the shape our people are in when we reach the mining operations. You may end up taking a pounding anyway before we can arrive."

Liz looked straight into Austin's eyes as she said, "If you must do this, then make damned sure you make it in time to make a difference. That's the message I'll give to our baby. I love you, Sam."

"I love you, Liz." Liz walked away from the screen without another word.

It didn't take long for people to start feeling like shit. Austin noticed that some of the people were starting to let their concentration slip and reminded them of the need to stay focused. Before the first hour was up, several people had already collapsed. Incredibly, they insisted on taking stimulants to keep working. They tried to do as many of the tricky calculations as early as possible, so that they'd just be implementing the plan by the time they reached the mining operations.

Austin had Albretti keep him up-to-date on the system she was developing, since he assumed that he'd be the one to operate the rail gun and maneuver *Pathfinder*. He was a qualified space pilot and the only one with combat experience. He thought back on a conversation years ago with Yabuno and hoped that his life-span would give him an advantage in staying alive long enough to do what needed to be done. In spite of his assumptions, he had Albretti keep several others up-to-date as well, in case Austin was wrong and couldn't do what had to be done.

Although there should have been relief over their having left the radiation field, they knew the damage had been done. Their ship was now too radioactive to protect human life; there was no place to hide from the invisible killer that lurked everywhere. As time wore on, Austin was aware of feelings he hadn't experienced in many years, outside of dealing with injuries. He knew he was feeling worse than he had even ten minutes earlier, and it would be even worse in another ten minutes. By the time they reached the mining operations, more than half of the people had collapsed, and no one who was left standing was in good shape. It would have been even harder if they would have had to force their faltering bodies to work within a regular-gravity environment.

The mining operations were a great source of pride for Citadel, being quite advanced by Earth's standards. As Albretti began to describe what it would mean for them as they approached the operations, Austin noted, sadly, her grayish pallor, with deep black stains under her eyes. "On the one hand, it's a big help for us that the facility is fully automated," she said, "since it means that I can call up various components that we'll need. Full automation also has a downside, though."

"What you mean is that no one's there to help with anything," Austin replied.

She shook her head as she said, "No one at all. The operations weren't designed to handle this situation, and there are still things to be done that need human interaction and muscle."

With a wan smile, Austin said, "I've picked out a few people still standing to suit up with me to provide the interaction and muscle."

"While you're out there, I'll keep an eye on the people who are retrofitting *Pathfinder's* power cores to supply the power for the rail gun," Gina said. "We don't have the time to transport the surface power plant on such short notice." Austin nodded as he headed toward his space suit and the airlock.

Austin and his team removed the projector from the asteroid where it was housed and strengthened it to withstand the enormous increase in stress factors from firing projectiles at high speeds. Another group attached improvised metal "cages" onto the rocks to serve as the counterparts to the converted gun. They worked with desperate fear that they were taking too long as they brought the mismatched components together. They used whatever they needed from the facility or took it from *Pathfinder* itself. It wasn't pretty, but they knew they wouldn't get a second chance to do it. Austin doubted it would last for more than a few shots.

Several people simply stopped functioning as they finished fumbling with the modifications. Some of those people were in their space suits outside, no longer caring whether they even made it back to *Pathfinder*. Others slumped around the equipment in the hold where the bizarre weapon took shape. Austin didn't have the luxury of time to try to collect people who were still outside. If they weren't moving, he stopped trying to rouse them and wished them peace as they drifted into the shadows. Those lives had to be weighed against the thousands of souls on Citadel.

There were only two people with Austin in the hold as he ordered *Pathfinder* to race toward Citadel at extreme speed while they completed their modifications. By the time Austin reached the hatch to stagger to engineering, there were only floating bodies left behind in the hold. He didn't want to give away their position by sending a message that they were on their way. Citadel, on the other hand, had no reason not to broadcast updates on the progress of the scout ship.

He'd done everything possible to save time. The rail gun was already preloaded with several asteroids. If at all possible, he didn't intend to slow down upon approaching Citadel. He wanted to add *Pathfinder's* speed to that of the rail gun to launch projectiles with no time for the scout ship to avoid them. He looked around engineering and saw that no one else appeared to be active.

"Gina, how are you doing?" he called out. He bit off any more words when saw her slumped over a control station, her work done. Other than some background noises generated by a few systems, the silence that greeted him suggested a ghost ship. He knew it wouldn't be much longer before he'd be joining the other ghosts.

Austin had the main display focused on Citadel, with a second one that was receiving images from Citadel's vantage. The quality of the images was degraded because of the damage from the radiation field. At first, there was no direct image of the scout ship on the second display. Long minutes passed as a tiny dot expanded into a familiar nightmare. As the distance closed, it became increasingly clear that the scout ship would have the first shot at Citadel. Austin swore in frustration but knew there wasn't anything they could do about it. *Pathfinder* was holding together with a lot of hope as it was, and there wasn't any way to increase its speed further.

Citadel's satellites noted and broadcast images of the scout ship as it approached and settled into orbit. They watched as the familiar probe began to glow and blast Citadel with a tremendous bombardment from the EMP weapon. Critical systems all throughout the settlements began to fail, including security networks for their homes. Without a way to repair those networks, the settlers would become prisoners within their homes—if they could even get back to them in time before the cheaters descended on them. One by one, the things that made their world a twenty-second-century society failed.

Austin adjusted *Pathfinder's* course slightly to place it on a direct line with the scout ship. Perhaps it was the course adjustment that alerted the scout ship to the danger, but their adversary began to shift its position in orbit. It also began to rotate slowly, moving the probe away from Citadel and coming into line with *Pathfinder*. Austin knew that if the scout ship's EMP weapon was brought to bear directly toward his ship, the rail gun would be useless. If that happened, he was determined that *Pathfinder* itself would be the projectile to blast the other ship into pieces.

Just before the EMP probe came fully into line with *Pathfinder*, Austin fired the rail gun. In rapid sequence, three asteroids were ejected at extreme speed toward the scout ship. No more projectiles would fire. He wasn't sure if it was because the rail gun had failed on its own or because of the EMP weapon. Austin was able to nudge *Pathfinder* off of the direct line of approach to the scout ship. For a few moments, he had the best seat around as he watched the projectiles smash into and vaporize several large sections of the alien ship. What was left of the ship erupted in a pool of flames even larger than what they'd seen when the helpless transport had been destroyed.

The destruction of the scout ship seemed to signal the end for Austin as well, as he could barely even sit upright. He didn't want his body to drift through space forever, a radioactive corpse entombed aboard a radioactive coffin. He managed to bring *Pathfinder* about and slow her enough to allow him to try to launch a lifeboat to land somewhere on Citadel.

He didn't want anything more than to find a field somewhere to lie at rest. Hell, he was entitled to *that* much! Austin could barely crawl into a lifeboat. With trembling fingers that hardly even responded, he jettisoned it from *Pathfinder*. The lifeboat didn't need to be piloted; if it could still function, it would seek out a gentle place to land. If not, there would be an insignificant crash somewhere. His last thoughts were of Liz and whether she'd ever know where he was laid to rest.

CHAPTER TWENTY SIX

The damage on Citadel from the EMP weapon had been extensive, but *Pathfinder's* arrival had distracted the aliens aboard the scout ship from completing the attack before everything had been destroyed. As it was, emergency teams spread throughout the settlements to try to stabilize the situation, aided by transports that returned from safer havens in the solar system. In some cases, they were back to using hand weapons for survival against opportunistic cheaters. Slowly, painfully, they forced the cheaters to give back the territory they had taken.

The main medical facility had been crippled, so they were using a secondary facility that had been located far way. As Liz was talking with a doctor, she couldn't help looking back at a figure in a makeshift isolation chamber.

The doctor continued, "There is simply no way that he could have gotten out of that lifeboat by himself. He couldn't have been conscious; in fact, he should have been dead before he reached the ground."

"He knew somehow that he needed to get out of the lifeboat," Liz said. "It was radioactive and would have killed him if he'd stayed inside it."

"It wouldn't have mattered, Liz. He had prolonged exposure to far more radiation than was needed to kill him."

"What are his chances, Doctor?" Liz asked.

"You need to prepare for the worst," the doctor explained. She waved her hand around the damaged facility, her tense fingers revealing frustration as she said, "As best as we could under these circumstances, we've completed the decontamination protocols to try to cleanse Sam's body as much as possible of residual radiation. He's in bad shape, and people don't recover from the levels of exposure that he's received. Even if someone survives for a while, the body can't keep going for long; there's a tipping point where everything starts to fail and nothing more really helps. His still being alive is itself a minor miracle. It would be another miracle if he survives the night."

"Can I visit with him?"

"Since you're pregnant, let's give him a few more hours to get the radiation levels down further. With some precautions, it should be safe for you to visit with him in around four hours. He's still unconscious anyway."

Liz spoke softly, partly to herself. "I've learned not to bet against anything that Sam does, so I won't bet against him making it through the night. Hang in there, Sam, so that you can hear my voice again."

Four hours later, Liz was next to him, wearing a suit to protect her from the radiation. She spoke to him softly through the night, although he never stirred. She won her bet that he'd still be there in the morning.

"What are the next steps for him, Doctor?" Liz asked the next morning.

The fatigue in the doctor's eyes showed she hadn't slept either as she said, "Please don't take this the wrong way, Liz, but I'm amazed that Sam is still alive; he should be dead by now. He hasn't gotten any worse, although he's still in bad shape. The good news is that his radiation levels are dropping faster than predicted, and we're not sure why. If this keeps up, you might not even need to wear the protective suit in a few more hours. This still doesn't change anything, though. People sometimes appear to have rallied from a terminal condition, only to lose ground over time. I wish it could be different with Sam, but my training tells me it won't. He'll still reach that tipping point I mentioned yesterday, and we won't be able to save him. The best thing you can do for him is to spend the time with him. At some level, that may be what's keeping him with us this long."

Later that afternoon, Liz's eyes were brighter as she talked with the doctor. "Sam seems stronger. I can't say for sure why I think so; he hasn't awakened, but his color seems a little better and so does his breathing."

The fatigue in the doctor's eyes had given way to surprise. She shook her head as she said, "Sam is much stronger than I would have imagined. The radiation levels have dropped almost to nothing. His breathing *is* getting stronger, and his color looks much better than it did even a few hours ago. You can stop wearing the protective suit and start holding his hand without wearing gloves. That seems to be the best medicine for him right now."

Liz stayed with Austin through the night again, caressing his face and holding his hand. When morning came around, she had fallen asleep from exhaustion. She started awake when she realized the hand she was holding was squeezing her hand back!

"Sam! Doctor! Sam!" Liz looked into Austin's smiling blue eyes and saw traces of the old energy there. The doctor rushed over, expecting to hear that Austin had reached his tipping point. Instead, she was amazed to see Austin awake and focused on her with intelligent eyes.

His voice was little more than a croak as he asked, "How long have I been out?"

"It's been three days since your lifeboat crashed," the doctor replied. "We were lucky that the distress beacon on it was still functioning, because we'd never have found you otherwise. Our monitoring systems weren't in any shape to track you."

"How bad was the damage from the attack?"

"They blasted the hell out of us, but you distracted them before they could take us out completely. We still have a lot of work to do to fix things around here, but we can probably avoid traveling back to the nineteenth century while we do it."

Austin's eyes were unflinching as he asked, "What shape am I in?"

Her eyes twinkled with a trace of black humor as she said, "You should be glowing-in-the-dark kind of dead, Sam. Instead, all traces of the radiation that you absorbed are gone. Although you're still in a hell of a mess, you seem to be fighting back against the damage you've suffered."

"I can't begin to thank you properly for what you've done for me, Doctor."

She snorted as she said, "We're good, but we're not *that* good. Whatever is responsible for your body's response to the radiation is coming from within you. I wasn't clear when I said you're fighting back against the physical damage you've suffered. The latest tests show that much of the physical damage has started to reverse itself. If these actions continue, you may be able to walk out of here on your own in two or three days. You'll still need some more recovery time, but you won't have to stay here for it."

Liz's face brightened as she asked, "Doctor, are you saying that Sam will recover fully from the radiation exposure?"

The doctor replied, "I'm not sure what would be a 'full' recovery for Sam, Liz. We'll know within a couple of days whether he really is on the road to recovery. Let's wait until then to make that assessment. In the meantime, I'd like to order some further tests."

Two days later, the doctor entered Austin's room to find him on his feet, looking worlds away from being a victim of extreme radiation poisoning. Austin smiled and with a strong voice said, "Well, Doctor, are you still prepared to give Liz a speech about my being at death's door, or are you ready to accept that I'm looking pretty spry, all things considered?"

The doctor smiled back as she replied, "I guess we're past those comments now, Sam. The tests show that your body is somehow repairing itself. The rate of repair seems to be picking up by the hour."

"What are the long-term consequences for Sam as far as any genetic damage and his ability to have children are concerned?" Liz asked.

Austin grinned as he said, "That's a polite way of asking whether my balls and other equipment will be OK!"

The doctor chuckled as she said, "We can't find any evidence of genetic damage. As far as whether Sam's sexual abilities have been affected by the radiation, it seems unlikely in view of his return to health."

"I guess you'll just have to take our word for it that if you don't hear back from us, there aren't any problems in that regard," Austin said with a gleam in his eye.

Liz had the same gleam as she said, "I guess we'll need to confirm that one in private."

Austin's smile faded as he said, "Doctor, I appreciate everything you've done for me, but I need to ask you to turn over to me all of your medical files on me, especially the ones relating to checking out my genetics."

The doctor said, "I expected that you would make this request, assuming that you survived, but I can assure you that your records would be kept in strict confidence."

Austin's eyes generated a cold blue fire as he said, "Promises of confidentiality have been made before, Doctor. Although it happened a long time ago, people important to me died because those promises were broken. I'll let you use the records if it becomes necessary for any future treatment, but they stay with me until then."

"All right, Sam," the doctor agreed. "I can understand your position. Your records will be provided to you once you are discharged from this facility.

Austin's eyes warmed considerably as he said, "Thanks, Doctor." Austin turned to Liz as he said, "I think we'll be ready to leave once I get changed out of these hospital duds into some real clothes. I guess the old ones are still glowing in the dark!"

Liz's eyes were wet as she said, "Matt has been waiting to see you, my love. Then you need to spend some time talking to our baby on the way and then making love to me. The rest of Citadel will have to wait for at least another day or so before it gets ahold of you. They may have to wait even longer."

Austin was subdued as he said, "One thing I need to do before anything else is to send out a message acknowledging the others that were with me on *Pathfinder*. We need to honor them for the sacrifices they made. Austin smiled tenderly. "After that, we'll make them wait as long as you want, my love!"

CHAPTER TWENTY SEVEN

The rest of Citadel did, indeed, wait before Austin met with them over his link. It didn't take long for the smiles from the greetings and good wishes to fade as they discussed the current situation.

"Thank God the *Keith Thomas* and the mother ship never crossed paths, Sam," Yabuno said. "Although the biggest tragedy would have been the loss of the people aboard her, we would have also been without our only ship with a reliable warp-field generator."

"Where are the remains of the scout ship?" Austin asked. A grim smile played out across his face as he said, "The last time I saw it, I didn't have much time to watch it get the same treatment it gave the yard."

"Our tracking capabilities were pretty much hammered, so we aren't sure what happened. It was in orbit when you blasted it, so our best guess at this point is that everything burned up in the atmosphere. We haven't found a single fragment from it."

"That's too bad," Austin mused. "Maybe we'd have been able to get an idea about their plans. It's interesting that the mother ship didn't stick around long after we clobbered the scout ship. It seems clear that only the scout ship was small enough to enter the system safely. Once the mother ship saw what had happened, they would have had to consider the possibility of being on the receiving end of more asteroids. Since they couldn't get to us, they must have decided that it wasn't worth hanging around further."

"We may be less in the dark than we realize regarding their plans, Sam."

"What do you mean?"

Yabuno frowned as he said, "The signals from our communications array at the entrance to the radiation field show that they were scanning the array. While we're not sure about everything they learned from the array, they appear to have checked out the beacons and seen the pathway to Earth."

Austin's eyes became cold as he said, "They may have decided to give our old stomping grounds a visit. I wouldn't want to take any bets on anyone there coming out on top from a fight with these creeps. The only thing that saved our asses is the fact the mother ship couldn't get past the radiation field. There's nothing like it back there. We'd better warn them, so that they can make some preparations for defending themselves."

"We can't do it," Yabuno said.

Austin's eyes narrowed as he demanded, "Why the hell not?"

"They trashed the array before leaving," Yabuno replied with a cold fury. "Even though we've replaced and rebooted everything we can think of, the communications side going to Earth doesn't work. They may have already made it to the next beacon and trashed it too."

"There may not be an Earth much longer, if that's where they went," Austin said quietly.

"Why, Sam? Earth has far greater resources to defend itself than we do. It also has the benefit of regular space-based patrols that should be able to do something."

"Our home system isn't militarized, Bret. For reasons that you should recall from your history lessons, we had a pretty damned significant incident when I was president. As a result, there isn't much support for anything that could be upgraded into a rail gun. Fortunately for us, I didn't allow that thinking to get in the way of our having somewhat more advanced mining technology available here. Unfortunately for them, although there's a shitload of mining technology back there, it can't be converted quickly into weapons. I don't believe that any patrol ships would be able to take on the mother ship without being blown away by that EMP weapon.

"Even though Earth's population is vastly larger than ours, they'd suffer hugely if they were to be on the receiving end of a sustained EMP attack. After the attack, without modern technology to help them, they'd be just as much at the mercy of the aliens as we would have been. It might take longer to wipe out everyone on Earth, but it could be done, especially if the aliens have biological weapons up their sleeves, assuming that they have sleeves. It would take much less time to wipe out people on the Moon or Mars, since it takes serious technology to keep things running there in the first place."

Austin's blue eyes were indescribably sad as he said, "We may end up being the last humans alive, if those aliens aren't stopped."

Liz asked, "Isn't that up to the people there to handle, Sam? We were barely able to get through contact with their scout ship."

There was a determined look on Austin's face as he replied, "We have something that Earth doesn't have. We can upgrade another asteroid projector into a rail gun and haul it to Earth in the *Keith Thomas*."

"That projector is the last one we have, Sam," Yabuno said. "No one is complaining over how you used the other one, but if the only functioning one leaves Citadel, we'll be completely defenseless against another attack, if they decide to return." Yabuno crossed his arms. "You're asking us to give up our security to help a people that told us to go to hell when we told them we were now our own state. We don't owe them anything."

With a calculating look, Austin asked, "Aren't you forgetting something? If they decide that they can take out Earth, then what's to stop them from deciding to have another shot at us anyway? If they lose again, then they might go somewhere else and leave both star systems alone. I believe our security actually depends on our helping out the folks back on Earth, regardless of whether they've shown us the respect we deserve."

A grim twinkle appeared in Austin's eyes as he continued, "Let's keep in mind that we need to buy some time. This is a temporary measure that may buy us that time. Once we've taken the steps necessary to establish proper defenses for our star system, then Earth, Mars, the Moon, and the others are on their own. If they can't figure out what to do to protect themselves from unwanted visitors, then there'd be little point in adding our own lives to their casualty lists."

"What happens if we get there too late to do anything except dig several billion graves?" Yabuno demanded.

"I'd rather find that out by trying to help them than sitting here in terror against the day they return," Austin replied quietly.

Yabuno shook his head. "You're asking people to give their lives for the sake of other lives, Sam."

There was a look of pride in Austin's eyes as he said, "That's the same thing I asked of the people aboard *Pathfinder*. The 'other lives' happened to be on Citadel. I've never been as proud of anyone as I was of those people. They knew it was a one-way ticket for them, but not one of them stayed behind."

Yabuno blinked. He looked away for a moment with a sigh and then turned back. "I've wanted to ask you something. What would you have done if the rail gun hadn't worked?"

Austin gave Yabuno a hard look as he replied softly, "I would have used *Pathfinder* herself as a guided missile if I thought there wasn't any other choice. I wouldn't rule out the possibility of doing so with the *Keith Thomas* if necessary, either, although I don't believe in throwing away people's lives needlessly. I have some ideas about how to handle that situation in a way that wouldn't be as deadly to the people aboard."

Austin's eyes were blurred for a moment in sorrow as he said, "As for ramming the scout ship with *Pathfinder*, I didn't have to worry about the impact on the rest of the crew, since they were all dead by that time. I wasn't about to let them give their lives only to have the scout ship survive because I was worried about my own life."

"Let's talk about those plans of yours, Sam," Liz said gently.

Austin, Liz, and Yabuno were having a pointed discussion about the voyage.

"I still don't see why you need to be the one to lead the *Keith Thomas*, Sam," Liz said. "Haven't you already done enough for us?"

There was a haunted look in Austin's eyes as he answered, "Gina Albretti gave her life because she wanted to make sure her four-month-old daughter would have a chance at life, Liz. I want to make sure that Matt and the baby on the way have that same chance."

"Let someone else do it," Yabuno said. "You were damned fortunate to have things work out the way they did. We have to assume that the mother ship must have seen what happened and won't be fooled if we try a repeat."

"Yes, that's probably true," Austin replied with a nod. "That's why I need to be the one to lead the mission. I'm the only one with training as a space pilot who also has combat experience."

"Sam, we've known each other a long time, so I'm going to say something that you won't like hearing," Yabuno said. "First, understand that a lot of people have serious questions about whether this is even a good idea. You're damned fortunate that the people have a hell of a lot of respect for you, because there isn't anyone else who could get the people to support this idea, or at least not withhold their cooperation. There are people who are wondering whether you want to be in charge of this mission because you feel guilty over not having died with the others on *Pathfinder*. Some are wondering if you have a death wish or are blinded by a need for revenge and are just trying to get the rest of us to cooperate so you can stick it to the aliens."

"What do *you* think about it, Bret?"

With sad eyes, Yabuno said, "I think the loss of the people on *Pathfinder* hit you hard, Sam. I can't imagine what it must have been like to have been the last one still standing as you approached the scout ship. I know that you're not the kind of man to throw away lives without good reason, but right now you might feel differently about your own life. I think you'd consider it a fair trade to exchange your life for the mother ship."

Austin stood up quickly, visibly agitated as he said, "There's nothing 'fair' about the exchange, Bret. Those creatures stuck their noses, if they even have noses, where they didn't belong and decided that our lives didn't mean anything. Good people are dead because of that decision, and there's a price that must be paid for those lives. No one who's unwilling to see that this price is paid has any business leading the *Keith Thomas* to Earth."

Bret stood up with some agitation of his own. "If that's the way you feel, why are you opposed to *my* coming along? I might be useful."

Austin nearly smiled at the word *useful,* saying, "Your usefulness for the trip is outweighed by the fact that you may be the smartest man I've ever met."

Bret brushed away the comment, saying, "That's a strange thing to say. For one thing, you're overlooking several other people on Citadel who are scary smart. For another, you're a hell of a lot smarter than you let on."

"I'm not under any illusions about the odds of being able to pull this off twice." Austin sighed. "If it doesn't work out, then Citadel will need a new leader and you're the best man for the job. You'll have to come up with another plan and get everyone to agree to it. Believe me, it isn't always easy. If you come along with me and don't come back, I'm not sure that any of what Citadel needs to happen will happen."

Yabuno smiled without humor, saying, "It isn't all that hard to figure out what Citadel would need to do if things don't work out, Sam. If that happens, it probably means that Earth is gone and further visits aren't on the table. Our focus would be on seeing to the security of our own star system, which will happen anyway." His face was cold as he continued, "We'll try to develop technologies that will give us a chance to do something other than run when we encounter these beings. While I'd do my best to do these things, there are others who can also do them. There may not be others who can work with you as well in the heat of the moment to take out the mother ship."

Austin shook his head slowly, followed with a wry grin as he said, "Damn it, Bret. I should have realized you were also smart enough to come up with a compelling reason why you should come along. We'd never have made it to Citadel at all if you hadn't been on our ship and figured out a way to keep the old generators functioning. We may need you to come up with a neater trick to save our asses after we reach Earth. I guess you've talked yourself into what may be a one-way ticket. It'll be interesting to see what's been happening with our people on Earth, assuming that we can deal with the mother ship."

"There's another reason why you want to return to Earth, Sam, isn't there?" Liz asked.

Austin replied, "Yes, I need to talk with some responsible people in person about Citadel's status and appointing a representative. That person would serve, in effect, as our ambassador."

"Who'd you have in mind, Sam?"

"I'm sure you can guess." Austin looked at his link and said, "Holy shit, it's late! I hope there won't be any trouble with Donna on my account."

A grin returned to Bret's face as he replied, "Fortunately, Donna has a soft spot for you and knows the importance of what's going on. Hopefully, she'll be willing to forgive you when she hears that I'm going to Earth."

Austin grinned back as he said, "Better get some sleep now while you can, because I want everything to be ready to go within days, not weeks!"

Later the next day, Austin and Liz had a private argument.

There was heat in his voice as he said, "Liz, there's no way you can come with me on this trip. It's far too dangerous."

She walked over to him and held his hand as she replied, "Sam, I lost you once already. The cause was worthy, but you were still telling me you were going to die. In a way, it was even worse when they found you and brought you in for medical help. At least if you'd died out there, you'd have simply died in saving Citadel and I would try to move on." A tear trickled down her face as she said, "When I saw you in the treatment chamber, I don't know how I kept from breaking down. I thought I'd watch you die as a shadow of what you were.

"When you recovered, I swore that I'd never again be apart from you for things like this. I know it's selfish of me, since we have Matt and a baby on the way, but I won't watch you go off to die again. I'd rather have everything end for us together than to have us torn apart again."

"What do you think it would mean for me to have to worry about your safety while I'm trying to direct an attack on another ship?"

"You decided to die when you knew my safety was at risk on Citadel, Sam. You know how to do the right thing regardless of the harm that might come to the ones you love."

"Neither of us has the right to place our baby on the way in danger. That life needs to be protected, and the only way to do it is for you to stay here."

She pulled her hand away as she said, "I won't raise him without his father. Either we all make it, or none of us makes it."

Austin was quiet for a moment. "Next thing, you'll be telling me that you want Matt to come along."

"Yes, Sam, that's exactly what I'm telling you," she replied, with her blue eyes on fire. "Our whole family is together on this one. If you don't like it, then find someone else to go in your place."

"What would happen to our home while we were gone? It would fall apart pretty damned quickly without regular attention."

Liz smiled as she spoke into her link, "I think we're ready to hear from you."

There were plenty of familiar faces in the screen, all of them smiling. Donna Yabuno spoke on their behalf. "Sam, what can we say to someone who was not only willing to sacrifice his life to save our lives but is willing to do it again? We know that we can't possibly repay you for what you did and what you will do, but that doesn't mean we can't try. We know what Liz wants to do, and we'd be honored if you'd let us look after your place while you are gone."

Austin couldn't speak for a moment. His eyes were moist as he finally managed to say, "Liz isn't playing fair, bringing all of you into this matter. I don't know what to say."

"Tell us that you'll let us say 'thank you' in this way. You know that we'll take good care of your place and we'll have it ready for you *when* you return."

Austin turned back to Liz and took her in his arms as he said, "All right, you win." Few of the faces on the screen had dry eyes at that moment.

CHAPTER TWENTY EIGHT

As the *Keith Thomas* made its way toward Earth, Austin couldn't help but be impressed at how smoothly she seemed to function. If he didn't know better, he'd swear she was humming.

"She's a hell of a ship, isn't she, Sam?" the captain asked. Captain Adams was a familiar face, in charge of the ship that brought Austin to Citadel originally. He'd insisted on being the captain for this trip, even though he knew he'd have to yield again to Austin's overall authority.

"She's a terrific ship," Austin agreed. His voice dropped a bit as he continued, "Captain, I was surprised when you volunteered to be the ship's captain for this trip. I know things may be a bit awkward in view of what happened when we first entered the Citadel system, but I hope you understand why it has to be the way it is."

Captain Adams smiled as he said, "The way I see it is that someone needs to get this ship there in one piece. You have plenty on your mind as it is without having to worry about actually running this ship during the voyage. I promise to give you a ship that'll do everything you ask of her, even if it means that there won't be a trip back to Citadel."

Austin's blue eyes shone with appreciation as he said, "Thanks, Captain. We'll be putting this ship through its paces when we get there, so it's good to know where we stand." He looked around as he said, "It's still going to take some getting used to the fact that we now have artificial gravity on this ship."

The captain laughed as he said, "It almost doesn't seem right, does it? However, I think I'll get used to it pretty fast. By the time we reach Earth, I'll probably be too spoiled to travel in anything that doesn't have it!"

Austin made his way to his stateroom. It was the largest one on the ship and had an office attached to it. Even so, space would be tight, especially once they needed a nursery. To ensure that Austin and Liz had some privacy, Matt had been set up in the stateroom next door.

Austin mused over the simpler ways kids thought about things. For Matt, the trip was the chance to travel on a long voyage and to visit Earth, which he'd only seen in pictures. He didn't understand that some or even all of them might not live through the trip. They might not even see Earth. Being the only child on board, Matt was hugely popular and became the ship's mascot. As the mascot, he received special privileges, one of which was to be indulged when it came to his curiosity about the ship. As a result, the ship's crew was only too happy to take Matt on an extended tour of the place, with follow-up trips as requested, time permitting.

Liz was waiting for him as he reached their stateroom. He had been wearing one of his resistance suits to speed up his recovery. As he removed it, he watched Liz slip out of her clothes. She had barely begun to show, although her breasts were getting larger. She looked at them and smiled. "It seems, once again, that I'm in space with fuller breasts. This time, something else is fuller, too." She took his hands and guided them to her belly, which he caressed tenderly. A mischievous gleam sprang into her eyes as she guided his hands to her breasts and said, "I intend to take full advantage of the fact that we have artificial gravity and don't need to use the love machine. I don't think I could have stood not making love with you for six months!" She pulled him out of his clothes and into the bed with her.

In spite of the somewhat Spartan nature of the quarters, the rooms were well insulated, and the sound of the giggling failed to carry to the passageway.

Austin, like everyone else on the ship, worried over the fact that they had no idea how long it would take the mother ship to reach Earth, assuming that it was headed there at all. He and Yabuno talked about it more than once.

"It's funny how we each have confidence in a part of the issue but are much less certain about another part," Yabuno said.

"I know," Austin replied. "I'm pretty damned sure the mother ship is heading toward Earth, but I've no idea how long it might take them to reach it. For all we know, they could have already arrived and killed everyone there. They could already be adapting the place for their own uses, or they could have gotten bored and left for home. On the other hand, you're certain that they couldn't get there much faster than we could, although you're not sure if they would even bother to do it."

"No one knows how their thinking works, so it's just a guess that they'd go to Earth. They've already lost the first round in the Citadel system, so I don't see why they'd want to take a chance on losing another round. If they assume that the beacons would take them to another planet with beings similar to us, they'd have to assume that there would be similar capabilities there. Those capabilities took out their scout ship."

Austin shook his head. "Those capabilities were damned fortunate to have the protection from a radiation field. Without that field, the mother ship could have entered our solar system. Although under that scenario, *Pathfinder* and her crew wouldn't have been deep fried from the radiation, and the mother ship would have been at its original size. We wouldn't have been anything more than a gnat for the mother ship to worry about. I'm not sure we could have thrown enough rocks at it to take it out before it torched Citadel."

He shrugged as he continued, "If they assume that there won't be a radiation field preventing their entry into Earth's system, then they'll know to deal with anything that looks like a rail gun first. They can then take out everything else. This brings us back to the question of how long it would take for them to get there."

Yabuno spoke with the tone of an instructor, "I've said it before, Sam; the size and shape of the mother ship is what convinces me that they couldn't get to Earth much faster than we could, maybe even not as fast. While it's clear that they have some form of warp field propulsion, getting it to work would have to be a bastard of a trick to pull off. We've already learned that it gets much more difficult to generate and sustain a warp field bubble with even fairly small increases in size. Their ship is so large that it must take most of what they have even to make it work."

"For all we know," Austin countered, "the odd shape of their ship could contribute to an improved efficiency."

"I don't buy it," Yabuno scoffed. "I get it that they're much better at this technology than we are, but based on what I think are the limitations inherent in scaling up a warp field bubble and manipulating space time around it, I think we stand a chance of getting there not long after they do, maybe even around the same time. The question is what do we do once we get there?"

"It's a good thing that we were able to clear out a lot of the passenger space to make room for our nice collection of asteroids," Austin said with a grin.

Yabuno's face showed dissatisfaction as he said, "I still wish we could rig them with delayed-action explosive devices. I'd like to watch their ship blow apart from the inside once some asteroids break through their hull."

Austin smiled, understanding the feeling. "That may happen anyway, depending on what the asteroids hit. Anyway, we don't want to make it easy for them to destroy the asteroids by detonating explosives long before they get anywhere near the mother ship. Also, it should be harder for them to detect a series of asteroids heading toward them if there aren't any foreign materials on them."

"We'll have the metal counterparts to the rails on the asteroids," Yabuno reminded him.

"We'll have to take the chance that they won't look much different from asteroids around that contain those metals. Hopefully, that'll do the trick and we won't have to rely on any special weapons you put together from the collection of junk you insisted we bring along."

"That 'junk' might save us if your rocks don't." Yabuno chuckled. "I'll let you know once I have a better idea how to put everything together into something useful."

"Just keep in mind that we have less than three months to be ready."

A few weeks later, Austin's gaze swept around the hold with a look that was a combination of bewilderment and skepticism. There was a strange collection of components that didn't all look as if they belonged together. He said, "There's a reason why I called it 'junk,' Bret. As I recall, those warp-field generators came from some of our original transports. We know those generators won't sustain a warp field bubble for long."

"We don't have to sustain a bubble for long, Sam. We just have to sustain it for *long enough*. The generators we brought along are the best ones we could salvage and use on such short notice. We know they won't last long, especially using them as we intend. I hope to hell that the rocks do the trick, but we'll need another plan in case they don't. That plan has to be something they won't expect."

"They've seen warp-field generators before." Austin frowned.

"They haven't seen a *Keith Thomas* class ship before or what it can carry. They may not have seen what we can do with extra warp-field generators, either. Even if they have better technology, if we do something they don't expect, then we'll have an advantage."

Austin smiled grimly at the pride in Yabuno's voice. "We'll need it."

CHAPTER TWENTY NINE

The Citadel Group was filled with excitement over the testing of their new transport. It was based on the designs provided by the folks on Citadel and was a big improvement over the previous generation. Captain Sara Choi was having a great time commanding the new transport as they put it through its paces. The artificial gravity made it much easier for her to stay in shape for her other passion in life, dancing. Although they hadn't yet taken the new ship on a long-term run with the warp-field generators, they had taken her on shorter runs, with no problems. The ship was nearly cleared for release from her yard bay, when an urgent message was relayed from their communications array.

"Choi here, Casey," she said. "What's going on?"

A visibly shaken Casey answered, "Captain, we have reports of an incredibly large spaceship that entered our system a short while ago. The reports indicate that the ship headed straight for a Mars mining operation among the asteroids and destroyed it with some form of EMP weapon. A second mining operation has now been reported as having been destroyed." An image appeared, showing a completely devastated facility, with no areas remaining that could protect humans.

Choi gasped. "Were there any fatalities?"

"We have at least five dead confirmed," Casey replied.

Choi frowned as she said, "I don't understand; aren't those facilities automated?"

"Yes, but some inspection teams were there on their regular inspection cycles. They tried to make contact with the ship, but no one responded."

"There doesn't appear to be much left at these facilities, Casey; how do we know what happened?"

"Remember that the operations are linked; the first one sent images to the other sites until it was clobbered. From the information that reached the other sites, it's clear that an extremely powerful EMP weapon was used. The second site was evacuated before the ship arrived, but since that site was linked like the first one, everyone saw it blasted as well. All of the other sites have been evacuated and the authorities on Earth, Mars, and the Moon have been alerted."

"Why would anyone give a damn about the mining operations?"

"We're not sure, but the asteroid projectors at both sites were hit first and the longest."

Choi was puzzled. "What's so special about the asteroid projectors? They aren't a threat to anyone. Who are these guys?"

"Our best guess is that they are a nonhuman species from outside our solar system."

"Why do they think these guys are nonhuman? Humans have had EMP weapons for over a hundred years."

Choi's eyes widened in shock as an image appeared on her screen. Casey replied, "Humans haven't had a ship that's over ten times the size of your ship and apparently can travel in some kind of faster-than-the-speed-of-light fashion. Even if we could build a ship that large, we couldn't make a warp-field generator that would work for it. Also, the reports show that the design and structure aren't remotely how we'd go about putting a ship together. Even putting aside the size difference, you know it couldn't have been built by humans. It's scary even to look at."

Choi grasped at a slender hope. "I guess there's no way this could be from Citadel?"

Casey shook her head. "You're in a ship that represents Citadel's most advanced design for a transport. If Citadel had had the design for the other ship lying around as the next generation, I think they'd have said something about it. Speaking of Citadel, another thing that worries us is that this ship showed up near the beacon to Citadel. As you know, we stopped getting messages from the beacons three months ago, and that's about how long it would take for your shiny new ship to get here. It may be that it's also how long it would take for that ship to get here from there."

"You don't really think Citadel was attacked by that ship?"

Casey shrugged as she replied, "We don't know, but if it happened it's pretty hard to see how Citadel could have survived an attack from this ship. They aren't protected by any system-wide defenses. They don't even have any particular planetary defenses. The only thing working for them is that radiation field, and it might not mean anything to this ship."

"Sam Austin is pretty damned resourceful," Choi said with some heat.

Casey nodded and said, "He sure as hell is, but even Sam needs something to work with. We have to face the possibility that Citadel may be gone, along with their mining and manufacturing operations. Their other technology may be gone as well, other than what they've shared with us since contact was reestablished. That means that while your ship is a terrific piece of technology, we may not be able to get the most we can from it by talking with the people who designed it."

"What about the space patrol, Casey?" Choi asked.

Casey shook her head as she replied, "Patrol ships were sent out to deal with the alien ship. They did the best they could, but with the weapons they had, their fate was predictable, with more lives added to the ledger. Their ships were damaged so badly that men and women were trapped inside what became their coffins as their heat, air, and other environmental support failed. Even some of their lifeboats failed. It didn't take long for Earth to order its remaining patrol ships to engage in rescue missions and avoid further contact with the alien ship."

In an unconscious move, Choi stood at attention as she asked, "What do you want me to do?"

Casey's eyes were sad as she said, "You're on a transport ship, Captain. You don't have any weapons, so stay the hell out of harm's way. Hide, if necessary, until we figure out what to do with you. If things go to hell here, scrounge up whatever you need from around the solar system and head for Citadel; if they survived and this system is history, then that's the only place left for you. Even if they didn't survive, being there is probably better than being here. Good luck. I hope we meet again."

The president of Mars, or more formally, President Amelia Gordon of the United Mars Settlements, was in emergency session with her advisors. As one of her advisors manipulated images on the massive screen in front of them, Gordon noticed, sourly, that there was more bad news than good news. She said, "OK, I get it that Mars is the closest of the interior planets to the alien ship and the most recent course change shows that it's heading straight for us. I also get it that the ship used an EMP weapon to blast the hell out of everything. My question is why that matters to us, considering that we've hardened the hell out of our own systems because of our location and the planet's history."

Gordon's chief science advisor, a woman by the name of Jeffries, replied, "We all know the science, Madam President. Because Mars lost its magnetic field many millions of years ago, the solar wind stripped away the atmosphere, leaving the place cold as hell and hostile to human life without using artificial means to sustain us. Within this environment, we're much more vulnerable to damage from the solar wind than Earth would be, especially when there are major spikes in solar activity. We've known it for many years, so we've put a lot of effort into 'hardening' our electronics against solar activity."

Jeffries continued, "That's not all we've been doing, of course. As we know, we've been working for years to channel massive amounts of energy to the planet's core from our solar collectors. Eventually, we hope to melt the core enough to reestablish a magnetic field. With the protection of a magnetic field, we'll import various materials from the asteroids in massive quantities to reestablish an atmosphere. This includes the use of what were once called 'greenhouse gases' in order to increase the temperature of the atmosphere to get it to within Earth ranges.

"We've known for over a century that there's an enormous quantity of frozen water trapped beneath the surface, ready to resupply the planet with liquid water once the temperature has been raised sufficiently within a replenished atmosphere. We already are able to melt a tiny portion of that water to meet all of our needs. Although we're still many years away from changing the name of the place from the 'Red Planet,' in time, we'll have a planet that looks a hell of a lot like Earth, with protection from EM issues that is at least as good as what Earth has."

"Thanks for the science lesson, Dr. Jeffries," Gordon said, "but I want to understand why all of the 'hardening' that we've already done isn't the answer."

"The problem," she replied, "is that the alien ship appears capable of subjecting a target to an incredibly intense EM pulse that is well beyond what our systems were designed to handle." The others gasped as images were brought up, showing a devastated planet. Jeffries held up a hand as everyone started to challenge the images. "We've done some exhaustive work in interpreting the damage caused by the attacks on the mining operations. If we don't do something to stop that ship, this is what Mars will look like not long after they pay us a visit."

She continued, "We don't have certain options that Earth would have in the event that things like life-support systems fail under the assault of the EMP weapon. Our people can't simply retreat into the countryside and hope to live out their lives in fresh air and warm sunshine. If our systems fail and the people can't be removed to safety, they will die."

Gordon objected, "We've long planned for a catastrophe involving an extreme level of sunspot activity that would crash our systems, Dr. Jeffries. This includes having sizable reserves of food and other supplies to sustain ourselves."

Dr. Jeffries brought up other images and replied, "We also have extensive underground capacity to house our people in the event of that catastrophe. In fact, one of the unintended benefits of our environmental situation is that it would be nearly impossible for the alien ship to introduce a biological weapon onto Mars that would be effective. With everything organized in self-contained units and little atmosphere to speak of, there is no way for a biological agent to be introduced and spread in the same way as happened on Earth over a hundred years ago during the Bio War. Radiation is also out of the question, as it would likely contaminate the planet to the point that it couldn't be used by the aliens."

Jeffries shrugged as she poured some cold water onto the positive news, "However, lasers or explosive projectiles directed at the enclosures would be deadly. Also, there are limits to the extent our manual systems could make up for the loss of our environmental systems and to our capacity to place the people underground." Jeffries nodded at a man in the room as she said, "I'll leave it to Secretary Castillo to address the military situation."

Defense Secretary Francis Castillo moved toward the screen and walked them through the military situation, saying, "We all know that one of the guiding principles when Mars was recognized as an independent nation was that it wouldn't be militarized. While we have self-defense resources, we do not have an offensive capability."

"Tell us what we have, Frank," Gordon said.

"We have satellite-based missile defenses, using conventional explosive, laser, and nuclear weapons. There are also various electronic countermeasures."

"How effective will they be against the alien ship?"

Castillo shook his head as he replied, "We don't know. For one thing, we don't know the effective range of the enemy's EMP weapon. If they don't have to come within range of our weapons in order to use theirs, then we're screwed. Even if they come within range of our weapons, we don't know how much damage we can do. We also don't know if they have other weapons available."

"What about the nuclear weapons? Won't they wreak hell with their ship, maybe even destroy it?"

Castillo left a large question mark on the screen as he answered, "We don't know how close we'll be able to get the weapons to the target before we detonate them."

"I don't understand."

Castillo frowned as he said, "Their EMP weapon will destroy the critical components of our nuclear weapons before they can reach their target. That will, of course, be a problem with any missiles we launch against them. We'll try to counter that advantage by detonating some nuclear weapons to hit them with our own EMP spike and then launching more weapons to get them before they can react. We hope they'll be blinded or even severely damaged by the EM activity, but we just don't know if it will work."

Gordon hadn't gotten to be the president by being afraid of tough situations. "OK," she said. "Frank, you and Dr. Jeffries will work out what we need to do to protect our satellite network and other orbiting operations as much as possible. Move them away from the planet if necessary. You will also move as many people to underground locations as possible, starting *now*. Reconfigure as much of our systems as possible so that they can be controlled from remote locations." Gordon pointed to a small image on the screen that was moving toward them. "We don't have much time."

According to the displays in the Situation Room, the alien ship only seemed to edge closer to Mars, although it was traveling rapidly in real time. President Gordon and her scientific and defense teams watched as the ship crawled closer to the imaginary line that would enable them to launch their weapons. Gordon didn't waste any time. Once the line was reached, she gave the order to launch a strike. The people in the room held their collective breaths as conventional weapons raced toward the invader at high speed.

At first, it didn't appear that the alien ship even noticed the change. Jeffries pointed to the screen as they saw that the probe had extended itself and begun to glow its dull glow. The scientist in her was fascinated even as the danger repelled her. She gasped moments later as the missiles changed from being weapons to being insignificant bits of debris that weren't even important enough for the intruder to avoid. They watched as the debris bounced off the ship, destined to continue forever into space beyond.

Castillo looked at Gordon and said, "We're not done yet." He ordered the launch of other weapons that gave the ship a wide berth, before approaching from multiple directions. From ports concealed within the ship's unsettling exterior, the aliens countered with the launch of something other than an EMP weapon, which targeted each weapon from Mars. Although there was silence in space, they had no trouble seeing the explosions from each of the weapons that failed to reach their targets.

Castillo said, "Although this isn't the best time, at least we have confirmation that that ship possesses other weapons." He looked to Jeffries and asked, "I make those out to be some form of laser, Dr. Jeffries."

Jeffries looked at another screen, before turning back and nodding. "Yes, we've determined that they're using a series of high-intensity lasers." They were silent for a moment as the screen showed the ship continuing toward them.

Gordon broke the silence by asking in a quiet voice, "What are our options now, Frank?"

Castillo replied, "It's time to use our nuclear weapons." He smiled without humor as he continued, "We've had some serious debates over the years over whether we should even have them here, but right now I'm damned glad we do."

"You've already walked us through what will happen," Gordon said, "so I'm giving you the go-ahead to launch."

Jeffries spoke up. "We've calculated the distances from which the other weapons were destroyed and reconfigured our nuclear weapons accordingly. These are 'smart' weapons that are designed to evade missile defenses."

Jeffries walked them through what was happening. As several intense bursts flashed through the main screen, the quality of the images deteriorated. She said, "Those weapons were intended to detonate well away from the alien ship but have generated both EMP effects and a temporary screen that should make it difficult to detect other weapons."

As if cued by Jeffries, additional nuclear weapons had been launched to approach the ship from multiple directions, including behind it. For the first time, the alien ship slowed. "What's happening, Doctor?" Gordon asked.

Her eyes gleamed with hope as she answered, "There may be some confusion on their part over the location of the multiple threats represented by our weapons. It's also possible that the EMP blast from the nuclear weapons has caused some damage to their ship."

The hope faded from her eyes as they watched several ports in the alien ship open, followed by the destruction of the other weapons before they could get closer to the ship and blast it.

In desperation, Castillo ordered the launch of their remaining nuclear weapons with the objective of creating a field of radiation all around the ship. He looked at Gordon as he explained, "We want to make it absolute hell out there and poison them no matter which way they move."

As they watched their last weapons detonate, they saw their enemy hesitate again. They began to feel hope that the ship had suffered some damage from the repeated EMP blasts nearby. The hope faded as they watched the craft shift its position until it was able to move past the area of contamination. Damaged or not, the ship continued toward Mars.

Jeffries shook her head with frustration as she said, "I think we caused some damage, but it wasn't enough. We simply didn't have enough weapons to complete the trap."

She looked back at the screen that still held the images she'd pulled up showing the widespread destruction predicted by the analytical models. Other eyes followed her glance as Gordon said, "Transmit to Earth everything we have on the alien ship. I don't know what good it will do at this point, but activate our disaster beacon for catastrophic situations. Let's make sure we've moved as many people into the shelters as possible before those bastards get here."

The ship made a final approach to Mars, entering into an orbit that took in broad stretches of populated areas. The probe was extended, emitting its dull glow once again. With nothing to interrupt it, the EMP weapon devastated systems throughout the planet, destroying power grids and anything else that required power or circuitry to operate. Although some systems held out initially due to their having been "hardened," most of them failed eventually against the relentless onslaught that was more powerful and longer in duration than anything they'd ever seen. As the systems failed, the aliens followed up with laser bursts that tore through structures, adding to the damage. With emergency systems down, any structure with compromised integrity rapidly became as lifeless as it had been when it was being built.

It took some time to complete the destruction, since Mars had a population in the tens of millions, spread out among multiple settlement structures on the surface. The ship seemed to move in a leisurely fashion as it passed over one population center after another, leaving a trail of explosions, rubble, and bodies. While some structures avoided the devastation, it wasn't from a sense of mercy, since the aliens didn't seem to have that concept. It might have been that there were too many to count, although it was probably because the aliens didn't think it was necessary. With all power out and therefore life support unavailable, it would be only a short time before everyone was dead anyway.

Whatever the reasoning, after the last settlement had received the same treatment, the ship moved back into space away from Mars and stopped. There was no way to know if the ship had suffered some damage, but any damage had clearly not been enough to save Mars from widespread ruin. For the ship, if there was any damage that needed repair, it would make sense to take care of it now. The prey on Earth had undoubtedly been alerted and would have some time to prepare itself for the intruder.

After some ten hours, the alien ship was on the move again, this time toward Earth. So far, the invaders hadn't encountered anything to lead them to believe that the outcome for Earth would be any different from what had happened to Mars.

CHAPTER THIRTY

Earth was in a state of high alert as the alien ship approached. Although Mars's communications network had been destroyed almost immediately, Earth had seen enough to know that they would be facing an enemy for which they were unprepared. One problem was that their defensive measures hadn't taken into account the possibility that a single ship could absorb terrible punishment and continue to deliver terrible punishment of its own.

The US Space Command had the primary charter for defensive actions in space, due to the somewhat complicated politics involved with the Allied Nations. While the AN was a vast improvement over the United Nations, which had gone out of existence over a century earlier, it was still a very imperfect organization when it came to handling certain matters. A key principle for member states was that military actions had to be subordinate to civilian authority. The problem was that no one believed that military actions could be run via committee, and the secretary general of the Allied Nations was not granted the authority to make those decisions on his own.

For over a century following the Bio War, the United States had been the largest nation on Earth by population and economy and had the sole veto power on the AN Security Council. With this background, including the fact that it was a strong democracy with an elected government that was accountable to the people, the decision had been made to entrust to the president of the United States the decision-making authority for the Space Command. For emergencies, the president was, in effect, responsible for the security of the planet from extraterrestrial influences, including both intelligent and natural sources.

In an eerie replay of events on Mars, President Courtney Harrington was in the White House Situation Room, meeting with her top military and scientific advisors. She turned to her secretary of defense and said, "What have we learned from Mars, Mr. Secretary?"

Secretary Rainey, a gruff man with steel-gray hair, replied, "We learned that it was stupid not to put in place more robust defense measures."

Harrington's eyes narrowed as she snapped, "I supported that approach, Mr. Secretary. I want you to limit your answers to dealing with the situation at hand."

Rainey's eyes flared briefly as he stepped over to the large screen and brought up several images. "My comment was relevant to the situation, Madam President, as it's a fact that our options are limited in the same way as on Mars. In one area, our options are even more limited, and in another, our options are more promising."

"Let's have the bad news first," Harrington said.

"We have less leeway than Mars did with respect to the use of nuclear weapons."

Harrington was puzzled. "We have a hell of a lot more warheads than Mars, so why are we at a disadvantage?"

"Their warheads detonated in a location that was outside the orbital path of Mars. In other words, Mars was moving away from that spot anyway, so it didn't matter that they were making that part of space a toxic hell. We've calculated the likely arrival point of the alien ship near Earth, and they'll be almost directly in our planet's orbital path. This means that if we try to do the same thing to them that Mars did, our planet will go right through the fallout and suffer massive contamination."

Harrington was shocked. "Won't our atmosphere filter out the radiation?"

Rainey shook his head as he answered, "Considering what we saw from Mars, we have to assume they have heavy enough shielding to do for them what our atmosphere does for us. Therefore, to foul up that part of space enough to poison them, it has to be something that won't be filtered out by our atmosphere. We'll only have a small window where we can use our nuclear weapons before it would be the same as cutting our own throats."

"What's the good news?" Harrington asked.

Rainey brought up a new image as he said, "We have a planet-based EMP device that can blast the hell out of anyone dropping into orbit. It's located in the middle of the country and has its own energy supply, capable of lighting up a city. That means the aliens are in for a rude surprise if they get past our space-based defenses."

"What about protection for the other side of the planet?"

"There is a sister operation based in Australia that is just as powerful as the one over here."

Harrington's eyes narrowed as she said, "Can we be ready before they get here?"

"We'd better be," Rainey replied quietly, before turning his head to look at the images from Mars.

As the alien ship came within reach of Earth's near-range sensors, they had confirmation that it was on an approach that placed it directly in Earth's orbital path. Since Earth was between Mars and the Moon, the assumption was that Earth would take the first hit.

The Space Command launched every large transport it could locate on short notice and sent them via remote operation toward the alien ship at extreme speed. Just before the probe started to glow, several of the transports were destroyed by extremely high-yield nuclear devices that had been placed in them, generating massive electronic spikes. It didn't matter that the electronics aboard the other transports were also fried, since they were already locked on their collision courses. Another hope was that the EMPs would create a screen that would protect the other transports from attack by the alien ship. If the alien ship couldn't see the transports, it couldn't attack them.

Long-range visuals were transmitted to the Situation Room. Harrington was only the second US president to order the use of nuclear weapons against an enemy in time of war, so there was an element of morbid fascination for her as she watched the drama unfold. At first, it wasn't clear whether any of the enemy had even survived. As the image cleared somewhat, she screamed in frustration over the sight. If the alien ship had been damaged by the nuclear devices, the damage didn't prevent it from moving before the transports converged on its location.

Harrington looked at Rainey, who shook his head. "We were right on the edge this time, Madam President. We don't dare try it again." Harrington looked at the image of the EMP facility as Rainey continued, "If we're going to survive, we'll have to rely on other weapons. We still have an arsenal of conventional missiles to deploy."

"Do it," Harrington ordered.

In moments, conventional missiles launched from satellites and ground-based stations raced toward the alien ship. The plan was to overwhelm the aliens with a high volume of missiles hurling toward them at extreme speed. To the dismay of everyone in the Situation Room, the result was always the same, with alien lasers finding each missile and destroying it before any damage was inflicted. The satellites themselves were destroyed, compromising much of the planet's communications capability.

Rainey warned what would happen next. "They'll likely enter into a stationary orbit over North America. It's the obvious place to target, since it has the greatest concentration of population. Fortunately, that puts them in our crosshairs for our own EMP surprise."

"Pull the trigger," Harrington said.

The North American EMP weapon had already been brought online. In moments, it targeted the ship with a blast powerful enough to knock it out of the sky. For the first time, the alien ship stopped and moved away from its target. However, while the ship seemed to shudder from the force of the weapon, it didn't stop from directing its own EMP weapon against the North American counterpart. The probe began what was by now a familiar dance. There was more good news as the EMP weapon from Australia began to pound the invaders as well, although the angle of attack from the Australian weapon wasn't as precise because of the location of the invaders, reducing the effectiveness of the second weapon. People began to cheer as they saw the ship venture further back into space.

They stopped cheering when they saw that what might be called tentacles had reached out and captured several satellites that had no more weapons to launch. The satellites were somehow fused together into a huge, misshapen ball with a nightmare of jagged edges and angles. With an almost delicate caress, the tentacles launched the monstrosity toward the planet. It didn't take long for them to figure out that the ball was heading for the Australian EMP complex in a trajectory that was calculated perfectly. People in that facility were frantic with fear as they tried to get away. Only a few succeeded before the terrified souls clogged every possible exit, clawing over each other to get away from the new menace that was heading toward them at extreme speed.

Some people had the courage to stay at their posts and try to increase the energy from the EMP weapon even further, in the hope that even at that extreme distance, the ship would be damaged enough not to be able to continue with the attack. Whether the ship was damaged was unclear, but the damage from the impact of the ball was devastating. The entire complex was blasted apart, with little left as a reminder other than a massive crater.

The North American weapon still worked, leading to a reprieve of sorts. Perhaps the alien ship was limited by internal damage in what it could do while it was pounded by the other EMP weapon. For a time, there was a standoff as neither side could take down the other.

Harrington turned to Rainey and said, "If that weapon fails, how long will our systems hold out?"

"Not long," he replied. "While our systems are a hell of a lot more hardened than they were a century ago, we never dreamed that our EMP weapon might not last long enough to take out anyone stupid enough to attack us." Rainey shook his head as he said, "I guess we should have done a better job of dreaming."

Their eyes returned to the screen as someone called out, "Our weapon is failing!"

One of the last images they saw on the screen was an explosion that ripped through the complex and could be seen from hundreds of miles away. Without the continuing impact from Earth's EMP weapons, the alien ship's EMP weapon began to take a terrible toll on North America. Soon, many critical systems began to fail.

The president's secure communications system failed, and her ability to lead in the crisis was crippled. She was evacuated from the Situation Room as it was overwhelmed by the EMP weapon. Much of the rest of the planet's guidance and communications infrastructure failed as well. It wouldn't take long before North America was a mere shadow of what it had been technologically. It wouldn't be much longer before the rest of the planet was in the same situation.

Perhaps it was the damage from the ground-based EMP weapons that had kept the alien ship from keeping track of what was happening around it in space. Perhaps the aliens had simply been distracted or careless. Whatever the reason, the ship wasn't prepared for an attack from a different direction. The *Keith Thomas* had reached Earth and was pounding the enemy vessel with asteroids that were launched at extreme speed from a rail gun. The ancient rocks tore through their target, wrecking large portions of the insane architecture and ripping huge holes as they burst through the other side like angry solar flares.

Austin, Yabuno, and others watched the carnage from the bridge of the *Keith Thomas,* savoring the moment. As Austin turned toward Yabuno with a grim twinkle in his eye, Yabuno held up his hand and said, "Before you say 'I told you so,' better take a look!" Austin looked back toward the screen, and the twinkle in his eye vanished in the frigid glare.

In spite of the substantial damage to the alien ship, it hadn't been destroyed; even the EMP weapon had managed to avoid contact with the asteroids. To show that it was still capable of dealing death, the vessel began to turn about to bring its EMP weapon to bear on the new threat. Before it could complete the maneuver, the *Keith Thomas* shifted and made its way at high speed toward the asteroid belt, placing itself out of range of the weapon. Although they had run out of asteroids, they could reload if they could get back to the floating rock pile in time. Normally, the alien ship would have been able to catch up to its quarry within an hour or so, but because of the damage, it was closing the distance only very slowly. That a pursuit was possible at all was remarkable, considering the pounding the ship had already taken.

Austin had stayed on the bridge for hours as the chase continued and the pursuers kept closing the distance. As each minute ticked away too slowly for anyone's comfort, the vessel kept taking up more space in the aft displays. Austin noted that what had once been a comfortable distance had been reduced to where they were only barely out of range of the weapon.

Finally, a particularly massive asteroid was coming into view up ahead. The *Keith Thomas* would have to veer around it to make it to the rest of the field in time. As they began to veer and pass from sight behind the asteroid, the pursuers, apparently having anticipated the maneuver, began to take a shorter path that would avoid the large asteroid altogether. The aliens took note of their prey as it appeared around the far side of the asteroid. The pursuers closed the distance rapidly, with their EMP probe extended and starting to glow.

Once again, carelessness caught up with the masters of the alien ship. A more careful view of the Earth ship would have shown that it wasn't carrying a rail gun. Another view would show that it had an EMP weapon deployed to the rear. The weapon started to pound the alien ship. As the pursuers made the decision to face down and overpower this new EMP weapon, their vessel was torn apart from behind by a new menace. The aliens had failed to note that the absence of a rail gun might mean that another ship was in the area. They should have turned their attention back toward their rear, off to one side behind the asteroid, where there was a ship identical to the one in front of them, but with the familiar rail gun. The rail gun was off to the side, as a new form of projectile had been deployed.

Austin smiled grimly at the display and said, "I think the junk in the hold has some real possibilities. Let's rip these guys a new set!"

"Glad to oblige, Sam," Yabuno replied.

He had combined some previous-generation warp-field generators with high-speed projectiles. The weapons were effectively launched toward the alien ship in their own warp bubbles and were impossible to track, which meant they couldn't be destroyed by lasers. The technology was untested, and there was no way to improve what was, at best, a rudimentary means of guidance toward the target. At the time the bubbles had collapsed, if everything worked properly, the projectiles would enter the ship through the massive holes created by the impacts from the asteroids. They would then generate new warp bubbles. The bubbles would be inherently unstable and distort and rip the ship apart.

In a way, it would be a return to when they were first developing the ability to generate warp bubbles and had ended up with ships and other structures that had been distorted grotesquely. In view of the insane nature of the alien ship architecture, the people on board the other ships thought the distortions might be an improvement.

The reality didn't go quite as planned. Several of the projectiles missed the ship completely. Others collided with undamaged portions of the ship's hull and caused only minimal distortions. Finally, several made it to their target as planned and entered the ship. Moments later, they watched as the ship was torn apart and then consumed completely by multiple explosions that seemed to merge into a single miniature sun.

Austin watched as the ball of fire consumed a malevolent intelligence that had tried to extinguish all human life in two solar systems. The two ships moved away from the fireball so that they could establish communications.

"Congratulations, Captain," Austin said. "You looked just like me!"

Choi grinned hugely as she replied, "That's probably the first and last time anyone will say that about me, Sam! We didn't have a chance to talk before, but you can't imagine how glad we are to see you. We'd been given orders that no one wanted to hear, which was to hide. The people on Mars and Earth had it far worse, of course, but it wasn't easy for us to have to sit and watch while our people were being destroyed."

The grim smile returned to Austin's face as he said, "Instead, you became part of the trap that destroyed them, Captain. If the timing had worked out differently, the aliens might have reached us and taken us out before we could do anything about it. Because you distracted the hell out of them, they weren't watching their backs as we set up our surprise."

"Bret's EMP weapon certainly caught their attention." She beamed. "We were happy to take it aboard. How did you happen to have one available?"

"They tried to use their EMP weapon to destroy everything in the Citadel solar system, so we decided to return the favor."

Choi's face went white as she asked, "My God, Sam, did they destroy Citadel?"

Austin shook his head as he replied, "No, but not for lack of trying. They destroyed our space yard and then tried to take out Citadel itself. Citadel took quite a beating from the EMP weapon, but we were able to prevent the aliens from completing the job. We took them out with some asteroids from another rail gun that we put together pretty much on the run. Citadel was repairing the damage to its systems when we left three months ago."

"I don't understand," Choi said in a puzzled tone. "That ship didn't seem to have any asteroid damage when it entered our solar system."

"That ship never entered our system," Austin explained. "The aliens must have been worried about the radiation and the fact their ship was too big to get into the system using the safe path. The best way to describe what happened is to say that a scout ship pulled itself apart from the alien ship and came into the system to do the dirty work. That scout ship was still three times the size of the *Keith Thomas*. We lost *Pathfinder* and some good people in taking it out."

"I'm so sorry to hear that, Sam."

Austin nodded briefly as he said, "We'll find the time to mourn them properly on Earth as we've already done on Citadel, but we should head to Mars right away. Earth has taken some ferocious hits, but Mars really needs our help. A lot of lives depend on systems that have been blasted to hell or are about to quit because of the pounding they've taken. If we can get there in time, we may be able to keep a lot of systems running long enough to last until permanent repairs can be made. I'll send a message to Mars letting them know that we're on our way. With a lot of luck, maybe we can keep the loss of life to a minimum. I'll send instructions to the rest of the Citadel Group operations in this system to drop everything and help out Mars."

As both ships raced toward the beleaguered planet, Austin was surprised to find that partial communications had been restored. He found himself talking to President Gordon. "Amelia, I'm delighted to see that you are unharmed and have communications back online. I assume that you were able to send some of your satellites away for safekeeping?"

Gordon greeted Austin with a small smile. "Yes, although much of the place has been wrecked. We could sure use some help right now, because we've already lost some lives and are going to lose some more due to lack of life support."

Austin's eyes were filled with blue fire as he replied, "We're already heading toward Mars at high speed, Amelia. Everyone on our ships will help you in any way possible. I've ordered both ships to be stripped of nonessential components where needed to bring your systems online and instructed the Citadel Group to collect and transport further critical resources to Mars. A lot of people are coming from our space yard, and they can repair practically anything. We may not be able to repair an entire planet, but we'll do our best to bring your critical systems online."

Gordon was overwhelmed by Austin's generosity and found she couldn't speak. She could only shed a few tears as she said, "Thank you."

Yabuno and his team lived up to their reputations and helped keep the ravaged planet alive. The *Keith Thomas* and her sister ship hauled people and supplies and served as repair facilities when nothing was available elsewhere. The work they were doing with the people on Mars wasn't pretty, and much more extensive repairs would be needed down the road, but they just wanted to save as many lives as possible.

Over time, as the initial problems were addressed, they were able to repair more enclosures so that people could return from their subterranean exiles. Although the solar collectors had been damaged, they'd been repaired, allowing power to be provided for critical needs, such as life support. While this meant that the terraforming activities had to be halted for a while, they were relieved to learn that the there was no meaningful cooling of the core during this period.

A few weeks later, President Gordon contacted Austin. Her smile was now broad and warm as she said, "We're finally ready to take things to the next step and complete our repairs, Sam. While I'll try to thank you for all of the lives here that were saved because of Citadel, I'm not sure there is really any adequate way to do it. I'll just say that we are forever in your debt. We stand ready to repay that debt whenever you need it."

Austin's smile was equally warm as he replied, "Friends don't keep score, Amelia."

"Nonsense, Sam. You will always have friends on Mars."

The *Keith Thomas* found time to visit the beacon at the entrance to Earth's solar system and repair the communications array. To their great delight, they learned that communications could once again be sent to and from Citadel. Although there was still nothing approaching virtually instantaneous communication between the two systems, in time, people at each end would know that the people at the other end were all right.

It was time for the *Keith Thomas* to visit Earth. As they approached the planet of his birth, Austin wondered whether the political will would be in place to upgrade Earth's defenses. If the past was any guide, after the emotions from the current situation had passed, the usual equivocations would reemerge and it would be hard as hell to get anything done. Austin was glad that fight wasn't his to worry about.

CHAPTER THIRTY ONE

Austin's stature as a former US president, as well as his recent role in helping to save two planets, granted him immediate access to the current president. For the first time in decades, he found himself in the Oval Office.

Austin smiled and asked, "I hope the Situation Room is functioning again, Courtney."

"Everything's back to normal," Harrington replied with a smile. She looked around the room and said, "Do you ever wish you had this job again, Sam?"

Austin grinned and said, "Not on your life! I was honored to serve for over forty years, and that was plenty. Besides, I already have a job, as the leader of Citadel. I think I'm the only person to have served as the president of the United States and as the head of another state."

Harrington's smile faded as she replied, "Yes, well, that's still a problem. You can understand why we can't agree to recognize Citadel as a sovereign state."

"Not really, Courtney," Austin said with a shrug. "For many centuries, colonization has long been recognized as a legitimate means of claiming territory and establishing governments. That's essentially how Mars was recognized as a sovereign state."

"Mars is different, Sam," Harrington countered. "We didn't recognize Mars as a sovereign state for a long time. Mars had to go through certain steps before that recognition was granted, including acknowledging that we had certain rights to approve their government and activities."

Austin's tone was wry as he replied, "I don't think you need to tell me about Mars, since my signature is on the treaty that granted that recognition. There were a couple of reasons for the delay. The first was that it took a long time for Mars to look like a community of settlements instead of a series of dormitories for miners. The second is that Mars had become dominated by a rogue element that tried to attack Earth. Everyone wanted to ensure that that situation couldn't arise on Mars again. Under the circumstances, Mars had to make some compromises to get what it wanted. Citadel doesn't."

Harrington made a dismissive gesture with her hand as she said, "Sam, Citadel has a population of what, eleven thousand? It doesn't make sense for a group that small to claim an entire planet for itself, even if we were in the business of parceling out rights to planets."

"The population is higher than that by now," Austin corrected, "but by your reasoning, no planet outside this system would ever have a population that would justify recognition as a separate state. Now that we've finally solved the problem with our transports and with our communications, the emigration will resume and possibly increase. It won't be long before our population is in the hundreds of thousands."

Austin's tone darkened. "Besides, we've seen what can happen when other people from Earth come along. They have this idea that they can simply take over a planet that we took the risks to reach, explore, settle, and adapt to productive use. One of the key requirements for recognizing a separate state is that there is a defined territory, with some ability to defend that territory."

Austin gazed at the president with a grim look in his eyes as he continued, "It seems to me that by that standard, we've done a better job than you have, since we fought the aliens off without any outside help. The fact is that no one has entered our territory successfully without our consent, and we intend to keep it that way."

"You also are very particular about the people you allow to go to Citadel. Some think that that decision should be up to the people who want to go."

Austin frowned as he said, "That's bullshit, Courtney. Countries have a right to decide what people they'll allow to 'join up'; the US does it. Besides, Citadel isn't a place for people who are looking for something fun to do or who are trying to 'find' themselves. We aren't a theme park, and we aren't set up to minister to people who need long-term help of some kind. It also isn't a place for the criminally mischievous or for social misfits. Frankly, a lot of people aren't tough enough to last on Citadel. It's a pioneering society, and we want the type of people who can fit in that society. We want people who are willing to make a long-term commitment to both the place and the values behind the place."

"You don't even have a formal government," Harrington noted. "Citadel is a business venture, with you as the leader. We don't recognize those types of activities as 'states.'"

Austin gave out a mild snort as he replied, "Once again, Courtney, I have the advantage of knowing better than anyone else what can be recognized as a 'state.' Business ventures are not and have not been excluded from that proposition. Mars was a business venture and so was the Moon. For that matter, the US wasn't pretty when it was first set up. Besides, I've felt for some time that we need a formal government in place. I've gotten a commitment from our people to set up a formal government once things have settled down."

"Even if every other issue was resolved to our satisfaction, we'd need to approve that government," Harrington stated.

Austin rose with fire in his blue eyes as he said, "No, by God, you don't! For far too long, this country has had the arrogance to believe it can simply dictate conditions to practically anyone on practically any issue. Although there were times when it was convenient to me to take advantage of that attitude when I was president, it was because I recognized that things were changing that I supported the recognition of Mars.

"This country and this planet have no say over what happens outside this solar system. We will control our own destiny and set our own rules for what happens in our system. If you want to learn about settling other worlds in other systems, you'll need to talk with us, since we're the ones who have figured out how to do it. That includes being the only ones who have figured out how to travel extreme distances successfully. The thieves who reached the entrance to our system could never have returned to Earth with what they stole, and one of their ships never arrived at all."

"We'll figure those things out, Sam," Harrington warned.

"Most things get figured out eventually, but what about for now? Besides, you have a more immediate problem."

"What do you mean?"

Austin's eyes were full of concern as he answered, "I have the benefit of many more years than you of having observed human nature. After this crisis has passed, while Earth may take some measures to improve its defenses, there probably won't be the political will to improve them to the point that Earth would survive another attack without outside assistance."

"What are you saying?"

"I'm saying that there were multiple reasons for our coming here to help this system. We wanted payback for the attack on Citadel and the lives that were lost in defending our homes. In addition, we wanted to stop the aliens from being able to come back to Citadel and possibly engaging in another attack on us. We also wanted to help fellow human beings avoid being wiped out."

"We're very grateful for what you've done," Harrington said with a somewhat forced smile.

"Are you? You may not realize several facts. The first is that we stripped our system of the only meaningful defense we had available so that we could help to defend this system. The original rail gun we used in Citadel against the aliens was useless for anything after we'd destroyed their scout ship. We only had one other unit remaining that could be adapted into a rail gun, which is what we used in this system. There was a huge amount of resistance to taking it away when it might mean the end of everything we'd just fought to save. If it hadn't been me making the argument, Citadel wouldn't have agreed to it, regardless of what you may think about the powers of the Citadel leader.

"Another fact is that I was committed personally to this mission in that I brought my family with me. If I failed, we would all be gone. I didn't want to do it initially, but Liz helped me to see that it had to be that way. Once we made the decision to come to this system, we had enough volunteers that we had to turn away people. When I listen to the arguments from people here against recognizing Citadel, I haven't seen those people making that kind of commitment to the security of this place. It seems to be easier to make those arguments when people are pretty damned comfortable."

Austin's eyes locked onto the president's eyes as he concluded, "The point I'm making is that I'm hugely glad that the aliens were defeated and that we were able to make a difference when it came to saving a lot of lives. However, as matters stand right now, I'm not prepared to make the same commitment to the security of this solar system again, especially at the possible expense of Citadel's security. One of the benefits of the current situation in Citadel is that our society has demonstrated that it has the will to make the changes necessary to our security to prevent another attack from being successful. I'm not so sure the same is true for you, Courtney. I hope I'm wrong. Good day, Madam President."

CHAPTER THIRTY TWO

Austin, Liz, and Yabuno found themselves meeting with a familiar face from the past. J.W. Preacher III rose to greet them warmly. "It's so wonderful to see you all again!" he said. He turned toward Austin and Liz and continued, "I was so delighted when I heard that the two of you were married."

A vigorous man in his fifties was next to Preacher, smiling as broadly as Preacher. The resemblance between them was striking, with the younger man's full head of hair already well on its way to the shade of white that was the only color that adorned the older man's equally full head of hair. Preacher turned to his son, J.W. Preacher IV, and asked, "What did I tell you about Sam and Liz after we met them?"

The son grinned broadly as he said, "You said these two would get married someday." He looked at the visitors and said, "Dad's never wrong about these things."

Liz smiled and said, "But I was engaged to someone else at the time!"

The son shrugged and said, "He didn't know anything about that. He knew what he saw in front of him and figured that what was meant to happen would happen in time. He figured out the same thing with a woman that I was seeing. The good Lord has blessed me with over thirty years of marriage to that wonderful woman and four grandkids for my dad!"

The elder Preacher said, "Bless all of you for coming back to Earth, even after the way they treated you over Citadel's status."

Austin smiled and said, "That's one of the reasons why we wanted to see you, J.W. I don't think anyone has any secrets in Washington that you don't know, so you must know how things went with my meeting with the president."

Preacher's face became more somber as he said, "I'd say that most of Washington knows how that meeting went, Sam. The president is ambitious and inexperienced and would benefit from having more of the kind of vision that you had when you were president. You still have it, for that matter."

Austin smiled his thanks and said, "I don't think that the subject's been closed. While I've been clear that I won't do the kind of dance that others have had to do in the past to get what they wanted, I'm not opposed to influencing the opinions of the people who can make recognition happen."

"While the president doesn't have the last word on the subject, Sam, her opinion carries a lot of weight. It wouldn't be easy to get what you want as long as she's opposed to the idea."

Austin's smile became broader as he said, "J.W., it has been said of you by many people, including me, that you are a wise man. What people sometimes overlook is that you are also a crafty man, which is something else. If public gratitude counts for anything, it should be at its peak right now. It seems to me that a man who is both wise and crafty could figure out a way to motivate the right people to listen to public sentiment in favor of recognition of Citadel as a sovereign state. I also want you to know that I intend to name you as Citadel's ambassador to the AN, if that can be done, as well as to individual countries, if you're willing to accept the job. To be clear, I want to name you as Citadel's ambassador even if things don't work out for now on the sovereignty issue, because I couldn't imagine anyone else being the right person for the job. If you think it'd be helpful, I'd be willing to name you as Citadel's ambassador today."

"I think tomorrow would be soon enough, Sam," Preacher said dryly. "I would be honored to accept the assignment. It would probably make my task easier, since it would avoid the appearance that we are begging for their blessings so that we can become a state. If we are already calling ourselves a state and naming an ambassador and doing other things that states do, it would help some people to get comfortable with the idea that Citadel is already a state. Among those other things that a state does is have trade agreements with other states, Sam." Preacher gave Austin a sly look as he asked, "I don't suppose that you have anything in mind on that subject?"

Austin returned the look, saying, "As a matter of fact, I do, J.W. I've brought some files along that have an outline of what I have in mind. Free trade is a cornerstone of Citadel's policies. But those who get with the program with Citadel sooner will find that the trade is freer than for those who take longer."

Preacher smiled and said, "I understand, Sam. What's even more important, others will understand and listen. When are you returning to Citadel?"

"The baby is due before we'd be able to return to Citadel, so we've decided to stay here until after the baby is born. We'll stay at our home in California. I'm looking forward to seeing the place again after these last few years." Austin nodded to father and son as he said, "Both of you and your families are always welcome to visit; we have plenty of room."

Preacher said, "We may take you up on your kind offer, but for now, we have some work to do regarding a certain state that isn't even located in this solar system!"

CHAPTER THIRTY THREE

Austin, Liz, and Matt approached the house with excitement, although for different reasons. Austin and Liz wanted to see how their home had changed. Matt simply liked the adventure of seeing something new. He was also looking forward to being able to wander around a place without having to be on the alert for danger, especially the four-legged variety.

The rest of Austin's family had decided that the couple needed a few days to themselves before they descended on the place. Liz thought back to the first day when she met so many members of his family and had been welcomed into that family as one of their own. She looked forward to Matt getting to meet plenty of aunts, uncles, cousins, and even nephews and nieces.

Liz noted that the family had taken good care of the place. The landscaping had been given the attention it needed, along with a few small touches that probably reflected some personal sentiments. The sentiments clearly showed that the place had received the love that a family can provide for a home.

The large window in the front part of the house
looked the same as always, which meant it was clear and
ready to display the beauty of the countryside. The deep
blue sky was mirrored in the window, with clouds and
birds moving around in lazy patterns. After taking some
time to get settled and to show the place to Matt, they
found themselves up at the lake. The water was as clear
and cold as ever. It didn't take Matt more than a few
moments to get out of his clothes and run into the water,
shouting with joy. It didn't take Austin and Liz much
longer to join him. Matt got to dive down deeper than
he'd ever been able to do on Citadel. Although he wasn't
quite sure how he'd manage it, Austin resolved that he
would do something to give Matt the chance to do the
same thing when they were back on Citadel.

As Matt continued to splash and swim in the lake, his
parents stretched out on their towels, keeping an eye in their
son's direction. Liz's belly was showing a lot more development now, and she guided Austin's hand over to feel for
the baby. They stayed like that for a while, with Austin's
head cradled against her breasts as he reacted gently to any
sign of movement within. Soon, a shadow flashed before
them as a small, dark-haired bundle of energy bounded up,
dripping clear, cold water over them. The bundle of energy
pointed at his mother's belly and asked how his brother was
doing in there. His parents smiled as they placed his small
hand on her belly to "listen." Every now and then, he gave
out little shrieks of delight as he "heard" something.

Later in the day, father and son went on an extended
tour of the ranch on one of Austin's silent transports.
Liz smiled as she watched them from the house, with

Matt's shrieks of delight wafting back gently over the breeze. While they were out, Liz sat down at the piano and played a piece for the first time in nearly five years. To her delight, she found that her fingers remembered how to caress the keys and coax from the piano the music that gave her great pleasure.

Later that evening, Matt's mighty engine had finally wound down, and he'd been put to bed. His father carried him and placed his limp body gently onto the bed, making sure he was tucked into the covers until the new day was ready to beckon him once again.

Austin and Liz went to their bedroom. As they got into bed, Liz snuggled next to her husband and placed his hand on her belly. He woke up first the next morning and saw the warm rays from the sun streaming across them. Perhaps it was just a trick of the light, but the light seemed slightly brighter as it played across Liz's belly and full breasts. Austin smiled at the sight as he got up to make breakfast for everyone.

They stayed in touch with friends and colleagues at the Citadel Group. "It's a shame the crew of the *Keith Thomas* won't be joining us for a while," Liz said. "I can understand their wanting to spend time with friends and family after having been away for years, though."

Austin grinned, saying, "While that also applies to Bret, it doesn't really matter, since he spends most of his time with his technical colleagues at the Citadel Group. It'll be time well spent, since he's been checking up on the status of the sister ships to the *Keith Thomas* and working with them on some upgrades that occurred to him during the trip here from Citadel. He thinks we might be able to cut future trips by a couple of weeks, if we're lucky."

"At least the crew from the sister ship stayed here for a few days," Liz noted with delight. "Sara Choi is an amazing woman."

"She is, and an excellent captain, too," Austin agreed. "She's asked to stay with the ship once it starts regular runs to Citadel."

"Angie says that the interest in Citadel among prospective settlers has increased. While there won't be any impact on the current groups that are training for their trip to Citadel, it's clear that there are still many people who are willing to make the commitment and have something to offer to the community."

Although they spent time relaxing while waiting for the baby's arrival, Austin stayed busy with several projects. He was delighted to note that the systems at the ranch had all survived the attack from the EMP weapon without any problems. He was determined to make sure that they would be able to withstand even more powerful attacks. He worked out several upgrades and had them incorporated into the existing systems and structures. Most of the changes were so subtle that no one else realized what was happening. He had always planned ahead and brought online some new defensive measures that he hoped would never be needed.

Preacher had joined Austin for a few days at the ranch, so they could both catch up on all things related to Citadel.

"I've been working on a draft of a proposal for a government for Citadel, J.W.," Austin said. "While history is filled with examples of far larger populations that have been led by one person, I don't want to add another one to the list."

Preacher chuckled as he said, "Be prepared for people being very comfortable with what you have now, Sam. You may have a job on your hands convincing people that they need more control over their government when what they already have works."

Austin sighed and changed the subject. "Tell me about the status of Citadel's recognition as a sovereign state."

"The president, whatever her faults, is no fool," Preacher said with a shrewd look on his face. "She knows that she and others were being manipulated to provide for recognition and has let it be known that she isn't happy with the situation."

Austin smiled, saying, "I'm not worried about her happiness. I'm getting close to two centuries old and can afford to take the long view about things. Over the years, I've outlasted plenty of others who disagreed with me on issues. I expect that the day will come when her opposition will be considered a mere footnote to the issue, if people remember it at all."

Preacher replied, "Fortunately, there's an enormous amount of gratitude toward you and the people from Citadel, both on Earth as well as on Mars and elsewhere. Everyone knows that Citadel lost lives in defending themselves against their own attack. You could have stayed in the Citadel system, but instead, you risked your lives to come here and take on the aliens again. The people on Earth are well aware that their defenses collapsed at the moment that you and the *Keith Thomas* showed up. They also know that the outcome for them would have been grim at best if Citadel's people hadn't placed themselves in harm's way to destroy the aliens.

"Everyone on Mars is deeply grateful for all the help that the Citadel people provided in getting their critical systems up and running. You also have a special history with them, since as president you endorsed their recognition as a nation. You didn't allow the attack from rogue elements on Mars to distract them from doing what was right."

Austin grinned as he said, "You're a master at acting like an ambassador at every possible opportunity. I won't ask how the hell you managed to receive an invitation to speak before the Allied Nations, with all of the courtesies normally granted to an ambassador."

Preacher grinned back and said, "It hasn't hurt that I've made a point of talking about negotiating trade agreements with various nations, with an attractive list of trade goods to offer. I've made it clear that I will only deal with nations as an equal, which means with nations that recognize Citadel as a sovereign nation." Preacher chuckled as he continued, "Of course, since Citadel has the only ships that can travel between the two solar systems, it's in the best interests of nations to reserve space on those ships for trade while space is still available."

"It isn't a surprise that Mars has been the first nation to recognize Citadel and to accept me as its ambassador, Sam. Mars is therefore the first nation to negotiate a trade agreement with Citadel. Although they've always been considered somewhat roguish in view of their history, their actions still matter and the pressure is on for an Earth-bound nation to recognize Citadel."

"Where do we stand with the AN?" Austin asked.

Preacher replied, "As you know, the admission of new members to the AN is in the hands of the Security Council, where the US is the only country with a veto. Privately, the president has let others know that she will use that veto if necessary to prevent Citadel from being recognized. However, Citadel has no need to join the AN; the interests of Earth's solar system aren't particularly important to the people of Citadel, other than perhaps security concerns. The real issue is recognition of Citadel. Once that happens, Citadel can enter into whatever treaties it needs with individual states."

A twinkle returned to Preacher's eyes as he said, "Besides, Harrington's posture and foot-dragging are coming back to haunt her. She should have tried to work a deal with you while she could."

Austin was puzzled. "What do you mean?"

"My sources tell me that tomorrow Congress will propose an amendment to the US Constitution, which will grant formal recognition by the US of Citadel as a sovereign state. It will also confirm that US citizenship will apply to the current inhabitants of Citadel who had been US citizens and to their descendants. I expect the amendment to be ratified by the states in record time."

Austin was stunned.

Preacher continued, "The people, and that includes me, are grateful for what you've done, Sam. Recognizing

Citadel is a way to show that gratitude. Also, people will feel better about recognizing Citadel if they know that doing so won't require you to choose between being a US citizen and a citizen of Citadel."

When Preacher was finished, there were two sets of moist eyes in the room.

President Harrington complained that the amendment would prevent presidents from being able to break diplomatic relations with Citadel should the United States decide it was necessary at some other date. It was an awkward position to take, since she argued in favor of being able to be hostile toward the very people who had risked everything to come to their defense. No one was willing to start over on the amendment to give Harrington that right. She fumed but had to accept that she didn't have any role when it came to Constitutional amendments. As expected, it was ratified within a couple of weeks.

The threat of a veto in the AN Security Council had been the last form of leverage that Harrington had to prevent others from recognizing Citadel. Once everyone understood that Citadel didn't want membership anyway, Harrington's leverage was gone. The only thing Austin wanted from the AN was recognition, not membership, and he was about to get his wish. Harrington saw that she'd been outmaneuvered and had even ended up looking foolish. She asked for Austin to visit her in the Oval Office.

Harrington tried to conceal her feelings as she rose to greet Austin. "Welcome back, Sam," she said. "I imagine you didn't expect to be back here so soon."

Austin smiled without rancor as he said, "It may come as a surprise to hear that this is pretty much what I expected, Courtney. Before we were attacked by the aliens, I told a friend that Citadel would be recognized as a sovereign nation before you left office."

Harrington's face became less friendly as she said, "I don't think there's any need to be rude, Sam."

Austin replied, "Please don't misunderstand me. I don't mean to be rude; I'm simply telling you that I expected this meeting to take place in the near future, although I didn't know the specific timing of it."

"Isn't it enough that you've embarrassed me and the United States over that shameless piece of theater that old fox Preacher orchestrated? He played that issue for everything he was worth in order to generate sympathy for what we both know is a bad idea. You don't need to rub my nose in it."

"Courtney, you're confusing your personal embarrassment with embarrassment on behalf of the United States; the two aren't the same. You've never been particularly interested in listening to my perspectives on much of anything. That is your right, of course, but it isn't always a good idea to invoke that right just to make a show of asserting your independence from me and my legacy."

With a dramatic wave of her hand, she said, "Everywhere I turn I'm reminded of your legacy. As far as the public is concerned, you can do no wrong. What's worse, your actions have now left me with a new legacy where my hands are tied when it comes to certain areas of foreign policy, which no president should do to a successor."

Austin shook his head and said, "You may find this hard to believe, but I didn't have anything to do with getting that amendment in place. While Ambassador Preacher has been making a strong case in diplomatic circles for recognition, he never suggested that an amendment to the Constitution was an appropriate step to take. The people of the United States made their own decision on the subject."

Austin's face took on a harder look as he continued, "Besides, you don't have anyone but yourself to blame. Sometimes the best thing a leader can do is to know when it makes sense to step out of the way of public opinion. You've been so stubborn over trying to preserve what you think are your prerogatives that you overlooked the importance of doing what was right. You tried to rub my nose in the notion that Citadel's actions were subject to *your* approval, despite the lack of any legal justification for your claims.

"As a leader, I've often had to make sure my decisions weren't being influenced by my ego, which is something you should have tried harder to emulate. What I *won't* do is be lectured on what is right and wrong by someone who hasn't begun to face the experiences that would have informed her about what those concepts really mean."

"With respect to experience, I'd say recent events have provided me with hugely important experience," Harrington countered.

"Yes, but up until now, you've had a fairly uneventful tenure as president, so you've been able to convince yourself that your judgment really *is* superior to everyone else's. This is one of the few times that you've had to face a significant challenge. The question isn't whether you did the right thing in ordering defensive measures to be taken to protect the planet. Any president would have issued the same orders. The question is what happens going forward. You can either pretend that things will stay the same as they did before or embrace the steps that are needed to provide for security in a new reality. I know what a wise leader would do."

Austin's expression softened as he continued, "As someone who's been where you are now, I want you to be successful, for the sake of the country, if for no other reason. What I don't want to see happen is for people to say that it's a shame that you weren't more of a leader and it's a good thing that you'll be out of office soon enough.

"We're getting a bit away from the immediate subject, although they're connected. You need to be enough of a leader to put behind you the embarrassment that you brought on yourself. What's needed now is a more far-sighted approach to relations between Citadel and Earth. We don't know what the future holds for us as far as the aliens who attacked us are concerned. Although I'd thought originally that a show of force and resolve in both solar systems would be enough, I don't think we have the luxury of making that assumption anymore. For all we know, this was only the first round, with more to follow. Our two solar systems would be much stronger while cooperating with each other than they would without cooperation."

"I don't agree," Harrington replied. "I think the aliens have had a double dose of defeat when it comes to dealing with humans and won't have any reason to come back to cause more trouble. As far as Citadel is concerned, there doesn't appear to be anything further I can do to prevent Citadel from being recognized as a new nation, although it has happened without my blessing. I predict you'll find that it's much harder to make it work than you think, and you may realize that you're better off rejoining the fold, so to speak. The cooperation you mentioned would be much stronger with both systems taking guidance from the same source. That source should be Earth, and I intend to do what I can to make it happen."

"I'm disappointed to hear that you feel that way," Austin said with a sad frown. "That attitude went out of style decades ago and may end up causing more than a little mischief. I'll note that history is filled with people who were opposed to change and tried to block it. If that's really how you feel, remember that your time in office will come to an end and you'll no longer have the power of this office available to further your objectives."

"History will vindicate my opinion, Sam."

The blue fire returned. "Do you really think so?" Even the president of the United States winced at the words. Austin continued, "I think history will judge your opinion and consider it to be shortsighted and wrong. For the sake of two solar systems, don't make the mistake of underestimating Citadel. Others have done it and failed. Good day, Madam President."

A couple of weeks later, Austin had a long talk with Preacher about Citadel, saying, "For many years, out of respect for the office, I've avoided making direct public comments on the actions of any current president."

Preacher chuckled as he replied, "It doesn't matter. Even with your silence, the public can't help but notice that Harrington placed a lot of her prestige behind defeating Citadel's claim for recognition and she lost. She's been too high-handed in her attitude toward other nations for any tears to be shed over her embarrassment. Who else knows the specifics about the conversation?"

"The Citadel Group team knows, since they need to understand where they stand with a key leader on Earth." Austin shook his head as he mused, half to himself, "I truly hope that her bruised ego will mellow and allow our countries to stay on cordial terms. While Citadel and Earth need each other, the relationship will only work if it is as allies and partners. It will be a failure if someone tries to impose a master-servant relationship."

Preacher changed the subject. "Turning to a more positive topic, practically every nation on Earth has now recognized Citadel as a sovereign state, including the US, thanks to the ratification of the new amendment by the states."

With a bemused look on his face, Austin said, "Remarkably, Citadel has been recognized as a nation without the usual preconditions about the type of government it has to have, etc. Since Citadel wasn't seeking to become a member of the AN, it didn't have to go through that vetting process."

Preacher smiled and said, "Everyone trusts that you will make good on your commitment to establish a government, even if they aren't quite sure what it will look like. A nice benefit is that you are now recognized as a new head of state, with diplomatic status."

Austin grinned and said, "Another nice benefit is that everyone has accepted your credentials as Citadel's ambassador. Even President Harrington had little choice but to accept reality as well as your credentials." He laughed and continued, "That ceremony was barely cordial!"

Smiling broadly, Preacher replied, "What kind of an ambassador would I be if I reacted to such things? Seriously, I'm having the time of my life in my new role and have decided to retire from my law practice and turn it over to J. W. Preacher IV."

Austin looked around the room with appreciation and commented on the beautiful residence that was now the Citadel embassy.

With a chuckle, Preacher said, "You know better than anyone else that many of the embassies in Georgetown were abandoned and converted back to private residences a hundred years ago after the collapse of many countries following the Bio War. As a result, I had no difficulty finding and acquiring a stately home on Embassy Row, to serve as Citadel's embassy." There was a twinkle in his eye as he continued, "We had to find the right place, since circumstances will prevent there being an enclave of embassies on Citadel itself."

Austin gave Preacher a wry look as he said, "This probably sucks for you, but everyone will deal with you here for anything that doesn't require my direct involvement, J.W. I can't imagine giving that trust to anyone else."

Preacher smiled his appreciation and asked, "We need to figure out what else will be protected as official Citadel operations."

"I'm going to declare that although my ranch will remain my property as a US citizen, it will also have special diplomatic status when it comes to the right of anyone to have entry to the place." Austin's face darkened as he continued quietly, "This should give me the best of both worlds when it comes to protecting my privacy, which hasn't always been the case."

Preacher bowed his head slightly for a moment out of respect for some of those times and then said, "I think we should designate the Citadel Group operations as having consulate status."

"Agreed," Austin replied. "I want you to come up with other steps aimed at protecting Citadel assets from being subject to possible adverse actions by other governments, including the US. It's one thing for the US to take actions against US citizens; it's quite another to take actions against duly recognized foreign embassies and consulates. While the international community might overlook the former, it would be another matter if Harrington were to be seen not to be complying with the law of nations."

Preacher nodded, saying, "I'll come up with a list for you."

Austin smiled again as he said, "You've done an amazing job of negotiating trade agreements with many nations, while steering clear of any attempts to pull Citadel into the politics that have always swirled around this solar system."

With a shrewd look on his face, Preacher said, "The first diplomatic lesson for the United States was that it wasn't entitled to any more favored status than other nations when it comes to trade agreements. While

Citadel is willing to give the US an opportunity to enter into trade agreements, there are plenty of other nations in line, so the US can either agree to reasonable terms or stand by and watch others benefit. Although Harrington was willing to cut off her nose to spite her face, Congress had other ideas and forced her hand." With a nod to Austin, he continued, "It is understood that you will take the treaties back to Citadel to be ratified through whatever means you set up."

"One thing that people inside and outside diplomatic circles have discussed is the possibility of some form of mutual defense arrangement being put in place," Preacher said. He chuckled as he continued, "No one has discussed the matter within earshot of President Harrington!"

Austin laughed and mused aloud about the future, "One day, the tables might be turned, where Citadel ends up approving Earth's defense measures as a condition to agreeing to a defense arrangement. After all, Citadel has the ships and has shown it knows how to defend against outside attacks." Austin smiled over the notion of Earth being the junior partner for a change.

CHAPTER THIRTY FOUR

Matt had been right in his assumption that Liz was carrying his brother. During a spectacular day at the ranch with a deep-blue sky overhead, Liz gave birth to Luke Austin, a beautiful boy with the same dark hair and blue eyes that his brother had. A few weeks later, Matt and Luke were being looked after by family members so that Austin and Liz could share some quiet time up at the lake.

They got undressed to go into the water, and the only sign that Liz had been pregnant was her fuller-than-usual breasts. As she looked across the lake, he stepped over to her from behind and wrapped one of his arms around her waist and the other one across her chest and held her close. She sighed and said, "I love that even after two children, you still want me."

As she turned around to face him, a familiar gleam came into her eyes. She smiled and said, "It looks like you want me as much as I've wanted you for the last few months. I'm awfully glad you're always trying to find ways to get me naked. The feeling is extremely mutual! I don't have to share you with anyone else for a while, and I'm going to make the most of it."

It was time to leave for Citadel. Everyone was on board the *Keith Thomas*, which would be escorting several new sister ships to Citadel, which were carrying plenty of settlers. Austin had managed to meet most of them over the past few weeks and felt that they'd be wonderful additions to their new community. Rather, it was now a new state! Just before they left, they'd received word from Citadel that Karen Thomas had gotten engaged to Gina Albretti's widower! Austin and Liz were happy for both of them. Gina's wish was for Sofia to have a chance at life, and now she'd have one with a new mother and a father who might be able to grieve a little less over their lost loved ones.

Austin stood in front of a monitor, which showed an image of the path they'd be taking. He was holding the baby in one arm and Matt with the other and managed to point to a star as he said, "Matt and Luke, there's a hell of a home waiting for you out there!"

TARGET CITADEL

The story continues in the next novel by Robert Adrian, *Target Citadel*. Under Sam Austin's leadership, the new nation has prospered, with trade booming between the two star systems. The times become even more interesting when an ancient derelict spaceship is spotted drifting toward Citadel. The vessel might hold extraordinary knowledge, but it doesn't come with an instruction manual.

The current US president still has no love for either Citadel or Sam. Polls show that she's in a losing battle to be reelected unless something drastic happens. She sees her chance to get re-elected by creating a conflict with Citadel over the derelict. As a bonus, she can use the conflict to undermine the upstarts.

All eyes are on the planet once again, eager to see who will end up with the prize and at what price. The problem with starting a conflict is that it might spin out of control, which is especially bad news if some of the interested eyes aren't even human.

Robert Adrian is the pseudonym of Robert A. Schmid. He has been an attorney for over two decades, working with Silicon Valley technology companies. Since childhood, he has had a passion for science fiction. He's combined that passion with an interest in other times, both historical and futuristic, by writing the Sam Austin Chronicles, a series about a character whose life spans multiple eras. Mr. Schmid enjoys projects that require the use of his workshop and is active in local musical events, where he met his wife. They live in the San Francisco Bay Area with their three children.